D1169260

Easy Kisses

Book Four in the
Boudreaux Series
Kristen Proby

EASY KISSES
Book Four in The Boudreaux Series
Kristen Proby

Copyright © 2016 by Kristen Proby

All Rights Reserved. This book may not be reproduced, scanned, or distributed in any printed or electronic form without permission from the author. Please do not participate in or encourage piracy of copyrighted materials in violation of the author's rights. All characters and storylines are the property of the author and your support and respect is appreciated. The characters and events portrayed in this book are fictitious. Any similarity to real persons, living or dead, is coincidental and not intended by the author.

Cover Art:
Photography by: Sara Eirew Photographer
Cover Design: Okay Creations

ISBN: 978-1-63350-013-6

This one is for Holly Pierce.

OTHER BOOKS BY KRISTEN PROBY

The Boudreaux Series:
Easy Love and on audio
Easy Charm and on audio
Easy Melody and on audio
Easy For Keeps

The With Me In Seattle Series:
Come Away With Me and on audio
Under the Mistletoe With Me and on audio
Fight With Me and on audio
Play With Me and on audio
Rock With Me and on audio
Safe With Me and on audio
Tied With Me and on audio
Breathe With Me and on audio
Forever With Me and on audio
Easy With You

The Fusion Series
Listen To Me and on audio

The Love Under the Big Sky Series, available through
Pocket Books:
Loving Cara and on audio
Seducing Lauren and on audio
Falling for Jillian and on audio

Baby, It's Cold Outside and on audio
An Anthology with Jennifer Probst, Emma Chase, Kristen Proby, Melody Anne and Kate Meader

PROLOGUE

~Charly~

"I'm such a pushover." I follow my brother, Beau, from the bedroom. He's pulling my suitcase behind him, grunting from the weight.

"You're a lot of things, Charly, but a pushover isn't one of them." He smirks and rolls his shoulder, and then narrows his eyes at me. "This is over the weight limit."

"I didn't want to take two suitcases," I reply with a shrug. "So I crammed it into one."

"They'll make you take stuff out."

I laugh and shake my head. "I'm taking the company jet."

Beau cocks a brow and leans his hips against the back of my couch. "I'll make you take stuff out, then."

"No, you won't." I kiss his cheek, and pat it, harder than needed, laughing when he scowls. "You love me."

"I'm excited to be rid of you for a couple of weeks," he replies and rubs his cheek. "You're mean."

"I can't believe Savannah talked me into this," I reply, rolling my eyes. "I don't need a retreat full of a bunch of desperate women to tell me what my worth is."

"Van says the guy's hot."

"I can look at hot guys at the gym. I don't need to fly all the way to the boonies for that."

"Then why are you going?" I stop pacing and prop my hands on my hips, facing my brother.

"Because I'm a pushover."

His lips twitch.

"Because I love Van."

"And you never do anything for yourself," he adds.

"My shop is for me," I reply. "My house. My car. All for me."

"But you don't ever take a vacation, Charly. I don't know why you even bought this house. You never leave the shop."

"Hi, kettle, I'm pot." I shake my head and lead Beau to the front door. "Thanks for watering my plants and stuff for me."

"Take the two weeks to relax. And you never know, you might just learn something about yourself."

Beau lifts my bag into the trunk of my car and looks at me dubiously. "Are you sure you don't want me to drive you? I don't know if you'll be able to lift that thing back out."

"I'm sure." I grin and kiss him on the cheek again. "Thanks for bringing my suitcase out, and for the chat."

"Text me and let me know you're doing okay," he says, always playing the role of the oldest brother.

"Yes, sir." I give him a mock salute before lowering into the seat of my new Lexus and driving away.

I love my car the way a mother loves her newborn baby. I worked my ass off for it and everything else I own. My shop, *Head Over Heels* is a success, and gives me the opportunity to buy nice things and enjoy a fabulous shopping budget.

My family's money doesn't pay for any of it.

Okay, so I'm taking the Boudreaux Enterprises jet to Montana, but that hardly counts.

I have enough time before my plane is scheduled to leave to stop by Ryan's house and say goodbye. Ryan and I have a long, but not terribly complicated history. We've never been in love. We've used each other for nothing but sex.

Because, let's be honest, it's the sex that keeps us both coming back for more.

We haven't slept together in a few months, but he's my friend, and he's had a hard time of things lately, with the loss of his mom. I want to check in on him before I leave.

I park my car and make my way up his front steps, but before I can knock on the door, I can hear voices through an open upstairs window. Before I can call out to get Ryan's attention, I hear his voice saying, "I swear, Pamela, I haven't slept with Charly in weeks."

Who the hell is Pamela?

"I don't care," a female voice says, clearly pissed off. "I want her *gone*. I know your past, and I know that as long as she's in your life, you'll be sleeping with her."

"That's not true."

Oh, that's so true. I smirk and nod because the angry Pamela is exactly right. The sexual chemistry between us is undeniable.

"You've said it yourself," she says. "You may not like her, but you love to fuck her."

I feel my jaw drop.

"I already planned to call her," Ryan says. "I'm going to tell her that we're over. For good. I don't need her in my life. *You're* the one I want, Pam."

I back away and walk briskly back to my car. I don't need to hear any more.

Jesus, I know that things between us have been complicated for years, but I thought that at the very core of it we at least respected each other.

Maybe this trip is coming at a good time after all.

CHAPTER ONE

~Charly~

"Okay, everyone, listen up!" Simon Danbury says at the end of day one of the *Lift* seminar. "I know you're tired and you probably want to go to your room and crash. I get it. But I highly recommend that you come downstairs for dinner. Or go out with a few other girls." His British accent is sexy, I'll give him that. It's not a bad thing to listen to all day. "Talk to each other. Trust me when I say that the friendships you make while you're here for two weeks will be ones you take with you. Have a good night."

"God, I'm exhausted," a woman named Heidi says as we gather our things and walk out of the conference room toward the elevators to our rooms. I opted for a private room, but some of the women offered to double up to save on costs.

All I want right now is my quiet room, a bottle of wine, and some Advil.

In that order.

Heidi rides to the same floor as me, and I'm surprised to find that she's my neighbor. "I'm so glad I got a private room," she says, mirroring my thoughts.

"Me too."

"Are you going down to dinner?" she asks, nibbling her lip. She's a pretty woman, in her mid-forties. She looks athletic and fun.

"I really just want room service," I reply with a tired smile. "Who knew that listening to someone talk all day could be so exhausting?"

"Well, he made us dance too," she reminds me. "I haven't danced in years."

I nod and smile at her as I reach my door. "He's good looking, but he's not a great dancer. Have a good night."

"You too!"

My room is blissfully quiet. I open my curtains and sigh at the view. Giant mountains frame a blue lake. Despite it being early June, there is still snow on the peaks.

I can't get over how late the sun stays up here. It's late afternoon, but the sun is high in the sky. As I watch, several women walk out of the resort and down the dock to a waiting tour boat that trolls around the lake.

I bet the views they get are amazing.

I sigh and kick out of my heels, stretching my feet on the carpet and text my sister, Van.

First day is done.

She immediately replies. *How did it go?*

Long. Lots of talking and information.

I'm sorry if you hate it, she says. Instead of reply via text, I dial her number.

"Tell me you don't hate it."

"I don't hate it," I reply truthfully. "There is some good information so far."

"And Simon isn't bad to look at," Van adds with a

smile in her voice.

Boy, you aren't lying. "No, not bad."

"Oh, stop it." I can practically hear her rolling her eyes. "He's hot and you know it."

"Just because the man looks like Henry Cavill doesn't mean I think he's hot."

"Liar," Van replies with a giggle. "At least you get to stare at eye candy all day."

"I should be working," I reply without even thinking about it.

"The shop is fine," she says. "It's in good hands, and you deserve some time away. Enjoy it. And keep me updated."

"Okay. Love you, sugar."

"Love you, too," she says and hangs up and I sit heavily on the bed, looking around the lodgy room. There is nothing about this room that's my style, but it fits the Montana motif. There's a gas fireplace framed by logs and rocks, and there is even a teddy bear on my bed.

Nice touch.

My other sister, Gabby, would love it here. As an innkeeper, she's always been fascinated by different resorts. I'll have to mention it to her, and suggest that she and her new husband, Rhys, make a trip up.

I'm starving. I could order from room service, change into my yoga pants, and relax the rest of the evening.

Or, I could take advantage of being here and go be social.

I'm good at being social. It was bred into me. I can talk to anyone, and sell them shoes.

"Suck it up, Charlotte, and go experience what you came here for." I nod once and slide my feet back into my heels, grab my bag and room key, make sure my name badge is on, and set out for the restaurant.

Once in the lobby, I run into Heidi again.

"You decided to come down," she says with a friendly smile.

"So did you."

"Well, I did pay to be here," she says with a sigh. "Might as well soak it all in."

"My thoughts exactly," I reply. "Would you like to join me for dinner?"

"I would love to," she says and we walk into the restaurant together. The lodge theme is carried through the place, with a stuffed bear and moose at the threshold of the restaurant.

"Two?" the hostess asks.

"Yes, please," I reply.

"This way." She leads us through the restaurant toward a table. I glance to my left, and sitting by the window is Simon, his assistant Todd, and a blonde woman I saw this morning named Shelly.

Simon's eye catches mine, and he stands. "We have two empty chairs here. Would you ladies like to join us?"

Heidi and I share a glance, then a shrug. "Sure."

We sit across from Simon, facing the lake and the mountains, and I can't help but sigh at the view. Both the man and the nature behind him are amazing.

"Tired?" Simon asks with a knowing smile.

"A bit," I reply with a nod. "And the view is incredible."

"No kidding," Shelly says with an annoying giggle, and I realize she thinks I'm talking about Simon.

For fuck sake.

"Actually, I was talking about the mountains," I add, stifling a laugh when Heidi knocks her knee against mine.

"The views here are unreal. When I saw that the conference was to be held in Montana, I just figured we'd be in the boonies, on a dude ranch or something with no wifi and hunting and gathering our food ourselves. I had no idea that this existed."

"It's one of my favorite places in the world," Simon replies with one of his insane smiles. Seriously, he smiles and the room lights up. He's changed into a casual blue T-shirt that hugs his shoulders and reveals the sleeve of tattoos down his left arm. In all of his public appearances, he wears long sleeves, covering the ink. It's sexy as hell, not to mention the lean muscle there. His dark hair is disheveled from pushing his fingers through it all day, and his eyes look a bit tired, too. "Where are you from, Charly? Is that the South I hear in your voice?"

I grin. "Louisiana," I confirm. "I'm from New Orleans."

"Another of my favorite places," he replies with a wink.

"Oh, I love it there too," Shelly says. "What do you do there?"

"I own a shoe store." I grin at the waitress as she fills my water glass.

"Well, that wouldn't suck," Heidi says and glances down at my feet. "I admired your shoes all day."

"Thank you."

"How long have you done that?" Simon asks, listening intently.

"Six years," I reply. "But I've lived there all my life."

He nods, and I can see in his eyes that he has more questions, but he shifts the focus to someone else, to my relief.

"And where are you from, Heidi?"

"Arizona," she replies and begins telling us about her business raising assistance dogs. She pulls her phone out to show us photos, and I melt.

"Aww, what a sweet baby," I croon when she shows me the yellow lab puppy she's working with now. "Puppies are the best."

"I think so too," Heidi agrees. Dinner is surprisingly fun. We spend the next hour chatting about our homes, what we do, and things that interest us. Simon is funny and charming, easily deflecting Shelly's blatant flirtations.

He's professional. I assume he comes down and has dinner with a different group of women from the retreat each night. It's a nice touch.

I wonder how many he sleeps with.

I bite my lip to keep from laughing out loud and scold myself. Why am I always the pessimist? Maybe he's just a good guy who likes helping women.

It could happen.

I glance up to find Simon watching me. His deep blue eyes are dancing with humor, and if I'm not mistaken, lust.

But he suddenly clears his throat, and it's gone.

I sign my tab, wipe my mouth, and stand.

"Thanks for asking me to join you," I say with a nod. "I'm heading up to bed."

"I'm coming too," Heidi says, joining me. "Good night, everyone."

We wave and walk toward the elevators.

"So, I think I've figured out why Shelly's here," Heidi says. "I'm sorry, but that girl needs to turn down the flirt level."

"Agreed," I reply with a laugh. "He's just a man, after all."

"Exactly," she says. "If she came here to stare at Simon all day, she could have saved a shit ton of money and joined a gym."

I laugh, already feeling like Heidi and I are going to be friends.

"He may come in a pretty package," I add, "but he puts his pants on just like anyone else. I'm sure there's someone out there who thinks he's a pain in the ass."

"Oh, I like you," Heidi says.

"I like you, too," I reply as we reach our rooms. "Have a good night."

****

Honestly, if I wasn't so in love with New Orleans, I would move here. The morning air is crisp as I make my way on the trail around the lake. The woman at the front desk told me that the trail actually goes all the way around the lake, but I won't make it that far.

Today.

But I will explore it on my day off this weekend. For this morning, I'm just jogging down about a mile and back. The cold air filling my lungs feels amazing, and the view continues to stun me.

Who knew that deep down I was a mountain girl?

Amazing.

Suddenly there's a clearing and a small beach leading to the water, so I stop running and walk down on the coarse sand. It's flat enough to stand here and move through a few yoga poses, so I do. The sky is the biggest and bluest I've ever seen, and the mountains are reflected in the water.

This is as peaceful as I've ever felt in my life.

It's a damn shame I had to come all the way to Montana to find this.

I stand and take a few deep breaths, but footsteps behind me have me turning, my hand poised over the bear spray clipped to my waistband.

But it's Simon.

Not a bear or a mountain lion.

So I turn back without a word and take another deep breath.

"Beautiful, isn't it?" he murmurs as he stands next to me. He's tall, probably as tall as my brothers, who stand at close to six and a half feet. And without my heels, I feel incredibly short next to him.

I glance up at him quickly and nod. "I love it."

"Glacier Park is nearby," he says, Britain falling off his tongue and making my stomach clench. His voice is like melted butter. Thank God he's not smiling at me right now. The combination could be lethal. "I've hiked through there many times."

"How long have you been coming here?" I ask and tip my head back so I can look up at his face. His eyes, the same color as the sky, are trained on the mountains.

"About three years," he replies. He looks like he wants to say more, but he doesn't. He glances down at me and smiles, and my stomach drops.

God, that smile could end wars.

"If you have time, I recommend taking a day up in the Park. If you think this is beautiful, it will astonish you."

"I'll keep it in mind."

He nods and shuffles his feet, crosses his arms over his chest, and we stand here, quietly, for a long moment, taking it all in. A bald eagle soars out of the trees, over the water, and suddenly dives down to pluck a fish from the water, then circles back to his tree.

"Did that just happen?" I whisper in awe.

"Indeed," he replies softly. And then, without looking at me, he whispers, "Why are you here, Charly?"

"Because my sister made me," I reply immediately and grin. "Childish, I suppose."

"She made you?" He raises a brow and looks down at me. "What would the punishment be if you refused?"

"Refusing was never an option," I say without thinking. "And Van isn't the type to hand out punishments."

No, she was on the receiving end of punishments for too long to dole them out.

We stand in silence again. It's true that I came because of Van, but I came for me, too. I'm woman enough to admit it.

I needed a break. And maybe I needed to step back and take stock of things.

"I don't know what I need," I say, surprising both of us. "But I do know that I'm here because my sister isn't strong enough to be here herself yet."

I look up into the bluest eyes I've ever seen and into an ocean of questions. Before he can press for more, I smile and back away.

"If I'm going to make it to a lecture in an hour, I'd better get back to shower and get ready."

"You look beautiful," he replies and I think he means it. I wrinkle my nose.

"I've been running," I remind him. "See you later."

And with that, I run away, from the sexy man standing at the edge of the water and the troubling thoughts he's stirred up in my head.

Damn him.

CHAPTER TWO

~Simon~

"Okay, now take a deep breath." I'm sitting on the edge of the stage, watching the women in the room. Some are seated at their tables with their heads down. Some are lying on the floor.

The room is silent, periodically broken by sniffles and soft sobs.

Today's exercise is always a difficult one, for them *and* for me.

"You are magnificent women," I say softly. "You are precious, just like the baby in the basket. You wouldn't hurt that baby. You would comfort her. Hold her gently. Say sweet words to her.

"So why then, do you abuse yourself as an adult? I want you to take another deep breath, and then sit up carefully. Today has been an emotional one. I never said this journey was going to be an easy one."

I smile as the room of women sit up and open their eyes, pinning them to me. Some are full of hurt and pain, and it twists my gut. This is the hardest day of the first week, and I save it for toward the end of the week. It's a lot to take in, and it's quite emotional. We will have a short lecture tomorrow, and then they'll have the weekend to reflect and enjoy some time on their own.

My eyes find Charly, as they've come to do often over the past five days. She's good at hiding her feelings behind her happy hazel eyes and smug smirk, but now she looks a bit haunted, and that's my fault.

"I want you to take the rest of the evening to yourselves. I know I usually encourage you to have dinner together and to talk about the day, and if you want to do that, go for it. But, if you'd rather take time in your rooms to meditate, write in your journals, or just be calm, I encourage that as well.

"You did beautifully today, and I promise you that the pain you feel today is just a stepping stone to where you're going to be a week from now, or even a year from now. Thank you for being brave and for walking through this journey with me. Have a lovely evening."

The room typically erupts into chatter and laughter at the end of the day as the attendees gather their things and leave for dinner, but tonight the room is quiet. I stand and make myself available to anyone who wants to offer me a hug, or ask a question. Before long the room is empty. Todd approaches to take my mic from my ear.

"Today was intense," he says quietly.

I nod. "It always is." I don't know how many times I tried using these same techniques with my ex-wife, trying to help her, to get through to her. But I never could, and it led to our eventual divorce.

So if it helps even one person at these seminars, it's worth every difficult moment.

"I never get used to it," he replies and stows the sound equipment away for tomorrow. "You're changing their lives, you know."

"No, mate, they're changing their own lives; I'm just giving them the tools." I clap him on the shoulder. "I'm not going to dinner tonight. I'm going to spend some time alone."

"I figured," he replies with a nod. Todd's been my friend since childhood and part of my team since the beginning. He knows me well, maybe better than anyone else.

"Have a good night."

"You as well," he says as I walk away. I return to my room to file my notes and pull out tomorrow's file. I toss it on the table and pull my shirt over my head on my way to the shower. I need to wash today off of me.

Rather than dwell on Amy and our horrible past, my mind wanders to a beautiful brunette.

Charly intrigues me. She's stunning, yes, but there's something else there that pulls at me. Her hazel eyes hide plenty, I think.

Then again, I could be an idiot and there's nothing there at all except a pretty woman and my wishful thinking. Although, what I'm wishing for, I have no idea because she's a client and I don't do relationships, so it would do me well to simply forget about her altogether.

The part that surprises me the most is that a woman hasn't turned my head in years. Not like this. I've had moments with pretty girls that ended mutually satisfyingly, but I didn't want to get to know them. Yes, I know that I sound like a sod for saying that, but it doesn't make it any less true.

Yet, despite my better judgement, I want to get to know Charly, not just in a professional way, and that's startling. I've mentored thousands of women, and I can honestly say that this is the first time I've wanted to kiss one so badly it makes me sweat.

I scrub my hands over my face, dress, then pace to the window to look out on the lake. There's still enough daylight left to take the boat out for a short trip. I could use the fresh air.

So, I grab a sweater and head down to the dock, waving at one of the dock workers as I climb into the boat I've rented during my time here and push away from shore.

The air is a bit crisper on the lake. I take a deep breath and glance to my right, surprised to see Charly sitting on a dock with her feet dangling over the side and her face tipped up to the sunshine, as if I conjured her up myself.

She's petite. Much shorter than my six foot three, and she looks like I could pick her up with one hand. Her dark hair is long and straight, framing a gorgeous face with golden-hazel eyes.

Without giving it much thought, I cut the engine and guide the boat to the dock. Charly opens her eyes and watches as I approach.

"You have a boat?" she asks in greeting.

"I rent it when I'm here," I reply with a smile. "Do you like boats?"

She smirks. "I grew up on boats."

Interesting. "Hop on. I'll show you the other side of the lake."

She seems to hesitate for a moment, but then she climbs aboard and I push away from the dock, start the engine, and set off down the lake. She's sitting in the bow, her face in the wind, eyes closed and hair whirling, and just enjoys the ride. We're not going terribly fast, but fast enough that we couldn't have a conversation without shouting, and I think we're both too tired for that.

When I slow down and cut the engine, she looks back at me and grins. "That was nice."

"I'm glad you enjoyed it," I reply and join her in the bow, sitting across from her. "How are you after today?"

"I'm fine," she replies immediately and crosses her arms, but she's not fooling me. Her eyes are sad.

I sit forward and brace my forearms on my knees. "Really?"

She looks back out on the water and swallows hard. "It surprised me."

Here we go.

"How so?"

"I wasn't expecting it to be so personal." She shrugs and looks back at me. Her eyes travel over my face, and I want to scoop her up and cuddle her, but I stay where I am.

"What were you expecting?"

"You don't want to know," she replies with a laugh and shakes her head.

"Try me," I reply.

"Okay," she says and crosses her legs. "I thought it would be a lot of frou-frou *you can do it* nonsense. I don't know, but I wasn't expecting it to be so deep."

"I'm rarely *frou-frou*, darling," I smirk.

"Well, one thing is for sure, it reminded me that Savannah is not ready for this. I don't think she would have survived today. She's a strong woman and everyone thinks that she's doing great, but she's struggling."

"Is that the sister you mentioned before?" I ask, enjoying the way the South sounds on her voice.

"Yes."

"What happened to her?"

Charly sighs and shrugs. "Let's just say that evil takes on many forms, and sometimes it worms its way into your family."

A man.

"Is she your only sibling?"

"God, no." My skin tingles when she giggles. "There are six of us. Three brothers and three sisters."

"That's a large family."

"You're telling me," she says with a grin. "But I love it. We're close."

"Do they all live in New Orleans?"

"They do," she says with a nod. "My daddy built ships, just like his daddy before him and so on. My brothers Eli and Beau and Savannah run the business now."

"They build ships?" She's more fascinating the longer I talk to her.

"Not with their own two hands," she says. "But they run things now."

"That's incredible."

"They're somethin'," she says with a smile. "My daddy would have loved this." She looks back out over the water and to the mountains. "He loved being on the water just about anywhere, but he would have sat here with me and said something profound that I would have rolled my eyes at but appreciated later."

"He's gone then?"

"Three years," she says with a nod. "Too long."

She swallows hard and her eyes are washed in tears, but they don't escape her eyes.

"I'm sorry, Charly."

"Me, too," she says and offers me a small smile.

"You're easier to talk to than I expected. I've said more than I usually do."

"And I feel like you've only scratched the surface."

"The surface is scratched all the same, and that doesn't happen often," she says and runs her fingers through her hair, watching me. "What about you?"

"What about me?"

"Tell me about your family."

"Ah." I sit back and scrub my fingers over my mouth. "I'm an only child."

"Where did you go to college?" she asks, her eyes holding mine. I like that she maintains eye contact during conversation.

"Oxford."

"I called it," she says and leans back with satisfaction.

"You did?"

"I pegged you for an Ivy-Leaguer."

"Where did *you* go to college?" I counter.

"Duke," she replies with a wide smile. "Takes one to know one."

"What did you major in?"

"Philosophy," she says with a laugh. "And I sell shoes for a living."

"I bet it's a bit more than that," I reply, enjoying her. "What are your favorite shoes in the world?"

"My pink stilettos. They're Louboutin. I've had them for five years and if the heel ever breaks on them I'll cry for a week."

"That sounds serious."

"I'm always serious about shoes," she says. "What's your favorite thing?"

This makes me pause and run my finger over my lips, thinking. "I don't know if I have a favorite thing."

"Oh, come on," she says and rolls her eyes. "There has to be something."

This. With you.

"I have an affection for my car."

"What kind of car do you have?" she asks with a raised brow.

"The fast kind," I reply with a grin.

"I have a new car," she replies. "It ranks up there with favorite things."

Before I can reply, she shivers, and I realize that the sun has just dipped behind a mountain, making the air colder. I reach under the seat for a blanket and wrap it around her shoulders, my face inches from hers. All I'd have to do is turn my head and my lips would be on hers.

Instead, I drag a knuckle down her cheek and tuck her hair behind her ear.

"This is the first time my professionalism has ever been tested," I whisper, surprised that the words are spoken aloud.

"What do you mean?" she asks. She licks her lips as she stares at mine, and I feel my blood flow directly to my cock.

Bloody fantastic.

"We should get back." Before I can move, she grips my forearm with her hand, keeping me still.

"What do you mean?" she asks again.

I shake my head, but not answering her is simply disrespectful. So, I clear my throat and cup her cheek in my hand as I look into her eyes.

"You're special, Charly, and I'm quite attracted to you. But you're a client. So I have to keep this strictly business between us."

She narrows her eyes. "Are you telling me that you

take women on your boat, alone, often, and keep it business?"

"No," I reply and sigh. "I'm never alone with clients."

"Breaking rules," she says in that slow Southern drawl of hers that makes me want to kiss the fuck out of her. "But I should remind you that I never said that I wanted you back."

I don't bother to reply; I simply smile and walk away, start the boat engine, and take us back to the resort.

***

"We need to go over some things," Todd says the next morning after I answer my door to him.

"Then you'll need to go for a run with me," I reply shortly. I slept like shit. I couldn't get Charly out of my head, and when I did sleep she was in my dreams.

Naked.

Fucking hell, maybe I just need to get laid.

"We don't have time for a run," Todd says with a scowl.

"You just hate to run," I reply and tie my shoes. "I need it today."

I need to burn off this sexual tension.

"Fine." Todd sighs in resignation.

"Let's go."

We walk through the lobby and out the back door toward the trail that winds around the whole lake. I break out into a slow jog.

Just as we turn a corner, I see Charly walking up ahead toward the clearing where I saw her the other day. I immediately turn the other way.

"Let's go this way."

Todd joins me, but looks over his shoulder toward Charly.

"That brunette, Charly, is a pretty girl."

"Is she?" I ask. *She's not pretty, she's fucking gorgeous.*

"You've noticed," Todd replies. He's already breathing hard and we've barely started.

"You need to run more," I inform him, hoping to change the subject, but without success.

"Did I see you come in from the lake with Charly last night?" Todd asks.

"So?"

"So, I'm just saying, you've noticed that she's pretty."

"Where are you going with this, Todd?"

"Okay, I'm just going to be honest because I can't breathe and don't have the lung capacity to beat around the bush."

"Fantastic."

"I've never seen you look at anyone the way you look at her. Even Amy."

"We don't say that name," I remind him, and wonder just how I'm looking at her.

"It's true," he continues. "And Charly is a beautiful woman, Simon. You *should* notice. I'd worry if you didn't."

"I'm so relieved that you're not worrying."

"You should take her to dinner or something."

"She's a client," I remind him. "This is work."

"Come on, you're a human being, Simon. If you wanted to pursue a beautiful woman, no one would fault you for it."

It's starting to piss me off that he keeps referring to Charly as beautiful. Not because it's inaccurate, but because he's obviously taken more than a passing notice.

"Yes, they would," I remind him. "I'm a public figure. Everything I do is under scrutiny. These *Lift* retreats are successful because we all maintain our professionalism. This is a safe place for the women who attend. I don't fuck with that, and I'll bust your arse if I ever find out that you do."

"I get it," Todd says and holds his hands up in surrender. "But there's nothing that says you can't call her when this is over."

He smiles smugly and I punch him in the shoulder, just for the hell of it.

"Ow! Bugger it."

"Can we talk about the reason we're here now?"

"Fine."

Todd begins talking about seating arrangements and plans for the cocktail party at the end of the retreat. I'm listening with only half an ear.

Starting up something—physical or otherwise—with Charly is impossible, no matter how attracted to her I am. It would be career suicide. And how can I ask the other women here to trust and listen to me, if I'm carrying on with one of their peers?

I'm supposed to be here teaching them. Leading them. Helping them.

Not fucking them into the mattress.

Which is what I want to do with Charly, and only Charly, repeatedly.

"Are you listening?" Todd asks as we approach the lodge.

"No," I reply truthfully. "I'm hitting the shower. I'll see you in an hour."

"You're a pain in my arse!" he calls after me, but I ignore him and march straight to the elevator.

And there she is, already waiting for one. The universe keeps throwing her my way, and I'm not complaining in the least.

"Good morning," I say, panting from the run. My shirt is soaked with sweat, and I can only imagine how I must smell.

"Good mornin'," she says with a smile. "Did you have a good run?"

"No," I reply with a laugh. "Todd insisted on coming with me and he talked incessantly."

Charly laughs and leads the way into the elevator when it arrives. "Which floor?"

"Four."

"Me, too," she says and pushes the button. "Thanks again for the boat ride yesterday. It was nice."

It was bloody amazing.

"You're welcome," I reply and lean on the wall opposite from her, willing myself to keep my hands to myself.

"Is it going to be another long day?" she asks as she leans against the wall, mimicking my stance.

"No. We'll be done by early afternoon."

"Oh, great." She grins. "I told Savannah all about yesterday."

"Really? Did she tell you to pack your things and run as quickly as possible?"

"No. She said it was good for me, but she was glad it was me and not her. So much for sisterly love."

I smile and curse silently when we reach our floor. When the door opens, three women are waiting for the elevator. Their eyes widen when they see me, and I want to roll my eyes.

Many women are not coy when they see a man they find attractive. We'll be discussing this next week.

When they're in the lift and the doors are closed, I

glance down at Charly and smile. "Do you have time for me to show you something?"

"We have to be in the conference room in an hour," she replies, but I can see the curiosity in her eyes.

"It'll be quick. It's the perfect time of day."

"Okay."

I lead her to my room, at the end of the hallway.

"Hey, if you think you can just lead me to your room—"

I turn to her and cut her off. "I said this would be quick, darling. Trust me, if I were bringing you to my room to seduce you, it wouldn't be quick. I'd be exploring you all day and night."

She doesn't act shocked at all. She simply raises a brow and smirks, like she did the first morning we were here. She's all but saying, "Sure. I don't buy it."

So I lean in and press my lips to her ear. "Don't press me, darling, or I'll drag you in here and prove it to you."

When I pull away, the smirk is gone, but the laughter is still in her eyes and I can't help but wonder what I would have to do to truly surprise her.

I open the door and lead her into my room, then grab my binoculars and step out onto my balcony. "I just found them yesterday."

"Found what?"

"Look." I hand her the binoculars. "Look into that tree there, where we saw the bald eagle just the other day."

She raises them to her eyes and is silent while she looks, then gasps.

"Oh my God! She's a mama!"

"She is," I confirm with a grin. "Are they sticking their heads up?"

"They are. Good Lord, they're tiny little things."

"And bald," I reply and have to catch my breath when she looks up at me in wonder, her hazel eyes wide and happy.

This is what surprises her? Not sexual innuendos, baby eagles.

"This place is so cool."

"I'm glad you like it," I reply and take the binoculars when she hands them back to me.

"I need to get in the shower and ready for class."

"Wait." I have absolutely no idea why I don't want her to leave. She *needs* to leave. I shouldn't have brought her in here to begin with.

"What?"

I sigh and shove my hands in my pockets before I do something monumentally stupid, like touch her.

Because once I start, I won't want to stop.

"Nothing," I reply and shake my head. "Thanks for letting me show you."

She watches me for a moment, then shrugs and walks toward the door. "See you in a bit."

"See you."

CHAPTER THREE

~Charly~

"I don't think I've ever seen anything quite like this," Heidi says beside me in the back seat of a Toyota 4Runner as we climb our way into Glacier National Park the next day. I'm in the middle, between Heidi and Violet, another member of Simon's staff. Simon asked Heidi and me to join them yesterday afternoon after class, and I couldn't resist my curiosity to see more of the area.

Simon's driving, and Todd finally shuts the radio off when there is nothing left but static.

"No radio for bears, I suppose," he says with a shrug.

"How big is this park?" I ask.

"Thousands of square miles," Simon replies. "We will just do a day hike today, then head back to the hotel this evening."

"Fun," Heidi says with a grin. "I hike a lot in Arizona. I'm what you would call *outdoorsy.*"

"I'm outdoorsy," I reply with a nod.

"You had to borrow a pair of my shoes," Heidi reminds me with a grin. "You can't wear heels to hike in."

"I'm outdoorsy in that I like to drink on the patio," I

reply, making everyone laugh. Simon eyes me in the rearview mirror and smiles. "Besides, I had my running shoes."

"You're going to like this." Simon winks, and just like that my stomach does that weird flippy thing again that he seems to provoke in me. And when he touches me? Holy bananas, it's intense.

Before long, we pull into a parking lot that's only about half full.

"Are all these people here to hike this trail?" Violet asks.

"Yeah, and there will be more," Todd replies. "This is a popular hike. It's good that we came early to beat the afternoon crowd."

"Well, with lots of people around, there shouldn't be many bears," I say optimistically and laugh when Violet's eyes go round.

"I thought he was kidding when he mentioned bears," she says.

"Nope," Todd says with a laugh. "But don't worry, this trail isn't well known for bear activity."

"Remind me not to go on the trails that are known for bear activity," I mutter to Heidi, making her laugh.

The guys shrug into backpacks, loaded down with bottled water, granola bars, and beef jerky.

"Let's go!" Simon says, his eyes shining like a boy on Christmas morning. This is clearly his thing. I can't get over how different the wilderness is here compared to Louisiana. Of course, there is no swamp here, thank goodness. It's warm, but it's a dry heat, so I'm not immediately covered in sweat. And the trees, these tall, beautiful evergreens, are so close together in some places that you can hardly see through them.

We cross the main road and walk down the clearly marked trailhead to the Trail of the Cedars and Avalanche Lake. The first part of the hike is easy, relatively flat, and gorgeous. Deep green ferns cover the ground, and according to placards along the trail, this is the only place inland from the Pacific Northwest with an active rain forest.

Crazy.

"How are you, love?" Simon asks as he joins me.

Good God, the English and their terms of endearment should have to register with a federal office upon entering the country.

"I'm great," I reply and clear my throat. "This is beautiful. And surprisingly easy."

He smiles and nods. "It's not easy for too long. We'll start up the Avalanche Lake trail in a minute."

I shrug. How hard can it be? If tons of people come here every day to hike it, it can't be that bad.

A few minutes later, we come to the trailhead and read the big sign that describes the hike.

"A five hundred feet gain, over two miles," Heidi reads. "That's not too bad."

"Gain in elevation?" I ask.

"Yes," she replies. "But it's over the course of two miles."

That's not too far. Hell, I walk more than two miles when I shop through the French Quarter. I got this.

"Let's do it," Violet says and smiles widely. She's a pretty woman, much taller than me. She has a lean body, jet-black hair, and eyes that match her name.

We all nod enthusiastically and begin to climb. There's a rushing river to our left, and when we get to the top of a small hill, we stop to watch it rage down through a canyon.

Todd and Simon are talking to each other, but I can't hear them over the loud water. It's cooler in here, under the trees and beside the river, and I just take a deep breath, soaking it all in.

Boy, if my family could see me now. They'd laugh their asses off, and ask where their sister Charly is.

The others begin hiking again, and I fall in behind them, bringing up the rear. Heidi and Todd are chatting away, showing each other photos on their phones, the hike not seeming to bother them at all.

And here I am, already winded. Jesus, I might die up here in the middle of the wilderness.

Simon and Violet are just ahead of me, chatting.

"So you're going back to school in the fall, then?" Simon asks her.

"I am. I took too much time off. I'm ready to be done with it already and start working."

"You took time to find yourself. There's nothing wrong with that."

"Except for the fact that I'm almost thirty and I don't know what I want to be when I grow up," she replies with a laugh, then punches him in the arm. "Unlike you, who seemed to know from the time you were in nappies."

What the hell is a nappie?

"That's not true," he replies, and I can't take my eyes off his ass. I mean, I might die on this trail, but at least this will be my last view. "I was at least sixteen when I decided."

"See?" she says.

"You'll figure it out," Simon replies and pats her on the back. My eyes are drawn to the sleeve tattoo covering his arm. It disappears into his grey T-shirt, and I can't help but wish that he'd take his shirt off so I can see if there is more to it. He's been wearing long-sleeved button down shirts during the classes, so getting a glimpse of the ink is a treat.

"How are you doing back there?" Simon asks and turns to look at me. "Whoa, are you okay?"

"Fine," I pant, ready to pass out. "This is harder than I thought."

"You're bright red," Violet says. "Maybe you should take a break."

None of you need a break. I'm not too proud to admit that I'm just being stubborn, but damn it, I'm not that out of shape. Surely I can handle a two-mile hike.

"I'm fine," I repeat and keep climbing, but finally I sit on a tree lying next to the trail. "Jesus, I can't breathe."

"Go ahead with the others," Simon says to Violet. "I'll stay with her."

"Just take it easy," Violet says with a grin and jogs— *jogs*—ahead to catch up with the others.

"Show off," I mutter, trying to catch my breath.

"We have all day, darling," Simon says and pulls a bottle of water out of his bag and offers it to me. "There's no hurry."

"I don't understand," I reply and gratefully accept the water. "I don't think I'm that out of shape."

"You have a lovely shape," he replies, his eyes suddenly hot. "But there's quite an altitude difference up here, and you're not in hiking shape."

"I run almost every day."

"Probably on a flat sidewalk," he says with a knowing smile.

"Okay, you're right." I take a deep breath, thankful to finally be feeling somewhat normal again and stand.

"Let's keep going."

"We can go back to the car," he offers, but I glare up at him.

"If you think I'm stopping now, you've lost your damn mind."

"My apologies," he says and gestures for me to go ahead of him, a satisfied smile on that handsome face.

The pace is slower now, but it's still up and down. The trail is rough, with loose rock and dirt, making it difficult on my balance. It's kind of like walking through dry sand.

A pain in the ass.

"Talk to me," I say, already beginning to breathe hard again.

"What would you like me to say?"

He's not breathing hard at all.

I hate him.

"Tell me about your tattoos." I take a swig of water. "If you talk, it takes my mind off of wanting to die."

"I won't let you die, love."

There's that love *again.*

"Good to know."

We turn a corner, away from the water. It's quieter now, and just a little warmer, but still pleasant. The terrain continues to dip up and down, which tells me that the trip back isn't going to be any easier than going in.

Damn it.

"I've only had the sleeve for about two years," he says, just as I begin to think that he'll ignore my request.

"That's not long."

"No," he says simply.

"Okay, I'll pull teeth. What made you decide to get it?"

"A woman."

"Ah, yes. A lot of men get tattoos thinking they'll impress a woman."

"Some do, yes, but that wasn't it."

I stop on the trail and take another sip of water. "What was it, then?"

"She scarred me," he replies simply. "And I decided to have the scars covered with the ink." He points to his bicep. "But one led to another, and before I knew it, it covered my arm."

"I think there's a story there," I say finally and lead him further up the trail.

"There's always a story," he says with a laugh. "But that's the gist of it."

And that's all he's going to tell me because the rest isn't any of my business.

"How do you know Todd and Violet?" I ask, wanting to keep the conversation going.

"I've known Todd since I was a boy," he replies. "He's one of my dearest friends, and I trust him implicitly. And Violet is his sister."

"No kidding." I frown. "They don't look much alike."

"No, Todd was adopted," Simon replies. "His wife just had a baby, otherwise she'd be here too."

"Oh, that's so great."

"Do you like babies?"

"Of course. I'm a red-blooded woman in my late twenties."

Simon smiles, a sadness in his eyes that makes me long to ask more questions, but suddenly he looks ahead.

"We're almost there," he says. "You've so got this."

"I sure as fuck do," I reply and push forward with

more confidence than I feel. But suddenly, we walk through a wall of brush and onto a beach.

"Holy shit," I say and stop in my tracks and just let the view wash over me. The lake sits in a bowl, surrounded by tall, jagged mountains. Waterfalls cascade down from the tops of the peaks. I'm surrounded by green and blue and brown, and I'm simply stunned.

"It takes my breath away every time," Simon says quietly beside me.

"I don't know if I believe that it's real," I reply with a whisper. There are other hikers here already, sitting on the beach, or on rocks in the water, soaking up the sun. Children splash in the water.

"Kids made it up here easier than me," I remark, suddenly more embarrassed than before, but Simon nudges my shoulder and shakes his head.

"You did great, Charly. You've never hiked something like this before. We have all day to enjoy the view and regroup before we head back out."

"Thank God," I reply. "I'm going to just go for a walk since we're no longer climbing up a freaking mountain."

"Good. Enjoy it. You won't be able to miss us." He nods over my shoulder and I turn to find Violet and Todd splashing each other in the water while Heidi looks on, laughing and encouraging them.

"I'm glad I came," I say, surprising myself. "I like you. All of you."

"We like you, too," he says and drags his thumb down my cheek. "Are you feeling better?"

"I am." It's the truth, but for some reason, I just need a little alone time. So I smile brightly and back out of his touch. "I won't be long."

I walk in the opposite direction as the others and slip my shoes off, stuff the socks in them, and carry them as I let my hot feet soak in the cold water. It feels amazing, and I don't even have to worry about a critter coming along to take my foot off for lunch.

It's different here. Relaxing. Quiet.

And it's made me long for home. Not the noise or the stress from work and responsibilities, but my family. I think they would like it here. Well, Eli would tolerate it. He's the definition of workaholic, but I remember times when we were kids and we'd splash in the water the way Todd and Violet are now as adults.

I love all of my siblings, but Eli and I always had a special connection. I'm the only one who was ever able to push his extreme serious side away to make him have fun.

Until his wife Kate came along. She's brought out more than any of us ever could. She made him see that while work is important, there are other things more important. He works a little less, and smiles a whole lot more.

I sit on a rock and tip my head up to the sun. I don't know what to do about this weird attraction I have to Simon. He's been professional, for the most part, and hasn't intimidated me at all, but I know that the attraction is mutual. Last night on the boat was intense.

While he was driving the boat, I was pushed back in time to an early summer day with my daddy, also sitting in a boat, floating through the bayou. I must have been about twelve, and it was just the two of us. My dad made sure to spend quality time with each of us kids.

"I like it out here," I said with a smile.

"Of course you do, darlin'." he nodded. "Boatin's in your blood."

"I don't know if I want to help with the business when I grow up," I replied carefully. "I know you love it, but I don't know if I will."

"Well, I think it's good, then, that in this country you can do anything that you choose."

"You won't be mad?"

"Why would I be mad at you for doing something you love, Charlotte? I want all of my children to be happy."

I felt so loved right then. Cherished, even.

"Maybe I'll get married and my husband will want to work for the company."

"Well, that might be so," he said thoughtfully. "But I don't want you to be in a hurry to get married, baby girl. You wait for the right man to come along, who makes you feel safe and respected and loves you like crazy."

"The way you love Mama?"

"That's right," he said with a wink. "I knew she was the one for me the minute I saw her. And you'll know too. So you just wait for that to come along. You won't regret it."

And so I've been waiting for the better part of thirty years to know the minute I see him, and *the one* is still eluding me.

"What is happening in that pretty head of yours?" Simon asks, startling me. I glance around and realize that I've wandered back to where he and the others are enjoying the water and the view.

"Not much," I reply.

"I don't believe you," he says and shoves his hands in his pockets, just like Eli would. He's taken his backpack off, and is standing before me in the grey shirt, shorts, bare feet, and a bit of scruff on his cheeks.

And for some reason, I have no problem confiding in this man, which is brand new to me.

"I was thinking about my family," I reply quietly.

"A bit homesick, are you?"

"A bit," I agree with a nod. "I've been away from home far longer than this before, but this time seems different."

"You're self-reflecting while you're here," Simon says gently. "Of course you're thinking about what matters most to you."

"Why are you so easy to talk to?"

"I like to think it's my charming wit and handsome features."

"Hmm." I narrow my eyes and tip my head back and forth, like I'm thinking very hard. "No. That's not it."

Simon bursts out with a loud laugh. "Come on, cheeky woman. Let's enjoy this view before we head back out of here."

"Oh God, more hiking."

"You're a pro already."

***

"Enjoy your time in town," the shuttle driver says with a kind smile the next day when he drops me off in the center of town.

"Thank you," I reply, tip him, and climb out of the old van and onto the sidewalk. *Town* is tiny, with just a three-block downtown area, but I've been told that there are fun shops and restaurants, and frankly some time away from the hotel, the woods, and Simon is exactly what I need.

I walk into a gift shop and browse around, deciding to get corny Montana T-shirts for the whole family.

Yesterday was exhausting. I haven't slept as well as I did last night since I was a baby. Maybe I should hike more often. It might help my insomnia issues.

It was also hard work, but fun. Heidi made us all laugh with stories of hiking through New Zealand. Todd passed around photos of his new baby. We spent a fun afternoon getting to know each other better.

I'm not sure why, out of the hundred women at the retreat, Simon chose to ask me and Heidi go with him, but I'm glad he did. It was a fun day.

But today, I get to shop, even if it is just for T-shirts with moose on them. The locals are friendly, asking me where I'm from, and then telling me stories of their own about Louisiana, whether they've been there or not.

Finally, I find a cute café for lunch and take a seat at the counter, next to an older man with thinning gray hair and a kind smile.

"You're not from around here," he says.

"How did you know?"

"Well, I know everyone here," he says. "And I surely don't know you."

"You're right. I'm Charly, visiting from New Orleans."

"Never been," he replies. "I just stick around here. I figure, there's not much out there prettier than this."

"You know, I think you may be right again. I've been all over, and this is at the top of my list for beautiful views."

"I'm Charlie, too," he says with a wink and holds his hand out to shake mine. "I recommend the steak sandwich."

"Sounds great." I place my order with the waitress and enjoy an hour of conversation with Charlie while we eat our lunch. "Were you born here, Charlie?"

"No, ma'am," he says. "I grew up in Los Angeles."

This surprises me.

"Moved here in the 60's. Found my Mary here, and raised our kids. Worked for the railroad until I retired about ten years ago."

"That sounds like a beautiful life."

He smiles softly and nods. "It sure has been."

I reach for my check, but Charlie plucks it up before I can.

"Thanks for having lunch with an old man today, Miss Charly. I'd like to buy your lunch."

"I didn't have lunch with an old man. I had lunch with a handsome new friend. Thank you." I reach for my handbag and shopping bags. "How far is the lodge from here?"

"Oh, I'd say it's quite a ways. I can give you a ride if you like."

"No, that's fine. I can use the exercise." *Especially after the hiking fiasco yesterday.* "Just point me in the right direction."

I'm pleased to hear it's not difficult to find and set off on the walk back to the lodge. Dark clouds have rolled in. I hope it doesn't start to rain before I get back.

But, of course, it does. And not just a sprinkle, but a hard, soaking rain complete with thunder and lightning.

Fantastic.

I hold my bags against my chest and jog for what seems forever. I can't see far ahead of me because of the wall of water coming down around me, but I know it's a straight shot, so I don't have to look for a street sign.

Not that there are many of those out here, since we're in the boonies and all.

Shit.

By the time the lodge comes into view, my lungs are on fire and my legs are exhausted and I'm soaked to the bone, shivering from the sudden cold.

Turns out, the weather in Montana can be a bitch.

I push through the double doors and into the hotel and stand dripping. I take stock, realizing with disgust that my silk top is ruined, as are my new Tieks flats.

I trudge toward the elevator with thoughts of a long, hot shower and a hot cup of tea when I suddenly hear, "What in the hell happened to you?"

My eyes close on a cringe, and I turn to find Simon staring at me in horror.

"Got caught in the storm."

"You're soaked through," he says, indignation dripping along with the accent off his tongue, and my back immediately comes up. "How long were you out there?"

"I don't know," I counter. "How long does it take to run here from town?"

"From town?" He's incredulous now. "You went to town alone?"

"Of course I did." I feel ridiculous. I'm standing here, dripping all over the hardwood floors, arguing with the sexiest man I've ever laid eyes on. I glance down and see that my black bra is showing through the ruined silk.

Perfect.

"I'm a grown up, Simon. Now, if you'll excuse me, I need a hot shower and a change of clothes." I turn on my heel and march to the elevator, relieved when I don't have to wait for it to arrive. I make it to my room before I start to shiver and feel tears threaten.

"Good God, Charlotte," I say in exasperation. "This is not worth crying over."

I have visions of that hot shower and tea, so I order room service and make my way to the bathroom for that shower when my phone rings.

"Hi, Van."

"Hey, mountain girl," she says with a laugh. Savannah's laugh was gone for so long that I don't mind hearing it in reference to me. "I have some news."

"Okay."

"Kate's preggers."

"Holy shit! That's great!"

"Well, it is, but she's at the doctor because she started to bleed. It's super early still, so this could be normal, or it could be bad."

"Do you need me to come home? I can pack up now."

"No. There's nothing you can do here. I'm sure she'll be just fine."

"But I really don't mind—"

"No way. I'll keep you posted."

There's a knock at my door. "Okay. I have to go, Van. I'll call later, okay?"

"Great."

We hang up and I answer the door, earning weird looks from the room service kid when he delivers my hot tea and cookies.

A girl deserves cookies after the day I just had.

I shut the door behind him, but before I can turn away, there's another knock, so I open it, expecting it to be the same kid, but it's Simon.

"I didn't mean to treat you like a child," he says, and my eyes fill with tears, completely pissing me off. "Hey, I'm sorry, love. I was just taken aback when I saw you and I was worried."

"I'm not crying."

"Okay." He steps inside and wraps me up in a big

hug, rocking us back and forth. His lips are on my head, and this could be the safest I've felt since I was a child and my father held me the same way. "What's wrong, darling?"

"I'm cold and wet and embarrassed. And my sister-in-law is pregnant, but she's bleeding, and Van doesn't want me to come home, and I'm worried."

"Shhh, love. It's okay."

It's so not okay, but damn this feels good.

"Why don't you go take that shower, and I'll fix you some tea?"

"Okay." I sniffle, mortified that I'm crying in front of him.

"How do you take your tea?"

"Lots of sugar," I reply.

"You got it." He steps back and waits silently as I gather some fresh clothes and walk into the bathroom. I lean my forehead on the closed door and take a deep breath before stepping into the shower. What is wrong with me? I never cry. Ever. I'm just going to chalk it up to being exhausted from yesterday's hike and today's wet run.

The hot water is heaven, and when I emerge ten minutes later, I feel better, but so tired. I really just want to curl up in bed and go to sleep.

I walk out of the bathroom and find Simon standing with his back to the room, looking out at the lake. My tea is steeping. One of the cookies is gone.

I might let him live.

"Do you feel better?" he asks without turning around.

"Yes." I step toward him. "Thank you."

"Don't touch me." His voice is perfectly calm, but his body is tense. "If you touch me, I won't be able to keep my hands off of you, and I'm going to keep my hands off of you, Charly."

I don't even know what to say to that, so I just stay where I am, staring at his broad shoulders.

"I didn't like the thought of you being out in the storm alone and something happening to you. I didn't like it at all."

"Okay."

"And I've worked for a long time at not giving a fuck."

I blink in surprise, not sure where this is going, exactly. He finally turns around and stares at me for a long moment. His face is sober, but his eyes are intense, almost tortured.

"But you give a fuck." It's a whisper.

"I give a fuck," he replies softly. "And I don't know what to do about that."

"Maybe there's nothing to be done." I'm leaving soon. I'm never going to see him again after this trip.

"Maybe." He crosses to me, stopping just short of touching me and stares into my eyes. His hands don't reach for me. Instead, he takes a long, deep breath and walks around me. "Drink your tea. Good night."

And, with that, he's gone.

What in the world?

I take a sip of my tea and sigh in happiness. It's exactly sweet enough, and just the perfect temperature.

Simon does tea well. Of course, he *is* British.

I grin and reach for my phone, wanting to hear Van's voice again.

"Miss me?" she asks.

"Madly. Have you heard anything?"

"Yes, I just spoke with Eli. Kate's fine. The doctor

said that this sometimes happens in early pregnancy, and she should be great."

"Good." I sit on the edge of the bed, relieved. "And you're sure that I shouldn't come home?"

"I'm positive. Everything is fine. Are you okay?"

"I cried in front of him," I say, surprising myself. Van laughs on the other end of the phone, and I sit here and wonder who the fuck I am.

CHAPTER FOUR

~Charly~

"I'm so damn hungry," Violet says the next day during our lunch break. She, Heidi, and I are at the restaurant in the hotel, waiting for our orders. "Who knew that thinking so damn hard could burn so many calories? No matter how many of these retreats I come to, it always surprises me how exhausted I am at the end of the day."

"I hear you," I reply and long for the burger I just ordered. "I've eaten more since I've been here than I do when I'm working a sixty-hour work week."

"It's all of this emotional stuff," Heidi adds. "I'm really looking forward to the dating advice later in the week."

"That's a fun day," Violet replies with a knowing smile. "Simon gets lots of crazy questions."

"I bet," I say with a giggle. "Women can be nutso."

"You have no idea," Violet replies. "I won't tell stories because that's a breach of privacy, but Simon has seen and heard it all."

"Is that Shelly chick still bugging him?" Heidi asks, and I remember the incessant flirting from Shelly that first night at dinner.

"No, she actually went home after Friday."

"Really? Why?" I ask, surprised.

"Because she finally realized that this wasn't a way to get a date with Simon," Violet replies. "But that's just between us."

"I don't know, Simon looks at Charly like he's interested," Heidi says, looking at me thoughtfully.

"He does not," I reply immediately and smile when our plates are set before us. "God, this looks good."

"Yep, that's how he looks at you," Heidi says.

"How?"

"The way you're looking at your burger."

We all crack up and dig in, sighing in delight. "So good," I say around a huge bite of burger and fries. "I should have ordered two."

"Back to the subject at hand," Violet says, ignoring my bad manners, "I think Heidi's right."

"Trust me, I have way more lust for this burger than Simon has for me."

"Whatever," Heidi says, rolling her eyes.

"Besides," I continue, "he's made it clear that this is strictly professional, and I already know that he's not right for me."

"You already know that?" Violet asks.

"Yep. I always know." And it's not just a little disappointing that I haven't found the right one yet.

"Now, this is advice I need," Heidi says and leans in. "Because I always choose badly. How do you know?"

"I can tell in the first five minutes if a man is *the one.* And trust me, Simon isn't him."

"How in the hell can you tell in five minutes?" Heidi asks.

"I just can," I reply with a shrug. "Sometimes it's based on the clothes they wear, or what they do for a living, or their opinion on food."

"Oh Lord," Violet says and laughs. "You can't be serious."

"Of course I am," I reply. "These are all deal breakers for me. And, Simon is out of the running based on geography."

"Now I'm intrigued. Do tell," Heidi says.

"He's international, and I live in New Orleans. It would never work."

"So, just like that, he's out." Violet nods. "Okay. How many times have you found *the one* based on this theory?"

"None," I reply with a frown. "But I'll know it when I do."

Heidi starts to speak, but my phone beeps with an incoming text from Eli. It's a picture of an ultrasound with the caption *You're gonna be an aunt again!*

"Look! My brother just sent me this. His wife is pregnant." I show the photo off proudly. "It's the most beautiful baby ever."

"Yep, it's a blob," Heidi says with a laugh. "I have three of my own, and they all started just like this. Congratulations."

"Thanks. I'm going to step out on the deck and call him really quick. I'll be right back."

"Take your time," Violet says with a smile. "We're in no rush."

I nod and dial Eli's number as I step out into the summer sunshine.

"Hello, Aunt Charly," he says.

"Hi, Daddy," I reply with a giggle. "Congratulations,

Eli."

"Thanks. We had a bit of a scare, but everything's okay."

"Van told me. I'm so happy that Kate's okay and that we're going to have a new bebe to love on soon."

"How are things there?" he asks, his voice serious again. "Are you learning anything valuable?"

"I'm learning all kinds of things," I reply. "And you sound like Dad."

"Well, that's good because I'm about to be one," he says. "Holy shit, Char, I'm gonna be a papa."

"You're going to be an amazing father, Eli. You're a wonderful man. This baby is lucky."

"Okay, let's not get too touchy feely here."

I roll my eyes.

"You're okay?"

"I'm okay," I reply, meaning it. "I'm enjoying it more than I ever thought I would, but don't tell Van. I'm going to let her think that she made me come against my will for a while longer."

"Women are mean."

"You beat your brothers up every day at lunch."

"That's called martial arts, and a workout," he replies easily. "Not the same."

"Whatever. Kiss Kate for me. I'll see you next week."

"Be safe, darlin'."

I end the call and look at the ultrasound again, smiling widely. There's a little baby coming to join our family soon. I can't wait!

"Is that yours?"

I spin to find Todd standing behind me.

"Sorry, didn't mean to look over your shoulder, but that's hard to miss."

"No, it's fine," I say with a laugh. "It's definitely not mine. It's my brother's. His wife is pregnant, and he sent me this to tell me."

"Excellent," Todd says, his accent as thick as Simon's, yet not quite as sexy. "Did you know that the baby is the size of a peanut right now?"

"Did you know tidbits like that during every phase of your wife's pregnancy?"

"Hey, I did my homework," he says with a wink. "Congratulations."

He pats my shoulder and walks away, and I gaze down at the photo one more time.

I love you, little peanut.

***

I'm late. I *hate* being late.

Despise.

Loathe.

It's my biggest pet peeve in life.

And here I am, struggling into my shoes as I yank my shirt over my head, no time to blow my hair dry, so it's in a bun on top of my head, and I have no makeup on.

My alarm didn't go off this morning, and I overslept. And I never oversleep. What is happening to me?

Just as I'm about to dash out the door to class, my phone rings, and like an idiot, I hit accept rather than ignore.

This is *not* my day.

"Hello?"

"Hey, beautiful," Ryan says with a sing-song voice, making me stop in the doorway.

"What's up, Ryan? I'm in a hurry." *And I don't ever want to talk to you again.*

"I was just thinking about you. I haven't seen you in

a while. Where have you been?"

"Remember when I told you I was going to a retreat for two weeks? These are those two weeks." I roll my eyes. Ryan rarely paid attention to details that didn't affect him.

"I didn't realize you were really going to that," he says, annoyance heavy in his voice. "I thought we said it was a silly thing to go to."

"No, *you* said that." I check the time. "What do you need, Ryan? I'm late for class."

"I want to see you," he says simply.

"You want to fuck me," I reply.

"Yes."

"No." I shake my head and sit on the edge of the bed. Who cares if I'm a couple minutes late?

"No? Are you seeing someone?"

"I don't have to be seeing someone else to say no to you," I reply, my voice strong. "But no, I'm not. However, *you* are."

"You must be mistaken."

"Nope. I'm not. I heard your conversation with Pamela, Ryan. You don't like me, but you like to fuck me. And if I remember correctly, you were going to call me and break it off for good. Which you didn't do. But let me just save you the trouble."

"No, there was no reason to call because I broke things off with Pam." He sounds panicked now. "There's no reason for us to stop seeing each other, Char."

"Yeah, there is." I sigh and shake my head. "You don't even like me, remember?"

"That wasn't true, baby."

God, I'm weak when he calls me baby like that. And he knows it. Bastard.

"Either way, I'm done, Ryan. It's time for both of us

to move on."

"Let's talk about this when you get home," he says soothingly. "Don't make any rash decisions."

"Whatever. I'm late. Goodbye." I hang up, turn my ringer off, and hurry out of my room. I'm *not* going to let him talk his way back into my pants again. I was okay with the friends with benefits thing, but I'm not okay with the *just benefits* thing. No way.

I rush into the room, already quiet, and cringe when a few people glance over my way. I hurry to my seat next to Heidi and get settled as quickly as I can.

"Are you okay?" she whispers.

"No alarm," I whisper back.

"You haven't missed anything yet," she says.

Simon isn't looking at me, which is good. It would only make me more uncomfortable. He's walking across the stage, talking expressively with his hands. He has a mic attached to his ear, so his hands are free, and I love watching him speak. He's an excellent public speaker. He's calm, comfortable.

Sexy as all get out.

"So, we're going to take a bit of a detour today, ladies. We've spent the past eight days talking about self-esteem, goals, how to achieve those goals, networking, etc. Today we're going to talk about your love lives."

"It's about time!" Someone calls out from the audience, making us all smile.

"Some portions of today are going to be fun, and others will be uncomfortable. That's okay. You can ask me anything, and I'll do my best to answer your questions."

Hands are thrown into the air, but Simon holds his own hands up in surrender.

"Hold off on the questions for a bit. First, I'd like to

speak a bit about expectation and self-worth."

For an hour Simon works the stage, reminding us all that we are worth so much more than what we're willing to settle for. Questions are asked and answered, and I sit here all the while, listening and getting angrier by the minute.

"If you don't want to be a side piece, or a friend with benefits, don't *settle* for that from any man." Simon is passionate as he repeats what he's been driving home all day. "If you want a man to be devoted to you, and to love you unconditionally, you have to do that for yourself first."

For the better part of ten years I've been involved with a man who didn't even *like* me. He just liked the sex. Because seriously, the sex was great. But now, as I sit here and listen to Simon talk about not settling for less than you deserve, I realize that this is exactly what I've been doing all of my adult life.

It's been my choice. I knew that until I found *the one*, I was content with casual relationships. But at the same time, it makes me feel cheap. And so fucking mad. At Ryan, at myself, and even at Simon for bringing all of this shit up.

Just before class is over for the day, I gather my things and leave. I can't listen to it any more.

"Charly!"

I stop halfway down the hall to the elevators and see Violet hurrying to me.

"Are you okay?"

"Peachy," I reply. "I need to be done with today."

"This wasn't fun for you." Her eyes are concerned and she pats my shoulder, and that's all I can take.

"No." My voice is flat. "It wasn't fun. I'll see you

tomorrow."

And with that I turn and rush back to my room. I want to call Ryan and scream at him, tell him that he can go fuck himself from now on, and how dare he treat me like something he can just throw away? He doesn't have to love me. I don't love him either.

But damn it, he sure as hell should have respected me.

I sit on my balcony for a while, silently fuming while I watch birds swoop through the air, a flock of ducks swim across the lake, and the sun hide behind clouds, then poke back out again.

How did I not see it? Am I too easy to trust? Or was I just blind, and assumed that he felt the same way that I did? Maybe I didn't read between the lines during the times apart. My arrangement with Ryan worked for me because I'd consumed myself with work and family for so long, I wasn't ready for anything more serious than friends with benefits. But I should have asked more questions. I should have paid more attention.

And maybe I'm being a little hard on myself and Ryan is just an asshole.

After a while, there's a knock on my door, and I know exactly who it is. He couldn't have come after me with a hundred women looking on, and I wouldn't expect him to.

Hell, I don't expect him to come after me at all.

Because as he's said over and over, this is just professional, and I already know that he's not the one for me, and the chemistry is just science.

Science is a bitch.

I stay where I am, rocking in my chair, even when he knocks again, and then for a third time.

"Charly! Open up."

And just with those three words, I'm all pissed off again. So I march to the door and swing it open, glaring at him.

"You don't have the right to be demanding with me."

"You don't have the right to lock me out," he counters.

"Fuck yes, I do." I stand on my tiptoes and stick my finger in his face. "You're not my boyfriend. You're not even my *friend*. You're a man that I know, that's it."

"That's not it," he says, beginning to breathe hard.

"Just because you give a fuck, doesn't mean that I owe you anything. Didn't you just lecture a whole room full of women about just that?"

He pushes his fingers through his hair and paces away, then turns back to me.

"I just want to—"

"And where do you get off, anyway?" I interrupt, pacing around the room myself. "Your life isn't all roses. *You're* single!"

"Charly—"

"If you know everything about dating, why aren't you doing it?" He props his hands on his hips and narrows his eyes on me, but I'm on a roll. "Are you one of those *do as I say not as I do* kind of people, Simon? Because I don't see you with a ring on your finger."

"You're bloody pissing me off."

"Yeah, well, I've been bloody pissed all bloody day," I reply and cross my arms over my chest. "And I don't even know why you're here! You keep repeating, like a broken record, that this is strictly professional and you're not going to touch me, and blah blah blah, which is perfectly fine with me, mind you. But then you go out of your way to be nice to me. Or maybe you treat all of the clients like this."

"You know better than that."

"I don't even think you *like* me very much." *Just like Ryan.*

"What in the hell are you talking about? Of course I like you. I can't fucking stay away from you!"

"That's just chemistry," I reply. "And trust me when I say that I've had my fill of that. It doesn't mean anything other than my junk likes your junk."

Now his lips twitch, and I can't decide if I want to kick him or kiss him.

Let's go with both.

"You haven't seen my junk, love."

"And what in the world is up with all of the *love* talk?"

"It's a term of endearment. Now you're just being difficult and stubborn."

"Well, that's who I am, Simon. I'm difficult and stubborn, and I'm no one to use terms of endearment on because *I mean nothing to you.*"

His nostrils flare as he marches toward me, letting the door slam behind him, and the next think I know, I'm in his arms and his lips are on mine. His hand glides up my back to fist in the back of my hair. He tips my head back to more easily assault my mouth, and I'm consumed by him.

Mercy, the man can *kiss.*

He whirls us around so he can boost me up against the wall, supporting me with his pelvis and the hard cock still confined in his pants.

His very impressive cock.

My hands are everywhere, in his hair, over his

shoulders, his back. I want his clothes off, *now.*

I grip the hem of his shirt and tug up. He leans back long enough for me to lift it over his head and throw it on the floor, and I'm stunned. The tattoo on his left arm covers the ball of his shoulder. I lean in and place a kiss there, where it ends, then bite his neck gently.

"If you're going to bite, fucking bite," he growls, and I comply, sucking the skin in my mouth and biting hard.

"Jesus," he groans and lifts my chin to devour my mouth again. He nibbles the edge of my lip before kissing me deeply. His hands are pressing into my ass firmly, most likely causing bruises on the skin.

I can't wait to see them later.

"I want you," he whispers against my ear then licks my earlobe. "I want you right now, and I'm bloody done with denying it."

"Yes," I pant, trying to catch my breath. I'm as out of breath as I was when we hiked the mountain, but for an entirely different reason.

He grabs my hands and pins them above my head, grinds his cock against my already wet center, and I'm about come undone from that alone.

I'm not even naked yet!

"Tell me you want it too."

"I do." *God, I do.* The fact that I haven't been with a man in forever is of no consequence. I want *this* man. Right now.

His hand dives down my pants and he cups me over my panties.

"Jesus, you're soaked."

"This is a little hot," I reply and think frantically which panties I'm wearing.

"A little?"

"Maybe more than a little."

"Love, this is about to get a *lot* hot. If you're not okay with that, say so now, because I'm about three seconds from being inside of you."

"Well, get on with it already."

CHAPTER FIVE

~Simon~

God, she makes me crazy. Her smart mouth, her firm body, the way she clenches my hair in her fists while I kiss the hell out of her. All of her.

And I want more.

I lower her to the floor and begin to strip her out of her clothes, not giving a fuck where I throw them. She's making quick work of mine as well, and when we're finally naked, I grab the complimentary condom on the wet bar, boost her onto the large bed, and cover her, my cock hard and pulsing. But I don't push inside her.

Not yet.

"We can't use that condom," she says, suddenly grinding everything to a halt.

"What do you mean?" I lift up, staring down at her, panting.

"I'm allergic."

"You're allergic?" Jesus, I keep repeating everything she says, but I have a serious lack of blood flow to the brain right now.

"Bad things happen down there when condoms are involved." She bites her lip. "I have an IUD, and I was with the same man for a long time. I haven't been with anyone else in months."

I narrow my eyes and take a deep breath.

"Trust me," she says, "this is no psycho trap or anything, I just don't want to deal with an uncomfortable crotch for the next week."

I chuckle and cup her face in my hands. The crazy thing is, I *do* trust her, and I haven't trusted a woman in a very long time.

"I'm clean," I say finally. "I'm very selective, and I see the doctor regularly."

A slow smile spreads over her lips.

"I thought you said you'd be inside me in three seconds."

"I was mistaken," I reply as I spread her wide and kiss her core, suck her lips into my mouth, then lick up to her clit and grin in satisfaction when she cries out and arches her back, grips the back of my head, and pulls me tighter against her, grinding herself on my face.

I love that she knows what she wants and isn't afraid to take it.

I can't stand it anymore. I press wet kisses up her torso, cover her mouth with mine, and slip inside her to the hilt. I want to stop and enjoy the wetness surrounding me, but her hips arch and I can't resist setting the pace, fast and furious, pumping in and out of her with frustration and pure lust.

She pushes on my shoulders, and I grip her ass and flip us and she begins to ride me like a woman possessed. She's breathing hard, her cheeks are flushed, and she's biting her swollen lips. She's planted her hands on my chest for leverage as she rides me, clenching that pussy around my cock each time she pulls up, and I swear to

God my eyes are bloody crossed.

Her tits are small with hard pink nipples just begging for my mouth, so I lift up and suck on one, then bite it and turn my attention to the other.

"Jesus," she groans, those hands in my hair again. "So good."

"Mm," I reply and grip her ass again, guiding her up and down my cock. I've never been so damn hard.

"Gonna come," she says and bites my earlobe. Hard. "Gonna come."

"Do it," I urge her and press my thumb to her clit just as she begins to spasm around me. "Go, love."

"Fucking hell," she groans and succumbs to her orgasm, clenching onto me with every muscle in her body. Fuck me, she's magnificent.

Just as she begins to come down, I reverse our positions again, pressing her back into the mattress and start to truly fuck her. Hard. Fast. Until I find my own release and crash to the bed beside her, out of breath and trembling.

"Fuck me," I whisper.

"I think I just did," she replies and pushes her fingers through my hair. I open one eye and find her watching me.

"So you did."

"Are you regretting it yet?" she asks, a smile on her lips, but her eyes are serious and vulnerable.

"Not even a little bit," I say and pull her against me, tucking her head under my chin. "That was magnificent, and I've been fighting it for nearly two weeks."

"That's a long time," she says, sarcasm heavy in her voice, and I slap her ass, then rub it in circles.

"You have quite the mouth on you."

"You have no idea," she replies. "But you might. If you play your cards right."

I chuckle and roll her onto her back again, content to lie over her and kiss her leisurely now, exploring her lips, rubbing my nose against hers. She smells fantastic.

And without the makeup she usually wears, she's stunning.

"What are you thinking?" I ask.

"I'm trying not to think," she counters and drags her hands down my back to my ass. "There will be time for that later, and this is too nice."

"Agreed." I glide my knuckles down her cheek. "I should go, but I'm going to be a selfish arse and say that I want to stay."

She bites that lip again before smiling and wrapping one leg up over my hip, and damn if I don't get hard again.

"Stay," she whispers.

"Are you sure?"

"Yes." She yawns and stretches under me, so I climb off of her, tuck us under the covers, and pull her against me. I haven't wanted to stay with a woman since my divorce, and I shouldn't stay now. But I don't want to leave her. This feels too good.

"Let's sleep for a bit, love."

"I don't know why I'm so tired," she says and nuzzles my chest, then kisses my tattoo and I'm amazed how my feelings for her can go from white-hot lust to tender in under two minutes.

"We just had quite a workout."

She smirks, but before long she's breathing long and slow in slumber, and to my surprise, I feel my own eyes close and I drift to sleep right behind her.

***

It's warm in here.

And someone is sucking on my rock-hard dick.

I come fully awake, blinking in the darkness. We must have slept for hours, because the room is dark and the full moon hangs high above the lake outside. Charly flung the covers off of both of us, and she's currently sucking my cock like a champ.

Holy shit.

"Charly," I murmur and rub her shoulders firmly, making her purr and sending vibrations through me that make me tingle.

And I've never been one to tingle.

It seems this is a night of firsts: first time I've slept with a client, first time to tingle, and certainly the first time to be pulled out of slumber by a blow job.

Her lips are firm, moving up and down, her hand working me as well. Suddenly she presses my cock to my stomach and licks down to my balls. I fling myself back to the bed, arch my back, and wonder what I did to deserve this.

To deserve her.

Because I'll gladly do it again and again, every day, for the rest of my life if this is the bloody result.

Holy fuck, Charly Boudreaux can suck cock.

She licks me again, back up to the tip, and in the moonlight, I watch her hazel eyes peer up at me as she bares her teeth and skims them over the rim.

"Fucking hell," I growl as she smiles and soothes the skin with her lips, then bites the shaft, gently, but with teeth all the same. "You like to get rough, don't you love?"

"Sometimes," she replies with a shrug, then sucks me all the way into her mouth, swallowing around the head and I can't stand it anymore. I have to touch her. I grip her head in my hands, careful to not hold on too tightly, and pump my hips, fucking her mouth in the perfect rhythm to send me over the edge in about six-point-four seconds.

"Gonna come, Charly."

"Mm," she replies, but I slow down so I can pull out, conscious of not coming in her mouth. She grips my hips and resists, sucking even harder, and I can't help it, I explode spectacularly, harder than before, and I didn't think that was possible.

She gently kisses my spent cock, my hips, my lower stomach, then smiles up at me.

"What was that for?" I ask, still panting and feeling as though electricity is shooting through my entire body.

"I woke up, and you're sexy, and—" She shrugs. "I just wanted to."

"I'll never complain about that," I reply with a smile, throwing one arm over my head. "I'll return the favor as soon as I catch my breath."

"No need," she replies and curls up next to me.

No need? Fuck that.

"Oh, there's a need, sweetheart," I reply and push her onto her back. I don't kiss my way down her delectable body. Not yet. Instead, I brace myself above her and kiss her forehead, her cheeks, her nose, and then make my way to her neck.

"That's one of my sweet spots," she says with a sigh. I nibble her there, and smile when she giggles. When I lick her from collarbone to earlobe, she sighs and circles her hips involuntarily. Her small hands are on my arms, kneading them, clenching them. Her nails will leave crescent marks on the skin, and I don't care.

I worry one nipple into a pebble, then kiss it, and before she can gasp, I flip her over, her stomach flat against the mattress and kiss her neck and shoulders.

"Oh God," she says and clenches the sheet in her fist.

"Another sweet spot?" I ask before nibbling my way down her spine.

"So far, everywhere you've kissed me is a sweet spot," she replies with a smile.

"Well, let's find some more." I drag my hands down her back to her hips. "Arch your ass up."

She complies, and I spread her perfectly firm cheeks open and kiss her pussy, loving the way she smells. She arches back further, crying out, and my thumb finds her clit.

"I can't do this," she says.

"You can," I reply calmly and bite her arse before returning to her core and sucking her lips into my mouth.

She comes apart beautifully, grinding herself against my face, mewling and moaning, and damn if she's not the sexiest woman I've ever met in my life.

She's gasping for breath and has gone limp.

"Can't move," she says.

"There's no need to." I kiss my way up her back and lie next to her, dragging my fingertips over her soft skin. "You have amazing skin."

"It's pretty thick," she says, then giggles, but I frown down at her. Finally, she opens her eyes. "What?"

"Why have you had to develop such a thick skin?"

"Oh gosh, for a thousand reasons, Simon. Being a woman is reason enough. I'm here for your seminar for a reason."

How did I almost forget? For a brief moment, she was just a beautiful woman in my bed, and the rest of it, the seminars and fame and money that go along with it, didn't exist.

But it *does* exist. And it's the reason she's here.

It's the reason we're both here.

"Are you okay?" she asks as she cups my cheek in her palm.

"Never better," I reply with a reassuring smile. "I really should go back to my room so we can both get some sleep before tomorrow's class."

"I can't believe it's the last day already," she replies, ignoring the part about me leaving. "It was a quick two weeks."

I take her hand in mine and kiss her fingers. "Thank you for coming here, Charly. I'm so happy that I met you."

"Is this goodbye then?"

"No," I reply and shake my head. It should be. But I know I'll seek her out tomorrow. "I'll see you tomorrow in class, and then at the cocktail farewell party."

"I might skip that," she says and bites her lip.

"Don't." I hate that it sounds like a plea. "I would love to dance with you."

"Okay. I'll stay for the party."

I grin and kiss her nose, then leave the bed while I still can. I pull my clothes on, thankful that my room is on the same floor and the chances of anyone seeing me leave her room are slim.

"Good night."

She raises up on an elbow, the sheet wrapped around her and her long dark hair falling over her shoulders, and I know that I've never seen anything more beautiful than she is right now.

"Good night."

***

The party is in full swing.

One hundred women are dressed to the nines, enjoying free drinks and music, a photo booth, and each other.

They've accomplished so much this week, and this is their reward. They get to unwind, relax, and have fun.

The music is booming, and I've been dancing non-stop, from woman to woman, spinning them around and thanking them for being here.

This suit is too warm, and all I want is to hole up in my room, alone, for about a week. I can speak to any room of people, and have, from twenty people to twenty thousand, but at the heart of it, I'm an introvert and this two-week seminar exhausts me.

Not to mention, I spent the majority of last night with Charly.

Which I'm definitely not complaining about.

Speaking of the sexy woman, I haven't seen her yet this evening. I hope she didn't change her mind and leave before the party.

I've reached the edge of the room, and as I twirl a pretty blonde in my arms, dip her, then set her back on her feet and turn away, I spy Charly standing by the wall.

Suddenly, the music, the other people, everything is gone and all I can see is her. She's in a curve-hugging black dress that plunges in the front showing off her cleavage. The hem ends just below her knees.

And the red fuck-me heels she's in make me want to sink to mine.

I cross to her, my hands in my pockets so I don't do something stupid like pull her in and kiss the fuck out of her in front of all of these people.

"Hello, Fred Astaire."

I grin. "I don't care if I'm bad. I like to dance."

"No one ever said you had to have rhythm to dance," she agrees and her gaze skims over the room. "Looks like the party is a success."

"You're stunning," I reply, happy that the music is loud enough that no one else can hear. "And I want to strip you out of that dress and fuck you senseless."

Her eyes flare and she licks her lips, then offers me a smile.

"I think that would be frowned upon right now."

"Later then," I reply.

"I'm sorry." She shakes her head, glances away. "I can't. I'm leaving in just a bit."

"When?"

"In a couple of hours. I just came by because I told you I would and I wanted to say goodbye to Heidi and Violet." She turns her eyes back to me. "And you."

"Charly—"

"Hey, no hogging him," a woman named Cheryl says and grabs my arm, pulling me back out onto the dance floor. I want to pull away, but Charly just shakes her head, smiles, and walks away. My eyes follow her as she walks through the room and out the door, and suddenly my stomach just aches.

She's gone.

"I'm sorry to interrupt," Todd says, smiling at Cheryl, "but I need to steal him away for a minute."

I smile at the woman and follow Todd outside where it's a bit quieter. Women are clustered in small groups, chatting and taking selfies. I wave at them as Todd leads me to a private area, then turns on me.

"You let her walk away."

I glance around to make sure that no one is listening.

"What would you expect me to do, mate? She has to go home, and I have to go back to London on Monday."

"You're being an idiot. I've never seen you look at *anyone* the way you look at her. Go after her. Ask her to stay the weekend. Spend some time with her when you don't have to keep it a secret."

"It makes no difference if we say goodbye now or in two days, Todd."

But fucking hell, I hate it.

"Take two days to enjoy yourself. You're a bloody workaholic and you deserve it. If you don't, I'll beat you to a pulp myself."

"Right." I blow out a breath and shove my hands in my pockets. The truth is, I'm not ready for her to leave. I would love nothing more than to spend the weekend with her, and Todd's right, I don't remember the last time I took two days to myself.

"I can't bail on this party."

"Yes, you can. You've been dancing with them for over an hour. Say something profound the way you always do, then cut out. Go catch her before she leaves."

I nod, and hurry inside, take the mic, and signal for the DJ to cut the music.

"Hello, you gorgeous women!"

The applause is deafening, and I motion for everyone to quiet down.

"This has been an amazing two weeks, and I can't tell you how monumentally proud I am of each and every one of you. Thank you for your hard work, and your dedication. Thank you for your honesty, and for keeping an open mind.

"Most of all, thank you for trusting me and my staff

this week. I will never take that trust for granted. Don't forget to check your email in the coming months for exclusive webinars just for you. Now, you've all bloody exhausted me, so I'm going to say good night."

They applaud again and I'm met with hugs and thanks as I make my way out of the ballroom. It takes me almost fifteen minutes to get to the elevator, and I'm practically running when the doors open and I make it to Charly's door.

She's still here. The *do not disturb* sign is on the door. Did she leave that there for me, expecting me to follow her?

Well, too bad. She should know better than to think that a simple piece of paper could keep me away.

I brace my hands on either side of the doorjamb and take a deep breath. I don't know if I'm hopeful that she doesn't turn me away, or that she does. Because let's be honest, this is not a good idea.

But, for this week, anyway, that doesn't seem to stop me.

So I knock three times and wait, still leaning into the doorjamb. Just when I'm about to knock again, the door swings open and I'm knocked back on my heels.

Holy Mary, mother of God.

She's taken her dress off, so she's standing before me in a black bra, black panties, and a mother fucking garter belt with stockings.

Her hair has been brushed out and is wild around her shoulders, and her face scrubbed clean.

"I hope you were expecting me, and not answering the door looking like that for room service."

A slow, satisfied smile spreads over her beautiful face.

"What do you need, Simon?"

CHAPTER SIX

~Charly~

That shell-shocked look on Simon's face does wonders for my ego. His lips are moving, but no sound is coming out as he takes me in from head to toe. I knew it was him at the door. He's the only one who would knock with a *do not disturb* sign.

And maybe I wanted to get this reaction out of him. I *am* a woman, after all.

"What can I do for you?" I ask again and cock my hip to the side, my hand propped on it.

"You can let me in before anyone else sees you like this and I have to kill them."

I roll my eyes and step back, letting him into the room, then close the door behind him.

"You always seem to catch me when I'm on my way to the shower." I walk past him and toss him a sassy look over my shoulder. I know what I look like from behind, and the look in his blue eyes is incredible for my ego.

"Lucky me," he says, swallowing hard. "You're packing up then?"

"I am." I toss my dirty jeans, folded nicely, into my

suitcase. "And you still haven't said what you came up here for. I'm sure the others are missing you."

"I don't care," he replies. His voice is rough, pulling my gaze away from the blouse I'm folding. "I want you to stay."

I knew it.

Of course I knew it.

I sigh and shake my head. "Simon, let's not do this. It's hard enough as it is. Just let me go."

"I'm not ready for you to go."

"What does it matter if I leave tonight or tomorrow when the others are?"

He lifts a brow and shifts his gaze to the bed. "I think you know the answer to that, Charly. But that's not what I mean."

"Awfully presumptuous," I mutter to myself and turn to face him again. "Okay, what do you mean?"

"Stay the weekend. I'm here until Monday evening. Stay until then so we can enjoy each other without the retreat happening at the same time. I want to be with you without any distractions or restrictions."

"I have to be in my shop Monday morning," I reply and bite my lip, trying to think of a way to make it work. I don't want to go either, but staying will only mean that I'll become more attached to him, and I don't want that either.

"Talk to me, Charlotte."

"Okay, I'm going to be brutally honest." I square my shoulders and prop my hands on my hips, and Simon's blue eyes immediately fall to my girls. I'd almost forgotten that I was standing here mostly naked. "I'm up here, Simon."

"Sorry," he replies with a self-deprecating smile. "Go

on."

"I'm not looking for something long term with you, Simon."

"I believe I suggested a weekend, love." He smiles when I glare at him. "Sorry."

"I'm not looking for something long term. But I'm not thrilled with the one-weekend stand either. You've taught me a lot this week, and even though it pissed me off, one of those things is that I've settled for the whole "friends with benefits" thing my whole life, and honestly, I've lied to myself."

"How so?" Now his eyes are glued to mine, listening intently.

"Because I always said that it was on *my* terms, so it was okay. I was content with that until I met the one that I'd be with forever. And I believed that."

"But you don't believe it now?"

"I don't know," I reply, frustrated now. "The sex with you is great, Simon. I won't pretend otherwise. But what you're suggesting is basically that we'll fuck all weekend and then go our separate ways."

"That's not what I suggested," he says and shakes his head. "You didn't listen well on the day about communication."

"How am I wrong?"

"I asked you to stay. You assume that means that all I want is a weekend of sex."

"I just told you that I don't want something long term."

"Bloody Jesus," he mutters and paces my room, rubbing his mouth with his fingers. "Sex doesn't have to be a part of the equation."

"Right." I snort and cross my arms. "Because we're so

not attracted to each other. You've undressed me with your eyes at least a dozen times since you've been in my room."

"It's not a difficult task, darling; you're practically naked already."

"Granted." I nod and sit on the edge of the bed. "So you just want to hang out all weekend?"

"Why not?" he replies and shoves his hands in his pockets. "I've enjoyed talking with you and spending time with you. I want more of that."

"And no sex," I reply dryly.

"If you prefer it that way," he says with a shrug. "I want nothing more than to fuck you for days, but if that makes you uncomfortable, we can take it off the table. I'm not an asshole."

"No," I agree and watch him for a moment. "You're not."

"I'll pay to have your ticket changed," he offers.

I bite my lip and consider him. I can call and let the pilot know that I won't need him for a couple more days, but I don't feel comfortable yet telling Simon that I have access to a private jet, so I just shake my head and reply, "That's not necessary."

"Is that a yes?"

"I have to leave Sunday afternoon so I can be at work on Monday. I've left my shop for too long as it is."

"Did you buy the red heels you were wearing tonight at your shop?"

"Of course."

He grins, a wide Cheshire cat smile. "Charly?"

"I'll stay." And I'll enjoy every minute of him, then go home and move on.

"Excellent." His eyes are hot as they travel over my

body.

"Sex doesn't have to be off the table." I smirk and stand, facing him. "I'm not a teenager. Let's enjoy the weekend. But don't play mind games with me, Simon."

He scowls and takes my hand in his, then raises my fingers to his lips. "It hurts my heart that you've had the kind of past experience that makes you need to give me that warning."

Oh God, this could be a bad idea.

The butterflies are back in my stomach and I feel my cheeks flush with pure lust. The things this man does to my body are *insane.*

"There's no love here," I reply softly. "But there will be respect and honesty, or I'm out the door."

"Deal," he says. "Both ways."

"Of course."

He slowly sinks his fingers into my hair at the nape of my neck and leans into me. "Thank you, Charly."

"Thanks for the invitation. Are we going to keep separate rooms?"

"Hell no," he says with a grin. "We'll move you into mine."

"Why yours?"

"Because it's bigger, and I'm staying longer than you."

"Good reasons." I can't breathe with him this close to me. He could have suggested that we'd be staying in a yurt and I would have agreed. "Should we move in now?"

"Fuck no, we're going to take that shower."

***

"You are a popcorn hog," I accuse Simon as we leave the movies the next evening. We saw the latest Marvel superhero movie, which I love.

"I am not," he replies and takes my hand as we walk out to the car. He's very affectionate and chivalrous, which is new to me. He always holds my hand, opens doors, and a whole host of other manners that I didn't even know existed outside of my own family.

He's dangerous for me, because I can't have him and I feel more for him than I ever did Ryan. Or for anyone, now that I think about it.

"You ate plenty of the popcorn," he continues.

"No, I just stopped putting my hand in harm's way. I thought for sure you might take it off."

"Okay, drama queen," he says with a laugh. "What now?"

"I have a sweet tooth," I reply. "Let's stop somewhere for dessert."

"My pleasure."

We find an ice cream place in town that's open late, so we stop in and each order a sundae, then find a table to enjoy our treats.

"What does cupcake ice cream taste like?" Simon asks me as he spoons up his chocolate.

"Here." I hold my spoon up to his lips and watch as he takes the bite and nods.

"Good."

"Yeah." I clear my throat and shift in my seat. "You have a sexy mouth."

"Keep talking like that," he says and takes another bite of his own ice cream. "I dare you."

"You dare me?" I raise a brow. "What will happen if I do?"

"I'll take you out to the car and suck your clit until you come all over my mouth," he replies without looking up from his ice cream, as if he's talking about the damn weather. "You're sweeter than this ice cream."

"God, Simon." Hello, wet panties.

"I won't warn you again," he says and meets my gaze with his.

"Tell me about your parents." I offer him an angelic smile and lick my spoon, changing the subject.

"Muriel and Charles Danbury," he replies.

"Are you close to them?"

"Very," he says. "They usually come with me to these seminars, but Mum recently had a knee surgery, and Dad is nursing her to health."

"How long have they been married?" Finished with my ice cream, I set the cup aside and lean on the table, resting my chin in my fist and listening to the British in Simon's voice.

"Thirty-three years."

"They had you quickly." I smile and watch the warm smile come to his face.

"And I was a handful. I was a sickly child." He pushes his own cup away and leans on his elbows. "I had apnea issues as a baby, so I was in the hospital for three months."

"You stopped breathing? That must have been terrifying!"

"I'm told it was." He nods and reaches for my hand. "Mum was always a stay-at-home mother when I was little, so she stayed at the hospital full time with me and Dad came around his work schedule."

"What does he do?"

"Aren't you the curious one?" He grins at me and keeps talking. I love his voice. "He's retired now, but he was a professor at university. After I went to high school, Mum went back to school as well to become a teacher, and she just retired last year from teaching primary school.

She retired early so she could enjoy it with Dad."

"That's awesome," I reply and rub the back of his hand with my thumb.

"Sometimes, when they join me on these trips, my dad will take one of the afternoon lecture sessions and teach it himself. He gets a kick out of it."

"I think it's wonderful that you include the people closest to you in your business."

"There's no one else I'd rather have with me," he says. "They're the ones I can trust implicitly."

"I can understand that. I have a small staff at the store, and I'm finally confident in who I have working for me. But it was a process. I had girls steal from me, girls who were lazy, girls who couldn't show up to work on time. A strong work ethic isn't necessarily ingrained in everyone the way it was in me and my siblings."

"No, it's not," he agrees with a smile. "And once you've been burned, you get very protective."

"Trust is hard to replace once it's gone," I add. "It's harder for Eli, Beau, and Van."

"How so?"

"Well, the shipping business is much bigger than my shop, and they deal with betrayal all the time. Just a couple of years ago, Eli's wife, Kate, was *poisoned* by a coworker."

"No way," he says, his blue eyes wide.

"It's the truth. The coworker didn't want to get caught embezzling funds, and she knew that Kate has a peanut allergy and fed them to her. It was horrible."

"What is wrong with people?" he asks with a frown.

"You're the expert. You tell me."

"I'm no expert on sociopathic behavior," he replies with a laugh. "But I can talk about self-esteem and flirting all day long."

"And you do," I say with a nod. "It's not rough, listening to you speak."

"I should hope not. Women invest a lot of time and money to do so."

"The information is good. And the package it comes in is also good."

"They do not come to see me just because they think I look good."

I cock a brow and smile at his obvious discomfort.

"I believe it was Shelly who went home a week early when she discovered that this wasn't a way to get in your pants."

When I realize what I've said, I dissolve into giggles and Simon looks on with a wide grin.

"You're funny."

"It's just ironic, is all."

"Shelly had no chance in hell," Simon says and kisses my hand. "And that doesn't happen often. Some women do flirt, but on the whole, they're just nice people who need help in certain areas of their life, and they come here seeking that help."

"It's a great thing that you do." Now it's my turn to kiss his hand. "When Van has had a chance to heal a bit, I'll recommend she come."

"If she's anything like you, she's stronger than you give her credit for."

I sit back, surprised. "What a lovely compliment."

"It's the truth."

I blink at him for a moment, then stand and throw our cups away. "Come on. Let's go for a walk around the lake."

"After dark?" he asks.

"Don't worry. I'm strong. I'll protect you."

***

"We haven't moved from this bed all day."

"That's not true," Simon says and drags his large hand down my back to my ass, then grips it tightly. "We stared at the baby eagles for an hour this morning and I answered the door four times for room service."

I stare dubiously at all four of the trays on the table by the window. "We should call someone to come get those."

"I figure we'll just order more food soon, so what's the point?" He plants his lips on my head and hugs me tight.

I'm afraid I've gotten used to all of this affection. Simon gives good hug.

"I should get up and start getting ready to go."

It's been hanging over me like a cloud all day. Each time I look at the clock, I count the hours that I have left with him.

Now it's only two.

Suddenly, I'm flipped onto my back and he's hovering over me, his arms flexed and strong next to my shoulders. His pelvis is cradled against mine, and my hands happily find their way down his spine to his rock hard ass.

God, his ass is ridiculously amazing.

"What are you thinking?" he whispers.

"I like your ass," I reply and watch with wonder as his face lights up. It does that a lot when he looks at me. "I'm not much of a deep thinker."

"I don't think that's true," he says and rocks his hips, making my eyes cross. He's growing against me and I can't wait to feel him inside me again.

"What are *you* thinking?"

"I'm thinking—" he presses his mouth to mine, but rather than kiss me, he just rests here, barely touching me, watching me. "That I'm going to make love to you right now, and then I'm going to spend the rest of the afternoon pampering you."

"That sounds nice," I reply, enjoying the way his mouth tickles mine. I feel him reach down to protect both of us, then he rears back and slips effortlessly inside me, then stops when he's buried balls deep. "God, you feel good."

"You feel bloody amazing," he says and leans back so he can brush my hair off my cheeks. His fingertips lightly dance over my skin. "You're beautiful."

I clench around him and arch my hips, but he doesn't pick up the speed.

"We always take things fast," he says and kisses me again. "But this might be our last time together, and I'm going to take it soft and slow, love."

My eyes want to fill at the thought of this being our last time, so I close them and bite my lip as he begins to move in long, slow strokes.

"You are simply breathtaking," he whispers. "Open your eyes, Charlotte."

I comply, relieved that the tears have passed and now I'm simply caught up in him, his body, his voice, his incredible eyes.

"You are amazing," I say and cup his face in my hands. *You're so much more than the sex.* But I don't say it, I just kiss him and am caught up in this unbelievable wave of lust and affection, and before long I have the most intense orgasm of my life.

"Fucking hell," he groans against my lips and falls

apart with me. We hold each other tightly for a long moment, and then without a word, he rises from the bed and walks into the bathroom. Before long, I hear the bathtub start and he comes back into the room wrapped in a robe and holding a smaller one out to me. "Follow me."

"*Now* you want me to be modest?" I ask with a laugh, but he just smiles.

"Trust me."

I do.

I shrug into the robe and follow him into the bathroom. The tub is filling with a delightful aroma of lilacs.

"There aren't any bubbles."

"It's oil, not bubble bath," he replies, but turns to me. "Would you prefer bubbles?"

"No, this is great. It smells wonderful."

"Have a seat." He points to the vanity chair, and I comply. "Face the mirror."

"You're terribly bossy."

He just cocks a brow, and I do as he asks. He moves up behind me and brushes my hair out as we wait for the tub to fill. I haven't had anyone else brush my hair since I was a child.

Well, my hairdresser doesn't count.

"You're good at that," I comment.

"You have pretty hair," he replies. When it's brushed thoroughly, he pulls it up into a knot on top of my head. "There, it won't get wet."

He's so thoughtful.

He takes my hand and leads me to the tub. He opens the belt and parts the robe, and lets his hands duck inside to tease my breasts and glide down my sides before slipping my robe off my shoulders.

He hangs it on the hook behind him, then turns and helps me into the tub.

"Oh, this is nice."

"Is it too warm?"

"No, it's perfect." I sink down and let out a deep sigh of contentment. We've had a lot of sex this weekend. That coupled with the walks around the lake and my muscles are weary.

This bath is exactly what I needed.

I close my eyes and lean back, listening to Simon bustle about the room, and the next thing I know, he's lathered up a washcloth and is dragging it over my body.

My eyes fly open to find him sitting on the vanity chair at the side of the tub, still in the robe.

"You're not joining me?"

"No, this is just for you."

I don't understand him. I've never known anyone so selfless. It almost makes me feel guilty, and that's something I'm going to have to think about later.

"You're good with a washcloth."

His lips twitch as his eyes follow his hand over my body.

"Tell me about the scars on your arm," I say.

"I already did when we were hiking."

"No, you told me the Cliffs Notes version."

He scowls, but he begins talking.

"My ex-wife was a difficult woman."

Ex-wife? I had no idea he'd been married.

"I won't get into all of her issues, because I'm enjoying this time with you and I don't want to fuck it up. The gist of it is, I found her fucking a friend of mine—"

I gasp.

"And when I told her that I'd be filing for divorce, she went crazy. Attacked me, and managed to drag her nails down my arm before I got her off of me."

"Holy shit, Simon."

"That was a while ago."

"When?"

He stops washing me and looks in my eyes. "Three years."

"Before all of this uber success?"

"Yes," he says and sighs. "The success has really only happened in the past year or so. It was a surprise to me, honestly."

"I told you last night, you have a good product, and a handsome package. I know, I've seen it." I grin, and he tweaks my nipple as punishment.

"Cheeky girl." He grins. "What I mean is, it happened fast. I went from giving small workshops in London to large seminars in the US, TV appearances, my own radio show, a bestselling book, and more."

"That's an impressive resume."

"I'm glad that the drama with Amy happened before the career exploded because I don't think I could have done both."

"You've done great," I reply with a smile.

"Thank you."

Finally, when he's done getting me nice and clean, and I'm both relaxed and turned on all over again, he leads me out of the bath and dries me off, wraps me back in the robe, and leads me to the bedroom.

Where a massage table has been set up.

"How in the world did this happen?"

"I arranged it," he replies, as if it's just that simple.

Then again, in Simon's world, it probably is.

He takes the robe again and motions for me to lie face down on the table. I don't know how long I lie here, but he takes his time massaging every inch of me, then flips me over and repeats the process until I'm a pile of mushy goo.

But then, his oily hands slip between my legs and he takes me for the most delicious ride. His movements are fluid, firm, and before I know it, I'm having an intense orgasm.

"Wow, so that's what a happy ending feels like."

He grins. "You're welcome."

"I'm going to be late."

"Stay. Just a bit longer. I'm sure you can fly out later this evening."

I drag my hand down his arm; my fingers glide over the scars there. "Well, I *am* hungry."

"I'll order room service."

"We might as well add another tray to our collection."

"There's that work ethic again."

CHAPTER SEVEN

~Charly~

"You look like shit," Gabby, my youngest sister, says as she leads Van and Kate into my shop just after opening the next day.

"I didn't get much sleep," I reply. That's an understatement. I didn't get *any* sleep. I just walked off the plane an hour ago.

"Well, we went to your place last night," Van says. "But you weren't home."

"Do *not* tell me that you were with Ryan the second you got back to town," Kate says.

"I wasn't. But enough about me." I rush to Kate and pull her in for a big hug. "Congratulations, sugar. I'm so happy for you."

"Thank you." She grins and rests her hands on her still-small belly. "We didn't think I could have kids you know."

"Well, it just proves that miracles happen," Gabby says then turns back to me. "So where were you last night?"

"Do you want the exact address?" I ask and turn away

to pull shoes off the wall. I'm going to build a new display today.

"You texted me Friday night to say that you were going to stay in Montana for the weekend," Van says and leans on my glass countertop.

"You're going to leave prints on that," I say.

"Answer the question," Van says.

"You didn't ask a question."

"Why did you stay?" Kate asks.

"Who is he?" Gabby asks gleefully.

"It was a women's retreat," I remind them.

"They have guys that work for them," Van says. "I've watched the videos and stuff."

"You totally got laid recently," Gabby adds.

"And her suitcase is back here!" Kate calls. I didn't even see her walk into the stockroom.

She's a sneaky one.

"Wait." Van holds her hands up and stares at me with shocked eyes the same color as mine. "Simon. You hooked up with Simon."

"I didn't say that."

"You're such a bad liar," Gabby says with a laugh. "You totally did."

"Maybe."

"Oh. My. God!" Van rushes to me and grips my shoulders in her hands. "Spill it. I want to know all of it. When is he coming to visit?"

"Why would he come visit?"

"Duh. Because you hooked up."

"Trust me, he's not coming to New Orleans." I shake my head and get back to work on the wall. "We had a good time. But it was just this weekend."

"Spill it," Kate says.

"I don't want to tell you every detail," I reply truthfully. "But he was awesome, and we had a good time. And now it's over."

"How did you leave things?" Gabby asks.

Awkward. Weird. Sad.

I stayed all night, agreeing to "change my flight" to super early this morning so I could squeeze every second I could in with him. And this morning, he walked me downstairs to the airport shuttle, hugged me close, kissed my forehead, and said, "Goodbye."

"Well, can you call him if you want to?" Van asks.

"We didn't exchange numbers," I reply and shrug.

"Why not?" Kate asks.

"Because it was just for the weekend," I remind them all. "There was no need to exchange numbers when we're never going to see each other again." Neither of us even brought it up, and I was fine with that.

I told myself I was fine with that.

"But what if you're traveling and you're in the neighborhood?" Gabby asks.

"Not. Seeing. Him. Again." I throw my hands up and walk a circle around my shop. "You guys aren't listening."

"We hear the words," Van says gently. "But your eyes are sad and you just look…*sad*."

"I'm fine." I grin and square my shoulders and make sure the sad is hidden well. "I learned a lot."

"I want to hear about that stuff too," Van says.

"You should go to one of the retreats," I reply. "I think it would be good."

"I'm going to sign up for later this fall," she replies. "And maybe I can get his number for you."

"You know what your problem is?" I ask as my door bell rings with an incoming customer. "Your problem is that you're all too romantic. You think romance should just happen to everyone."

"Nothin' wrong with a little romance," the customer says as she joins us in the salon. "Sorry, I overheard."

"That's okay," I reply with a smile. "I'm Charly."

"Mallory," she replies and waves at all of us. "Mallory Adams."

"Are you visiting?" Gabby asks.

"No, ma'am. I own the herb shop a few blocks over. I've been dying to stop in here. I need shoes for a wedding in a few weeks."

"Is it the shop over by Jackson Square?" I ask.

"Yes'm." Mallory is beautiful with blonde hair and green eyes, a curvy body. She's not much taller than me.

"I've been in that shop!" Kate says excitedly. "I shopped in there when I lived above you for a few months. But you had long black hair then."

"I remember now," Mallory says. "Yeah, I like to change things up with my hair."

"Well, I love your store."

"Thank you. I wish I still had you living upstairs. The guy who moved in not long ago is a pain in my ass."

"Really?" We all grin at her with delight. "What's he like?"

"I've never actually seen him, but he's constantly complaining. He's gone most of the day, but in the evenings, if I'm processing new herbs and such, he calls down to complain about the smell. I mean, it's an *herb* shop! What does he expect me to do?"

"Sounds horrible," Gabby says and hides her mouth behind her hand to chuckle.

"And he's always accusing me of making all kinds of noise in the middle of the night. I *do* sleep. It's not my fault that the place is haunted."

"Haunted?" Kate asks, swallowing hard. "It's haunted?"

"Oh, for sure," Mallory confirms.

"How do you know?" Gabby asks.

Mallory bites her lip and shrugs. "I've just heard things too."

I don't believe her.

We all look back and forth between each other.

"What am I missing?" Mallory asks.

"Nothing important," I reply. "I think it's my brother that's living above you."

"Nothing important?" she repeats and shakes her head. "I just basically called him a jackass right in front of you."

"Well, Beau *can* be a jackass," Gabby replies. "So it's okay."

"I lived in a haunted apartment," Kate says, still stuck on the previous conversation.

"It's okay, sugar, she's not a bad ghost." Mallory pats Kate's shoulder. "Ah, you're going to have a baby."

"How do you know that?" Kate demands with wide green eyes. "I've only told my family."

"I'm sorry," Mallory says, but she smiles and pats Kate's shoulder again. "I just know things sometimes. It's going to be a beautiful baby. You don't have anything to worry about."

We're silent for a moment, and then Kate breaks down into tears and hugs Mallory tight. "Thank you."

"You're welcome."

"I want to hear more about the ghost," Van says.

"Let's talk about that while I show you some shoes," I suggest, happy to have the focus off of me. "How does that sound?"

"Sounds great to me." Mallory focuses on Savannah and her eyes are suddenly sad, but almost before it was there, it's gone again and she smiles widely. "You're an interesting group."

"You have no idea," Gabby says with a laugh.

***

"I can't believe I let you set me up," I say into my phone two weeks later.

"Who better to set you up than your brother?" Eli asks. "Your favorite brother."

"We'll see how you rank in brother status after this date," I reply and smirk. "And seriously? His name is George? Is he ninety?"

"No, he's thirty, and you can't decide you don't like a man based on his name."

"Clearly you've never tried to date me before," I say. "I could decide I don't like him because his fingernails are too long."

"Well, of course. That's disgusting." I hear Eli chuckle on the other end. "George is a good guy. Call me later and let me know how it goes."

"Okay," I reply with a sigh and hang up, check myself in the mirror, and decide that the purple dress with white accents is a good choice for a first date. It's not too tight, but it's flirty around the hem, floating around my knees.

And the lime-green heels make it perfect.

I smooth on some lip gloss and walk the few blocks from my house to a pretty café where George said he'd meet me for dinner. I haven't been there in a while, but the last time I was there the atmosphere was casual and the food delicious.

When I turn the corner and the café comes into view, I'm not disappointed. It hasn't changed. And standing on the sidewalk is a tall man in a suit. He has dark blond hair and blue eyes, not quite as blue as Simon's.

Stop comparing every man you see to Simon!

"You must be Charly," he says as he approaches. His smile is warm and when he takes my hand in his, he's gentle.

"Guilty," I reply. "George?"

"That's me. I've heard good things about this place."

"I like it," I confirm and walk ahead of him inside. After we've been seated and ordered, he grins at me. "So how do you know Eli?"

"I work with him," he says. "I am the head of his marketing department."

"That's interesting," I reply, already encouraged by George. He's handsome, has clean fingernails, and a great sense of style. "How did you get into that?"

"I was originally an art history major," he replies with a laugh. "But I soon realized that appreciating art wasn't going to bring home the bacon."

"Enjoying art isn't a bad thing," I point out and smile at the waitress when she delivers our food.

"It is when you have an affection for old cars and love to travel," he replies and stares down at his sandwich. "This is huge."

"That's what she said," I reply immediately, and we both laugh. I like him, but he's definitely not for me even though he's a nice guy, and I'm enjoying myself.

"So tell me about your little store."

My teeth clench at *little store.* "I own a shoe store in the Quarter called Head Over Heels."

"My sister has told me about that store," he replies

and shoves some chips in his mouth. "She loves it in there."

"I'm glad. I like it too. How do you get that much food in your mouth?"

I should be horrified, or at the very least insulted that his manners are so horrible, but all I can do is laugh. He's funny.

"Talent," he replies with a wink. "Sorry, I was hungry."

"I have three brothers," I remind him and shrug. "I've seen worse."

"And this is just the first date. Just wait."

Oh, I don't think there will be a second date. He's good looking, but my brain is screaming *Abort, abort!*

He's not the one for me.

"How did you come to own a shoe shop?" he asks.

"I'm a shoe-whore," I reply and lean over to slap him on the back when he coughs on his food, then he breaks down in laughter.

"I hear that acknowledging you have a problem is the first step."

"Oh, I have a problem, and I don't plan to ever fix it. I knew I didn't want to go into the family business, and I love shopping. Few things beat the look in a woman's eye when she finds a pair of shoes that she loves. Sometimes, it's better than sex."

"Really." He sits back and smiles at me, but there is no spark in his blue eyes. "Well then, I'd say they weren't having sex right."

"Or the shoes are just amazing," I counter and take a sip of my sweet tea. "That's basically it. I just love shoes."

"Not a bad reason to start a business, I guess."

"I don't think so either." I push my plate away and

order the peach cobbler when the waitress arrives.

"I'll have the same," George says.

"So tell me about your family," I say, leaning on my elbow.

"I have two sisters," he replies. "My mother passed when we were kids. Dad lives in Florida now in a retirement community. He loves it. Golfs all day, plays bridge in the evenings with friends. It works for him."

"Are you close to your sisters?"

"Not really." He shrugs, as if it doesn't mean anything, and there's just one more reason that he's not the one for me. "We don't *not* get along, but they have families of their own, and I don't see them often."

"I see."

"But from what I can tell, you're close with your family."

"Very. I don't know what I would do without them."

George smiles and takes a bite of his cobbler and we fall into silence as we eat our dessert. Finally, when the dishes are cleared, he leans over and takes my hand, and I feel…*nothing.*

"You're not really feeling this, are you?" he asks.

"I'm sorry, George. You're a nice guy, and you're handsome, but I just don't think there's any chemistry here."

"Whew," he says and leans back in his chair. "I feel the same. I'm glad you said it first. But I do like you."

"I like you too, but it's more of a friends thing for me."

"Sounds good," he replies with a decisive nod. "Just friends."

"And just to be clear, not the friends with benefits kind of friends," I add firmly.

He sits back again and studies me for a moment, then shakes his head.

"I don't usually have sex with my friends."

I cock a brow, not a little surprised. George is simply a nice, normal guy who's grown out of the fuck-buddy phase.

"What are you thinking?" he asks with a smile. "You have a funny look on your face."

"You're like the Easter Bunny."

"Excuse me?"

"You're just a nice guy. No gimmicks. No strings. An adult man who doesn't have to sleep with a woman to be friends with her."

"Okay."

"I've never seen one of you in the wild," I explain and smile when he bursts out laughing again. He has a great sense of humor.

"Your brothers seem to be the same."

"Yes, but I wouldn't consider dating my brothers."

"Good plan."

George reaches for the check.

"I can pay for mine."

"Even if we're not going to date again, I'll still pay for this one." He winks and passes his card to the waitress. "It was a pleasure to meet you, Ms. Boudreaux."

"Likewise."

***

It's late and I can't sleep. Rather than going to the shop after my date with George, I came home to get caught up on housework and filing. I would rather be in the Quarter, with the noise and activity always happening there. It's too quiet in my house.

But that's not why I can't sleep. I'm too busy

thinking about a certain sexy British motivational speaker.

I miss him. It's really that simple.

And I'm sure that if I sent an email to Violet through the website, I could ask for his number, or ask her to pass along a message.

But why would I do that? Nothing long term can work out for us. The distance would kill me, and we said goodbye in Montana. Besides, if he wanted something more with me, wouldn't he have tried to contact me by now?

No, I won't humiliate myself by trying to contact him. We didn't exchange numbers, and stalking him is just... desperate. I need to concentrate on forgetting him altogether.

And I definitely need to stop comparing every man I know to him. That's just not fair, to them or to me.

My phone rings, making me jump.

"What's wrong?" I ask immediately. "Is it Kate?"

"No," Eli replies. His voice sounds tired. "I've been waiting up to hear from you."

"Why?"

"Because you said you'd call."

I pull the phone away from my head and stare at it for a second. "I'm almost thirty, Eli."

"I know, but I set you up with this guy, so I want to know."

"First of all, I'd like to remind you that you set me up with a man named *George*."

"Is there a list somewhere I don't know about full of names that you don't like?"

"And second, you set me up with someone who works for you."

"So? Half of New Orleans works for me."

"And third, what kind of update did you want? Did you want to hear about the earth-shattering, chandelier-breaking sex we had?"

"Now you're just trying to piss me off. I told him not to touch you."

I pinch the bridge of my nose and pray for more patience than I was born with.

"You set me up on a date, but told the guy he wasn't allowed to touch me?"

"Of course. I'm your brother. Ben might have threatened him too."

"Great." I sigh and sit up in my bed. "Well, you'll be happy to hear that he was a gentleman. He's a nice guy, but there was no chemistry."

"I see."

"And Eli? Don't try to set me up anymore. It's too weird. What if you set me up with someone I actually want to have sex with, but he's terrified of getting beat up? That's not sexy."

"I didn't try to set you up with someone sexy," he replies.

"Exactly. But I love you for trying."

"I just love you, Char," he says and tears fill my eyes. Why am I so prone to crying these days? Damn feelings.

"I love you too."

"I know you're a little lonely, and I know that you work too much."

"Takes one to know one," I murmur.

"Exactly. And now that I have Kate, I just want you to be as happy as we are."

"Someday," I reply. "Daddy always told me that I'd know him when I saw him."

"I don't believe in that love at first sight bullshit."

"Why not? It happened for Mom and Dad and they were together forever, and they were blissfully in love every day."

"Blissfully?" Eli chuckles. "They loved each other, but I think there were days that Mom would have happily killed him."

I frown and wonder if Eli remembers the same parents that I do. "You're wrong."

"No one has a perfect marriage, Charly. That's not realistic."

"I don't need perfect," I reply. "I just need perfect for me."

"He'll come along."

"Yes, but you don't have to deliver him to me."

"You're so ungrateful," he says with a smile in his voice. "Get some sleep."

"You too. Love you."

"Love you."

CHAPTER EIGHT

~Simon~

"Is this the first night without the baby?" I ask Kelly and Todd as we sit down to dinner in one of our favorite restaurants in London.

"I wish you'd brought her," Violet says with a pout. "I haven't seen her in days."

"Well, it's the first night Todd and I have been away from her together, so this is a treat," Kelly replies and takes a deep breath. "I missed you all while you were in the States. Todd filled me in, but did the two of you have a good time?"

"Montana is always beautiful," I say and set my menu aside.

"So was a certain—"

"Well, hello there."

All four of our heads whip up to see my ex-wife standing near our table with a smirk on her undeniably beautiful face.

"Hello, Amy," Kelly says, always the peacekeeper. "How are you?"

"I'm wonderful," Amy says and tosses her blonde hair

over her shoulder. "Aren't you going to say hello to your wife, Simon?"

"Ex wife," I reply and offer her a cold smile. "Hello."

"It's so nice to see the old gang together," Amy says, her eyes turning cold when they land on Violet. "I've missed my friends."

"We're not your friends," Violet says, her hand balled in a fist on the table. There's no dramatic, sordid history between the two; Violet just hates Amy. Passionately.

"I see." Amy turns her attention back to me and sets her hand on my shoulder. Her touch makes my skin crawl. I would shrug her off, but I don't want to cause a scene, and with Amy, things could escalate to horrific display in a matter of seconds. "How are you, darling?"

"I'm good."

"Simon's great," Violet says. "His business is growing by leaps and bounds. Didn't you see him on the telly recently?"

Shut up, Violet.

"No, I must have missed it. I did hear about your book hitting the New York Times."

"Six weeks in a row," Kelly adds, raising her glass in salute.

"Most of his television appearances have been in the US," Violet says, nodding. "That could be why you missed them. You should look them up on YouTube. He's become quite the sensation."

"That's enough," Todd says quietly to his sister. "Have a good evening, Amy."

"Well." She clears her throat, her gaze still on mine, and then as if she's gathering herself, she puts on a dazzling smile for the group. "Yes, I should join my friends. I don't want to be rude."

"Too late," Violet says and waves goodbye as Amy walks away. "I hate her."

"Rubbing Simon's success in her face doesn't do anyone any good," Todd says immediately.

"It was really more of a *he's doing much better without you* dig," she clarifies and takes a long gulp of her wine.

Todd and I share a long look. He's the only one in the world who knows everything about my tumultuous relationship with Amy and what she put me through during our marriage. The others just know how it ended, and that's bad enough to make them want her to suffer.

"How can you *not* gloat a bit to that bitch?" Violet asks.

Because the result would be far worse than just ignoring her.

"Because she's not worth it," I reply with a shrug. "She's not even on my radar anymore."

"So let's stop talking about her," Kelly says. "I'm baby-less, with some of my favorite people and I don't have to make a bottle or change a nappie. So tell me more about Montana. Were there some fun women there this time?"

"It was a great group," I reply before Violet can, making her scowl at me. "It was fantastic."

"Simon met a girl," Violet announces as quickly as she can between my comments. "That's the most important thing."

"Remind me again why we bring you to these things?" Todd says, rubbing his temple. "You're a pain in the arse."

"No, this is important, and you seemed to leave it out," Kelly responds, watching me with surprised brown eyes. "Who is she?"

She's the most incredible woman I've ever met in my life.

"She was a client," I say instead and wince. "I'm not proud of that part."

"I know you," Kelly says with a shake of the head. "You didn't flaunt it in front of the others, and you were professional as well. I doubt you have anything to be ashamed of."

"She's right," Todd agrees, surprising me. "You were discreet and Charly is great."

"Her name is Charly?" Kelly asks. "Tell me more about her."

"She lives in New Orleans where she owns a shoe store."

"My kind of woman," Kelly says with a wink.

"She's funny, and strong, and we enjoyed each other while we were there."

"And that's it?"

"That's it."

"He's a stubborn arse who won't call her," Violet says, shaking her head at me.

"We didn't plan to see or speak again," I reply, my gut twisting. I didn't realize how much I would miss her.

"What did you think of her?" Kelly asks Violet.

"Oh, we got along brilliantly. She has a strong loyalty to her family, and she's definitely smart. She wasn't showy or pushy, just a nice girl who we would be friends with."

"How lovely," Kelly says. "I think you should call her, Simon. Just the mention of her name makes your face soften. You deserve to have some happiness in your life. You work harder than anyone I know. You should enjoy some of it."

"I love you for looking out for me," I say and lean over the table so I can kiss her cheek. "You're one of the sweetest people I know. Why in the world did you marry this bloke?"

"Well, I'm rather fond of him," she says and kisses her husband softly. "And don't think I didn't notice that you changed the subject."

"You're a smart woman."

"I need to go to the loo," Violet says, motioning to Kelly. "Join me?"

"Sure."

The women leave, and as soon as they're out of earshot, I turn to Todd.

"How can I feel nothing for her?"

"Charly?"

"No, Amy. How can I look at her, have her hand on me, and I feel nothing for her at all. No emotion. I don't hate her. There's just…*nothing*."

"It's been a few years, Simon," he replies and pushes his hands through his hair. "She put you through hell for most of your marriage."

"Yes, so you'd expect that I would hate her."

"No, I expect you to move on, and that's what you've done. It hurt for a while, even before you left her. By the time you ended it, you'd already grieved and come to terms with it all."

"I don't want to go through life numb."

"You're not numb." Todd laughs and claps me on the shoulder. "You're a human being. If there had been children, or if she still had to be in your life for some reason, the bad feelings might still be there. But she's gone, and you're living your life. She's not a part of it."

"It's rather nice to get advice instead of give it out for a change," I inform him and drink my water. "And you may be right. I didn't feel numb in Montana."

"She makes you happy, Simon. I've missed seeing you happy. I won't pester you like the girls, but I will say this: what's wrong with going after something that makes you happy? Consider contacting her. Maybe she's missing you just as badly."

"Who says I'm missing her?"

"Oh, mate." Todd laughs. "I've known you most of your life. You can't hide things like this from me."

"I'll consider it."

"Good."

"What did we miss?" Violet asks as she and Kelly return. "Are you still talking about Charly? I can get you her number, you know."

Trust me, I've thought of that about six dozen times over the past six weeks.

But I just shake my head. "We are talking about the retreat this fall," I say. "I need you to start calling applicants so we can get our guest list narrowed down."

"How many did we get?" Kelly asks.

"Over five hundred," Todd replies.

"And how many are we taking?" Violet asks.

"One twenty five," I say. "So I'll need you and a few others on staff to call and interview the applicants, narrowing it down to our limit."

"Do we have a location yet?" Kelly asks. "I've never heard of people signing up for a retreat when they don't even know where the location will be."

"I'm looking into it," I reply. "I'll make a decision by next week."

"I'm going this time," Kelly announces. "I'll bring the baby. Women love babies."

"Wild horses couldn't keep her away again," Todd says.

"I wouldn't have it any other way."

***

I'm standing at the window of my London flat, staring out at the city. I'm in a high-rise in a sought-after part of the city. This flat is just one more thing that the new success has afforded me. The city is quieter at this time of night, lit up and beautiful.

But all I can see is Charly.

I was with her for such a short time, yet she occupies way too many of my thoughts. In the six weeks since I saw her, I've been to New York, LA, Paris, and back to New York. I've done television appearances and small group workshops. It's been a bloody busy six weeks.

And still, in these quiet moments, she's all I can think about.

The sex was incredible. I'll never deny that. Her body was seemingly made for mine, and I couldn't get enough of her.

But it was when we were quiet together that's at the front of my mind. Her laughter would brighten the darkest day. Her sweet smile and quick wit enamor me.

I simply miss her.

I press my hand to the cool glass, immediately reminded of our last morning together. I walked her down to the airport shuttle, and everything in me was screaming at me to ask her for her number, to suggest we meet again.

But I didn't. Instead, I kissed her forehead, and watched helplessly as she climbed into the van. As it pulled away, she looked back at me with sad eyes and pressed her hand to the glass. Was it her way of reaching out? Of wanting to connect with me, just one more time?

I don't know. But I'm going to find out.

***

It's a gorgeous sunny morning less than a week later when I pull up to Head Over Heels and cut the engine. I love New Orleans, and I can already tell that Charly's shop is something for her to be proud of.

The sign hanging above the door is wrought iron, blending with the historic French Quarter feel, and the name of the store, Head Over Heels, is written in a whimsical, fun font. The building itself must be at least a hundred years old, but it's been recently painted and is well maintained. The display windows are large and decorated for the season, with beach umbrellas, sunglasses, magazines, and a sign that says, *Only amateurs wear flipflops to the beach.*

I grin and walk into the shop, triggering a bell, announcing my arrival. I'm nervous as fuck. She might tell me to get the hell out. But she might be happy to see me.

I didn't call ahead. I decided to just surprise her.

"I'll be right with you!" Charly calls out, then returns to the man she's talking to. Her back is to me, so she hasn't seen me yet. I hang back and wander through the racks of shoes, but my eyes are pinned to her. Her hair is up in an intricate knot on top of her head; she's in a soft pink dress with killer black heels.

I want to find out what she's wearing under that dress.

"You know I love you," the man says, shaking me out of my daydream.

"I love you too, you big lug," she says and he folds her into his arms, hugging her tightly.

What the fuck? Did I just walk in on an intimate moment with a new boyfriend? Maybe I should have called after all. This is humiliating.

"You have a customer," he murmurs, and Charly whips around with an apologetic smile on her face, then stops cold when she sees me. Her face pales and the smile slides off of her face.

"Simon."

"Hello."

"Do you know him?" her man asks, and Charly nods and wipes her hands down her hips, as if they're suddenly sweaty.

"I'm sorry, yes. Ben, this is Simon Danbury. Simon, this is Ben."

"Hello," I say and shake his hand, then turn back to her, feeling gutted and so bloody disappointed. "I'm sorry for intruding. I'll go—"

"No, that's okay. I was about to leave anyway," Ben says and winks at Charly. "It was nice to meet you."

"Likewise," I reply, never breaking eye contact with Charly. The bell dings as he leaves, and we are suddenly left in silence. "I should have called."

"No! I mean, yes." She shakes her head and walks behind the counter. "I mean, no. This is fine. You're fine." Finally she stops, leans her hands on the counter, and shakes her head. "You surprised the bejesus out of me."

"I wanted to surprise you."

"Well, you did." She sighs and stares at me with those whiskey colored eyes. "Why are you here?"

"To see you," I reply.

"You flew all the way to New Orleans just to see me?"

"Why does that sound unreasonable?" I can't stand it anymore. I reach over and drag my fingertip down her temple to her chin. "Your skin is even softer than I remember, and I didn't think that was possible. Are you with Ben?"

"I'm sorry, what?"

"You heard me."

"Ben's a friend of the family." She bites her lip as I let my finger glide down her throat and to her collarbone.

I cock a brow.

"Seriously, if Ben is in love with any of us, it's Savannah. He's loved her since we were kids. He just needed some advice."

"I see."

"Were you jealous?"

"I didn't like it," I reply honestly. "I know I don't have a claim on you, and I have no right to be jealous, but seeing another man's hands on you didn't feel good."

"I don't think you'd be here if you didn't give a fuck," she replies, reminding me of what I said to her in Montana.

"And I give a fuck."

She sighs and watches me for a moment. "Did you come to town for a weekend of sex?"

And just like that, she's pissed me off.

"No, Charlotte. I didn't come to town to get off. If that were my goal, I could do that just about anywhere. That's not my style."

"Okay."

She cocks a brow and braces her hand on her hip, and I've never been so fucking attracted to anyone in my life. Strong women are incredibly sexy.

"I'm here because I missed you, and I wanted to see you."

"I'm surprised you didn't call."

"I'll be honest. For a while I was just stubborn, and convinced myself that you didn't want to see me again."

"I'm not sure I do."

I still. Her eyes are happy, and her body language is open. Am I misreading this?

"But then I realized that I missed you and I wanted to come find you, even if it was just to take you to dinner to see how you are."

"You came for dinner?"

"You're making this quite difficult."

Her lips twitch and I feel just a bit better.

"I really wanted that phone call, not that I would have admitted it."

"I'll add you to my phone right away."

She bites her lip for a moment, and then suddenly runs around the counter and launches herself into my arms, holding on with all her might.

"I'm happy to see you."

"I'm glad. You scared me there for a moment. I thought you were going to kick me out on my arse."

"I just—" She leans back far enough to look me in the eye. "I'm still learning."

"It seems we both are, darling."

"How long are you in town for?"

"A week," I say and return her wide smile. "I'm thinking of bringing this fall's retreat to New Orleans, so I thought I'd look at possibilities and spend some time with you, if you'll give me some. My agent is going to book a couple of radio shows while I'm in the area, and I can do my other radio show from here."

"You're bringing your business to New Orleans."

"Just for the week, so I can see you. I can't take the week off completely, Charly. I'm sorry."

"No, don't be sorry." She shakes her head and hugs me again. "Are you exhausted from the flight? Hungry?"

"Both." I grin as she pulls away and finds her cell phone. "What are you doing?"

"Calling in some help. I'm taking the rest of the day off. I'll help you get settled."

"Are you certain?"

She simply winks at me and listens as the phone rings against her ear. "Hello, Linda? It's Charly. I could use some help at the shop today. Would you be willing to come in and stay until closing?" She nods and adjusts a display as Linda talks. "Perfect. No, that's just fine, sugar, thank you. I'll see you in an hour."

Bloody hell, her accent just about brings me to my knees.

She hangs up and turns to me. "Are you really here?"

"It appears so."

"Linda will be here in an hour. Are you already checked into your hotel?"

"No, I came here first. Why don't I go do that while you get things handled here, and I'll pick you up in an hour?"

"I'll come get you. Where are you staying?"

I cross to her and pull her in my arms, rest my forehead on hers, and say, "If you come to me, we won't leave the hotel room, love."

She shivers. "Okay, you pick me up. I'm hungry. And I'm not that easy."

I kiss her gently. "I'll see you soon.

CHAPTER NINE

~Charly~

He's here.

Simon is in New Orleans. The minute I saw him, my tongue was stuck to the roof of my mouth and I was just…*numb*.

I haven't felt like an excited teenager over a boy since… Well, ever. I've never felt quite this way before, and I'm not quite sure what to do about it.

And I'm not going to overthink it now.

Because he's *here*.

"Thanks for coming in, Linda." I smile at the other woman and finish the display I'd started when Ben came in. "It's been pretty tame today."

"Oh, I don't mind at all." She grins and ogles a new pair of orange sling-backs. "Being surrounded by beautiful shoes is never a bad thing."

"That's the truth."

The bell over the door dings, and in walks Simon. His dark hair is damp from a shower, and he's changed into a Henley T-shirt and cargo shorts and good God, I want to climb him like a tree.

He flashes a smile at me, and I hear Linda gasp.

"Is this why you need the rest of the day off?" she asks, not bothering to whisper.

"Yes."

"Good girl." She offers her fist for a bump, which I accept with a laugh and wave at Simon.

"I just have to grab my bag."

"No problem," he replies and admires the display. "You did all of this while I was gone?"

"It doesn't take long." I shrug and duck into the workroom to retrieve my things. "I plan it out ahead of time, so putting it together goes relatively smoothly."

"It's a work of art," he says, his hands on his hips as he stands back and stares at the wall. "The way the colors flow, how you have them arranged. I like it."

"It's just a shoe display," I reply.

"Charly isn't good at taking compliments," Linda says and I feel Simon's gaze turn down on me. "Just smile and say thanks, honey."

"If you need me, I have my cell," I reply, ignoring her comment. "Call for anything at all."

"I've got this," she says, shooing us away. "Have fun."

"Shall we?" Simon holds his arm out for me, and I slip my hand through, loving the feel of his strong bicep under my hand.

Good God, what he does to me.

"Did you eat?" I ask when we're on the sidewalk.

"Nope, I waited for you."

"Good, I'm starving." I stop and glance around. "Where's your car?"

"I walked."

"You must be staying nearby?"

"A few blocks away." He takes my hand and links our

fingers. "Lead the way to something delicious."

Café Amalie.

I haven't been there in ages, and I just heard that they're serving lunch on the weekdays.

"I know a place." I wink up at him before slipping my sunglasses on my face.

"I'm sure you do." He takes a deep breath. "I thought it would be hotter."

"Have you been here before?"

"Once, but only briefly." He shakes his head and stops to look at some artwork in a storefront window. "It's a beautiful city."

"It really is," I reply with a nod. "It's been a mild summer. The afternoons will get hot, but it cools off nicely at night. In another few weeks it'll be miserably hot most of the time."

"Are you okay in those shoes?"

I glance down, surprised at the question, then chuckle. "I'm fine. I'm on my feet in shoes like this ninety percent of the time."

"The sidewalks are a mess."

"I'm holding onto you," I remind him. "I'm pretty sure you'll catch me if I start to fall."

A few minutes later, we come to Café Amalie. "I love this place."

He looks down at me in surprise and then starts to laugh. "Would you believe me if I said that I'm staying right across the street?" He points to the bed & breakfast with the cornstalk fence just across the street and I grin.

"I've always loved that place." *It's haunted.* I don't mention that to him. "This restaurant is amazing. Come on."

The hostess meets us. "Would you like to sit inside,

or in the courtyard?"

"If Joe is working, I'd like to sit in his section," I reply.

"Oh, I'm sorry. Joe doesn't come in until dinner." She smiles at me, then glances up at Simon and her smile widens, her flirt game turned up high. "But I'm happy to help you with anything else you might need."

"Great," I reply and smile sweetly. *I will cut you.* "Let's sit outside."

She seats us in a corner, under a magnolia tree so we have plenty of shade from the sun, and leaves us be.

"This is a beautiful place," Simon says and leans over to kiss my cheek. "Are you sure it's okay that I came?"

"I'm honestly shocked," I reply and set my menu aside, already knowing what I want. He follows suit and takes my hand, but before he can ask me anything further, the waiter comes to take our order.

"Tell me how you're feeling," he says after we've ordered.

"Like I said, I'm surprised. Maybe a little overwhelmed. I didn't expect to see you again."

"I know." He nods and sips his water. "I should have asked you for your number."

"Why?"

He blinks, perplexed. "So I could call you."

"It would have been less expensive than flying to New Orleans. Were you all the way in London?"

"I was. I've been all over the States in the past month, and I had just returned home for a few weeks. I don't have anything pressing at the moment, and to be quite frank, I just couldn't stop thinking about you, and I knew I had to come find you."

That could be the sweetest thing anyone has ever said to

me.

Our drinks are delivered with the promise of our food coming out shortly, and I take a long sip of my lemon drop martini.

"Is there anything special you want to do while you're in town?"

"I'm here to scope out a place for the retreat this fall, and spend time with you."

"Are you telling me that you don't have people who can find a place for the retreat? I don't believe that you do that yourself."

"Not usually," he concedes. "But I'm here, and it's convenient. I don't expect you to take the whole week off of work, so I'll work too."

"Well, after this we should walk over and get some beignets. It'll be the best thing you ever put in your mouth in your life."

"No, that's happened already," he says, his voice perfectly calm. "When you were naked."

And just like that, my body is on high alert all over again. I take a deep breath, then let out a gusty laugh.

"You certainly know how to turn me on."

"Likewise." He sips his own dirty martini. "All you have to do is look at me and I want you."

"And you might have me. If you play your cards right."

He smiles and kisses my hand. "I like it when you're sassy."

"Good, because I'm always sassy, darlin'. I have a degree in sass."

"I thought it was philosophy?"

"I minored in sass."

"Good to know." He's looking at me with such

humor and lust, I just want to fucking climb him right here and now.

"Well, hey there."

"Gabby!" I stand and hug my sister tight and whisper in her ear. "He came."

"I know, Ben called all of us."

"Hi, Aunt Charly," her son, Sam, says and hugs me around the waist. Ailish, her little girl, is sitting on my mama's hip, grinning.

"Hey there, sugar. It's been a minute since I saw you. Looks like you grew a foot."

"I'm a growing boy," he reminds me.

"I'm Gabby," my sister says to Simon and I shake my head.

"I'm sorry, I'm so rude. Simon, this is my sister Gabby, her children Sam and Ailish, and my mother."

He stands and shakes their hands and kisses their cheeks. "It's a pleasure to meet you. I've heard a lot about you."

"Well, you're new to me," Mama replies and glances at me with shrewd eyes. "But it's a pleasure all the same."

"Cha cha!" Ailish says and reaches for me, so I take her and prop her on my own hip, kissing her smooth cheek.

"This perfect angel is Ailish." I brush her light hair off her forehead.

"She's not an angel," Sam says. "She ruined my Lego thing that I spent all day building."

I laugh and glance at Simon. He's staring at me with hot eyes. Not with anger, but with lust and something else I can't quite figure out.

"What are y'all up to?" I ask my family.

"Well, yesterday was Sam's last day of school, so we

decided to come into town and take Maman out for lunch," Gabby says.

"Is Rhys gone already?" I ask, then turn to Simon. "Gabby's husband is Rhys O'Shaughnessy. He plays baseball for the Cubs."

"I've heard of him," Simon says.

"You follow baseball in England?"

"I follow all sorts of things," he replies. "Would you like to join us?"

"Oh no," Mama says, but I can tell that she has an arsenal of questions for him. "But I would love it if you came to dinner before you leave town."

"It would be an honor," Simon replies and kisses her hand, and for the first time in my life, I see my mother blush.

"Aunt Charly, are you still taking me on the gator tour this weekend?"

Crap. I forgot.

"You don't like gators," I reply, teasing him.

"I do too! And you said that you'd take me to celebrate school getting out. You've never gone to see 'em! I have to show them to you." His face is earnest and excited, and there's no way I'm going to tell him no.

"You know, I've never seen them either," Simon says, surprising me.

"You'd want to go with us?"

"Well, it sounds like something I should see while I'm here," he says and winks at Sam. "And you promised him."

"Right on!" Sam exclaims and high fives Simon.

"Sounds like we're going to see the gators this weekend."

"Better you than me," Gabby replies and takes Ailish

from me, who reaches her little arms out for me and pouts. I kiss her fingers.

"I'll see you soon too, love bug."

"Call me," Gabby says.

They say goodbye and go inside to their table and I sit back down and finish my meal, feeling Simon's eyes on me with each bite.

"Go ahead and ask."

"Ask what?"

"Whatever it is that you're thinking because it's really loud."

"I don't know if it's a question as much as an observation."

"Okay."

"A few observations, actually."

I laugh and sit back to sip the rest of my martini, watching him.

"Go ahead."

"You and your sister look a lot alike."

"We do, yes. And Savannah looks similar as well. My father's genes were strong."

"And your family is closer than I realized."

"We are incredibly close." I nod and tilt my head. "What else?"

"Her children adore you."

"They adore all of us." I smile and think about my brothers with Ailish. She has them wrapped around her tiny finger. "Let's be honest, they're adorable."

"They are." His eyes smolder again as they find mine. "And you're bloody gorgeous with a baby on your hip."

I cock a brow and ignore the fluttering in my stomach. "Am I?"

He nods once and finishes his drink, then waves the

waiter over and gives him his card.

"I need to walk off some of this energy," he says after he signs the check.

"Let's walk over to Café du Monde," I suggest. "I could use some sugar."

He takes my hand and leads me down the street. "Me too." He kisses my head, and I know he's not talking about the same sugar I am.

I grin and hold his hand tightly, enjoying our banter and our conversation.

Enjoying *him.*

***

"I'm so damn tired." I'm in his car later that night, my head leaning back. I roll my head on the headrest so I can look at him. "You're really here."

He glances at me and grins. "I'm here."

"Crazy. Turn left at that light." It's dark now. We spent all day in the Quarter, eating, shopping.

Wandering.

We talked endlessly and laughed more than I have in years. I loved showing him my city.

"I'm up here on the right. The yellow house." I point to my place and smile. I know that I'm not home much, spending most of my time at work, but I love my house.

"This is a beautiful neighborhood," Simon says as he pulls into my driveway. "Where's your car?"

"At work," I reply and yawn. "I'll get it tomorrow."

"What time do you go to work?"

"I'll leave here around nine. That gives me an hour to settle in at the shop before I open."

He nods and pulls himself out of the rental, circles the car, and opens my door.

"Help." I hold my hand out to him and he practically

pulls me out and onto my feet. "I think I'll sleep well tonight."

"Good." He kisses my nose and follows me up the steps to my front door. I unlock it, but before I can push it open, he turns me around and kisses me chastely, and pulls away.

"If you're going to kiss a girl, kiss her right." I grip his shirt in my fist and pull him back to me, kissing him the way I've wanted to all day. Our mouths are hungry for each other, devouring lips and tongues. My leg climbs up around his hip, and the next thing I know, I'm boosted up against the door, his hand is up my skirt and on my bare ass, and I'm ready for him fuck me right here, in front of all of Louisiana.

Suddenly, he lowers me to my feet, kisses my forehead, and backs away, panting and swallowing hard.

He pushes his hand through his hair and smiles. "Good night, Charlotte."

"Good night?" I'm shocked. "You're not coming in?"

"No." He shakes his head. "I told you, I'm not just here for sex."

"Let's be honest, Simon, we're both adults and the chemistry is off the charts."

"I took you out today, and I loved every minute of it. We have chemistry, yes, but it'll still be here in the morning."

"You're seriously going." It's not a question.

"While I still can." He reaches out to touch me, but thinks better of it, and walks down the steps toward his car.

I watch him pull away, then walk into my house. This is not what I expected *at all*. I thought we'd spend the night together and I'd be dead on my feet tomorrow from lack of sleep, but blissfully aware of every sore muscle in my body from the workout Simon would give me.

I'm torn between being offended and grateful.

I walk up to my bedroom and immediately shed my shoes and dress, then pull on yoga pants and a tank and wash my face.

He didn't stay.

My body is still on fire as I crawl between the sheets and flip through the photos we took today on my phone. Selfies in the Quarter. Both of us smiling happily at the camera. In one, Simon kissed my cheek.

He's here. He's not staying tonight, and he's completely knocked me off my feet.

***

My doorbell is ringing.

I come abruptly awake and wake my phone to look at the time.

Eight-thirty. Damn it, I was supposed to be up an hour ago.

I've also missed one call and three texts from Simon.

I pad downstairs, not in any hurry, and open the door, blinking against the sunlight and a fresh-faced Simon, smiling and holding a brown paper bag and a drink carrier full of delicious-smelling coffee.

"Good morning, love," he says. "I was getting worried when you didn't answer this morning."

I yawn again and step back, giving him room to come inside. I close the door behind him and lead him back to the sunroom off the kitchen. The furniture in here is colorful and comfortable, and this is where I like to start every day.

"Are you not speaking to me?"

"Not awake yet." I scrub my hands over my face, stretch my arms over my head toward the ceiling, then touch my toes.

"I'm beginning to get the message that you're not a morning person."

His voice is dry, but his eyes are warm as I stand and they leisurely travel over my body.

"I didn't fall asleep until about three," I reply and gratefully accept the coffee he offers me. "And then I slept so hard, I didn't hear my alarm or your call. I'm sorry."

"I'm the sorry one for waking you," he replies and sits on the couch, then takes my hand and pulls me down with him. He pulls me into his arms and hugs me close, nuzzling my temple and kissing me softly there. "Waking up like that isn't fun."

"I'll be okay." But I don't move away. It feels too damn good to be in his strong arms. "You must have gotten up early."

"I usually do, and I'm a bit jetlagged." He reaches for the bag of food and sets out toasted bagels with cream cheese and fruit. "I hope this is okay."

"It looks delicious." My stomach growls and I immediately reach for a handful of grapes. "You didn't have to go to all of this trouble."

I take a sip of my coffee. My head whips up to stare at him in wonder.

"You remembered how I take my coffee. And you're British." *And we only had breakfast together once in Montana.*

"British people don't remember things?"

"No, they don't drink coffee."

"Some do." He sips his tea and smiles at me. That smile *kills me.* "I remember just about everything about you, Charly. In case you missed it, I'm quite taken with you."

I haven't missed it. But it surprises me, and I want to ask why.

But instead I smile and munch on my bagel.

"Thank you."

"You're welcome. I'll drive you to work since I left you stranded here last night."

"Thank you again." I could argue, but why? If he wants to give me a ride to work, who am I to complain? "How is your bagel?"

"Fair. Once you've had bagels in New York, you get a bit spoiled."

"True. And we're a beignet town."

"I'll remember that."

"You seem to remember everything."

He simply smiles and sips his tea, and we settle in to enjoy the sunny morning, our food, and each other's company.

CHAPTER TEN

~Simon~

"We need confirmation that you can be in LA on the twelfth of next month to appear on Kimmel and Ellen, and then on the fourteenth, we have you scheduled with Hoda and Kathy Lee."

"That's fine," I reply to Todd and mark it out on my calendar. I keep a real paper agenda, mostly because I'm on the phone when I get the information, making it difficult to add to a phone calendar, and I used to forget to mark things down. "I have a deadline of September first for the next book, and my editor already gave me a three month extension, so don't schedule me anything else in July and August."

"Nothing?" he asks, surprised.

"I'll still do the weekly videos and the radio show. We'll be present on social media. But I can't travel, Todd. I have to write the book."

"Understood," he says. "I also want to roll out the new webinar programs next month."

"That means extra video time," I reply with a sigh and scratch my chin. "We'll have to do that the week after

I return to London."

"That was my thought as well. Have you done any scouting for the retreat later this year?"

"I did yesterday," I reply. "I'll email you some information this afternoon. I think I found the perfect hotel, but they're rather expensive. Let's see if we can't get them talked down. I don't want to have to drive the price of the retreat up for the ladies coming. It's already expensive for them."

"I agree," he says, and I can hear Kelly speaking in the background. "I'll be right there, darling."

"I can let you go. I think we've covered it all."

"One last thing," he says before I can hang up. "How are things going with Charly?"

I sigh and rub my eyes. I'm not ready to get into this with him yet.

"You don't have to give me all the details, man, but I need to know something."

"Things are good," I reply. "We're taking things slow."

"Slow? For fucksake, mate, you're only there for the week. Don't take it too slow."

"Thank you for that, relationship expert."

"Hey, my best friend *is* a relationship expert. I've learned a few things over the years. Don't take it too slow."

"Have a good evening," I reply, rather than entertain him further, and hang up the phone.

I actually haven't seen as much of her as I was hoping since I've been here. Yesterday, after our breakfast together and I drove her to work, we went our separate ways. I did the retreat research, and by the time we were both finished last night, we simply spoke on the phone for an hour, then called it a night.

And again this morning, I had to take early calls from London because of the time difference and I wasn't able to take her breakfast the way I did yesterday.

I miss her.

And Todd is right; I'm only here for a week. I need to make the most of it. Today is Charly's Friday, as she takes Sunday and Mondays off, and I plan to take advantage of it. No more nights alone, no more only getting an hour here or there. I'm going to spend some true, quality time with her.

I knew I admired her, and was so fucking attracted to her I ached with it, but now that I've seen her at work and with her family, I'm just completely taken with her. I need to know more.

I'm quickly realizing that this isn't just a job for me, or a casual relationship. I want it to be so much more. Where that might lead, I'm not sure, but it's time I take the kid gloves off and begin actively pursuing this woman.

I set my tray from breakfast outside my door and gather my wallet, sunglasses, and keys and set off for Charly's shop.

"Hey there, sugar," she says with a big smile when she sees me walk through her door a short time later.

"Good morning." Without skipping a beat, and not giving one fuck about the customers in the store, I walk to her and pull her in, kissing her firmly. My hands glide down her back to her ass and I grip her tightly for the brief embrace, and then I pull away. "I missed you yesterday."

"I see that," she says and covers her lips with her fingertips. "I might have missed you back."

I cock a brow and feel my lips twitch.

"Such a sassy girl."

"Do you sell those?" a young twenty-something asks, interrupting us.

"Do I sell what?" Charly asks.

"Hot men who kiss like that."

The girls laugh and Charly looks up at me with happy hazel eyes. "No, sorry, this one is already claimed."

Claimed.

I love the sound of that.

The customer shrugs and turns away. "A girl can try."

"What can I do for you?" Charly asks me.

"I need your house key."

She looks up at me in surprise. "What for?"

"Trust me." I lean in and kiss her cheek, and then her ear. "Just trust me."

"Okay." She shrugs and pulls her keys out of her bag, twists her house key off the ring and hands it over. "You're awfully mysterious today."

"Not at all." I kiss her once more and then pull away before I yank her into that stock room and strip her bare. "I'll see you when you get home this evening."

"It's a date." She winks and then returns to her customers. I walk outside and stand on the sidewalk, watching her for just a moment. She's truly excellent at her job. It's no wonder that her business is thriving.

Just before I turn to leave, she catches me staring and smiles, tossing me a wave, and then blows me a kiss.

I nod and leave, anxious to get my plan set in motion.

***

Candles lit? Check. Flowers? Check. Food on the way? Check.

I'm ready for her, and she is on her way home. For

the first time since I was a boy, I'm nervous for a date with a woman.

I hear her car door slam, and a few moments later, she walks in and stops cold, staring around the room and then at me.

"Wow."

I've turned the lights off, leaving the space cast in the glow from the two dozen candles scattered all over. Vases of roses in all different colors are also spread about, giving the room a rich flowery smell.

She walks over to me and hugs me around the waist, then looks up at me, leaning her chin on my chest.

I love how short she is.

"This is so beautiful."

"Not nearly as beautiful as you are."

She smiles, but I can see the fatigue in her eyes. She works herself to the bone. Today was almost twelve hours long, just like the two before it.

"I have another surprise," I inform her and take her hand, leading her upstairs. We walk through her bedroom to the master bath and she gasps. "Simon, this is just…*indulgent.*"

"You deserve it." I've filled her tub with hot water and lavender oil with rose petals floating on top. "I'm going to help you in, but don't fall asleep. Dinner will be arriving soon."

"Oh God, I'm hungry," she groans, and then sighs in delight when her body is enveloped in the hot water. All I can think about is how fucking amazing she looks, naked, soft, in the water. I want to join her and fuck her senseless in the water, but I hold myself back. This is all about her. "Goodness, a girl could get used to this."

That's my hope.

"Should I come check on you in a few?"

"No, I'll be down in a bit," she replies and smiles softly. "Simon?"

"Yes, love."

"Thank you. This is amazing."

"You're welcome." I kiss her forehead, trying to keep my eyes off her incredible body. I haven't seen her naked in almost two months, and fucking hell, I crave her.

And I'll have her before long.

The food arrives, and I arrange a delicious, casual picnic in the middle of the candles and flowers.

Just as I'm about to walk up to see if Charly did, indeed, fall asleep, she comes down the stairs wearing nothing but a robe. Her cheeks are flushed from the water, her eyes are heavy.

"You're the sexiest woman I've ever seen."

She tilts her head to the side. "Ever?"

"Ever."

"Wow. I'll take baths more often."

"Come on, sassy, let's eat."

"Oh God, is that Italian?"

"The Americans' version of it, yes."

"Perfect." But before she sits down, she leans into me, on her tiptoes, and presses her lips to mine. "This is perfect."

"I'm glad you like it."

She sits at a plate and waits patiently while I dish the food, giving her more than she thinks she wants.

"How was your day?" I ask and settle in to eat. The hot bread is delicious, as are the pasta and red sauce.

"It went well. We were busy, so that's always good." She spoons up some spaghetti and closes her eyes with a sigh of delight. "This is just *so good*."

"Watching you eat is like watching someone have sex," I reply and run through baseball stats in my head.

"It is not," she says with a laugh. "I just like food."

"Almost as much as sex," I agree and offer her some bread. "So work went well. How is your family?"

"Curious." She butters her bread and licks her finger. "I've now heard from all of the siblings. They're curious to know more about you, and to hear how I'm doing."

"That sounds normal enough." I reach over and tuck a piece of her hair behind her ear. "They love you and I'm a stranger."

"I get it," she says with a shrug. "And I've never been one to bring men around."

"What do you mean?"

"I don't think any of them have ever met anyone I've dated. Certainly not the boys. Actually, now that I think about it, Van and Gabby met Ryan once."

The mention of another man's name sets my teeth on edge, but I keep my cool as she continues talking. This is what I've been waiting for: Charly relaxed and telling me more about herself.

"But I just don't date seriously. Ryan and I had a mutually satisfying arrangement for the better part of ten years, but it wasn't serious."

"You had a friends with benefits for ten years?" I ask, completely thrown. She's amazing. Who would be satisfied with that?

"Yeah. Well, no. It's complicated."

"I have nothing but time," I remind her.

"We met in college. The sex was always great, and I thought we were friends too. Not long ago, I discovered that he doesn't even really like me all that much. It was *just sex* for him, and I'm done." She shakes her head and takes another bite of food. "He's called a few times, but not in a while now. I hope he finally believed me last time when I said *don't call me again.* Being an adult and entering into a mutually respectful physical relationship is one thing, but when there's no affection there *at all*, well, that's a problem for me."

"And other than Ryan, there haven't been any serious relationships."

"No." She shakes her head again and shrugs. "I'm busy with the shop and my family."

"So you're saying you don't have time for a relationship?"

"No, I'm saying that I don't have time to go and seek one out. Dating isn't easy. You know this; you deal with it every day."

"I do. I get it." I nod and can't help but feel a bit sorry for her. She's never been in love, or had her heart broken. She's never had a relationship.

That's about to change, and she doesn't even know it yet.

"You know, I was mad at myself when I was in Montana."

This brings me out of my reverie and catches my attention.

"How so?"

"I was just so pissed that I let Ryan use me for sex for all of those years. Granted, it was mutual, and it was exclusive. If either of us wanted to see other people, our physical relationship stopped. We were honest about that, and I believe he told me the truth."

"Okay, that sounds reasonable."

"But I was blind too, because I honestly believed he was my friend. And then we had the day in Montana when you drove home that we need to know our worth, and not settle for anything less than we deserve."

"You deserve so much, Charly."

"I know." She nods and pushes her empty plate away. She ate every bite. "My dad reminded all of us frequently that we deserved a person who loved us the way he loved our mom."

"You do."

"And I just convinced myself that Ryan was *good enough* until something better came along. It wasn't really fair to either of us."

"And how do you feel now?"

"I'm not angry, and I've broken it off completely with him, so there are no more games."

"So now that you know that you were participating in unhealthy behavior, you've taken steps to correct it, and you've purged the toxic relationship from your life."

"God, you're good at this," she says with a laugh. "Yes, I would say all of that is true."

"You did learn something from me." I smile proudly at her and stand to gather what's left of our meal. I stow it all away and come back to find Charly lying on the floor, half asleep.

"The candles are pretty." Her voice is soft. "I like the way they cast shadows on the walls. And the flowers smell so good."

"I'm glad you like them." I gather her into my arms after I blow the candles out and carry her up the stairs.

"You're strong."

"You're small." I kiss her nose. "How about a massage?"

"My feet could use it," she says with a yawn. "I've abused them this week."

"I can arrange that."

I place her on the bed and strip her out of the robe. Her skin is soft and still a bit dewy from the bath. She's on her belly, and it takes everything in me to not strip down and sink inside her.

I want her.

Now.

But I've been patient so far, and I can wait a few more minutes. I retrieve some lotion from the bathroom and begin massaging her feet, her legs, and over her perfect arse. She arches a bit and moans when my thumbs find the small of her back.

"Mm, so good."

"I love your skin." I work my way up her back and shoulders, her neck, and then down again. The feel of her beneath me, the small moans, is making me lose control faster than I wanted to.

I strip quickly out of my clothes and return to her. Kissing her now, where my hands have been. She grows quiet, and just when I drag my hand up between her legs, she snores.

Snores.

My poor girl is completely knackered.

Part of me is as frustrated as it gets. My cock is throbbing for her, and I want nothing more than to wake her and fuck her, but that would just be selfish.

Not that I can't be a selfish bastard at times, but not now.

Not with Charly.

I arrange us under the blankets and pull her into me, holding her close. She wraps her arm around my chest and settles in, sighing deeply, and soon her breathing is slow and deep in sleep.

As much as I was dying to be inside her tonight, this is excellent as well. Nothing feels as good as Charly wrapped around me. I missed this with her.

I bury my nose in her hair and breathe her in. Her arms tighten around me, and soon I'm falling asleep myself.

CHAPTER ELEVEN

~Charly~

"Charly."

Someone is whispering in my ear and dragging his hands down my naked body, deliciously following every curve, every dip.

"Charly, wake up darling."

"If I wake up, will you stop doing that?" I whisper back, not opening my eyes. I arch my back as his hand covers my breast and gently grazes over my nipple, waking it up.

Waking all of me up.

"I want to see your beautiful eyes," he replies and buries his face into my neck, biting the tender flesh there. "I want you to wake up."

Rather than reply, my hands take a journey of their own, down his back, his chest, stomach, and finally his impressively stiff cock.

"Is this for me?" I ask, sleep still heavy in my voice.

"Mm," he murmurs, his mouth wandering expertly over me. I blink my eyes open, and there he is, leaning above me, smiling down at me with lust-filled blue eyes.

One hand trails down my stomach and between my legs and his thumb finds my nub, making me inhale sharply. "But this is for me."

"I'm sorry I fell asleep last night." He was incredibly sweet last night. I don't think I've ever been pampered the way he pampers me.

"You can make it up to me," he replies and kisses me, bites my lower lip, and follows his hand down my body to my core. "I think I need to finish waking you up."

"I think you're right." I reach above me and grip onto the headboard, grounding myself because I know exactly what Simon does to me with that mouth of his.

And oh, how I've missed it.

But he teases me, nibbling on the inside of my thighs, the crease where my leg meets my center, my pubis, and even my lower stomach.

"Simon," I moan, circling my hips.

"I'll get there, love." He circles my pussy with a finger, then slowly slides it inside of me and places a kiss on my nub. His tongue tickles me. "I missed this. Your taste. The noises you make. The way your body comes alive for me."

"You should come with a warning label," I inform him and let out a squeal when he sucks hard on my lips. "May cause random explosions."

He chuckles and flips me onto my stomach, then slaps my ass and kisses up my spine as he guides his dick inside of me and then I can't think anymore at all as he sets an almost punishing pace, fucking me hard. He's so deep from this angle.

"Am I hurting you?" he groans in my ear.

"No."

"Good." He grips my hair in his fist and pulls. "I

don't want to hurt you, but I do want to fuck you, Charlotte."

I bite my lip as he picks up the pace, pumping his hips harder. He reaches around me to tickle my clit, and I'm done for. The combination of sensations sends me into a tailspin.

When the world rights itself again, Simon is at the side of the bed, gathering me into his arms and carrying me into the bathroom.

He starts the water in the shower, sets me down, and leads me in.

"I've wanted to get you in the shower since I've known you."

"You could have joined me in the bath," I remind him, but he shakes his head.

"It's not the same." When we're both soaked, he lathers up his hands and takes his time exploring my skin. "You're beautiful."

"I'm turned on," I reply honestly and reach for the soap, returning the favor. "And you're sexy."

I cup his still-hard cock in my fist and work him over, my hand slippery from the soap. His breath catches, his eyes claim mine, and he pushes me against the wall.

"I'm not done with you."

"I figured." I rinse him off and bite his lower lip. "Please tell me you're going to fuck me in this shower."

"I'm going to fuck you in this shower." He lifts me against the wall and lowers me onto him. The tile is cool against my back, the water and Simon hot and steamy around me, and I can't look away from him. His arms are strong, holding me steady as he pushes into me over and over. "I don't want this to be over yet."

"It's not." I push my hand through his hair and make

a fist, keeping his face close to mine. "It's not over yet."

"I don't think I can hold out much longer." His eyes close as he whispers *fuck* and he tips his forehead against mine. "You're better than I remembered, Charly. Fucking hell, you're going to be the end of me."

I smile and hold on tighter, gripping him with everything I have, and watch in fascination as he comes apart spectacularly, shivering and groaning my name.

There are few things more empowering than making a man come apart at the seams.

He plants his lips on my shoulder as he collects himself.

"Did you sleep well?" he asks after he finds his voice.

"Better than I have since…" *Since Montana.* "For a while."

He raises his head and smiles at me with those ocean blue eyes. "Montana." He knows.

"Yes."

"Good."

He kisses me soundly and lowers me to the floor. "What's for breakfast?" I ask.

"I had a delicious breakfast about twenty minutes ago." He winks and flips the water off, wraps me in a towel, and begins drying me off. "But I could go for some protein."

"I don't have much here in the house. I'll take you out."

"I'll take you out." He backs away to dry himself, then slings the towel low over his hips.

Simon Danbury is in my bathroom, well sexed, mostly naked, looking at me like I'm the best thing since Earl Grey tea.

Whose life is this?

"Are you going naked, then?" He asks, one brow raised.

"Next time," I say, shaking myself out of my reverie and walk to the closet. "Do we know what we're doing today?"

"Not all of it. Why?"

"So I know what to wear."

"Just be comfortable, love. Nothing fancy today."

I smile and reach for my favorite shorts and peach colored tank. My body feels well-used.

Thank goodness.

***

"How long have you owned The Odyssey?" Simon asks my sister-in-law later that evening. We decided to have dinner with my brother Declan and his wife Callie at the last minute.

"Well, I inherited it from my father about a year ago," she replies with a smile. Callie is gorgeous. She's tall and thin, with a full sleeve of tattoos, different from Simon's but just as many. She's all class with a sexy edge. It's no wonder my brother fell hard and fast for her. "But I've been in the business all of my life."

"I'd love to see it," Simon says.

"Come back with us after dinner," Declan says with a smile. Declan is my youngest brother, and the most laid-back of the three. "I'm playing tonight."

"Charly has told me about your talent," Simon replies. "I'd love to hear you."

"Perfect." Callie smiles. "How long are you in town for, Simon?"

"I have about four days left," he replies and my stomach falls just a bit. The thought of him leaving again makes me sad. I don't want him to go, and yet, I knew from the beginning that he wasn't going to stay forever. He never lied to me.

"Charly told us about your retreat after she got home," Declan says and takes a sip of his beer. "It sounds like what you do is pretty intense."

"It can be," Simon says with a nod. "Some of the days are more lighthearted, but yes, a good portion of it is intense. My clients are learning to trust themselves."

I hadn't thought of it like that, but he's right. When you boil it down to the heart of it all, it's about trust.

"That's a good way to describe it," I say with a nod. "I like that. I've already talked Savannah into going."

"Good." Declan covers my hand with his and gives it a squeeze. "If anyone needs to learn to trust themselves, it's our Van."

Savannah is Declan's twin sister. I've often been jealous of their bond over the years, but I realize now that it's not something either of them has control over. They're not choosing each other over the rest of us, they simply have a connection that we don't have.

And it's really quite beautiful.

"I'd like to meet Savannah," Simon replies. "I've heard a lot about her."

"She's so great," Callie says with a wink. "She'll keep you on your toes."

"I'm beginning to learn that the whole family is a force to be reckoned with." Simon laughs and finishes his drink. We finished eating long ago. The bill has been paid. We've just been chatting for the last half hour.

"Should we head over?" I ask.

"Yeah, I need to set up and Callie will want to make sure the place hasn't burned down." He turns to Simon. "She's a bit of a workaholic."

"Takes one to know one," Callie replies and kisses her husband on the cheek. "And you get me, so it works."

"Oh, I get you, all right." He kisses her lips and his hand is traveling up her side, and I immediately put the brakes on that spectacle.

"Okay, we get it." I cover my eyes. "Y'all have sex. You don't have to rub it in my face."

"What are you, nine?" Declan asks with a laugh as we stand and leave the restaurant.

"No, I'm your sister. There's no need to get gross in front of me."

"Being affectionate with my wife is not gross."

"That's your opinion, pal."

It's a beautiful evening. There's not a cloud in the sky as we walk the block or so back to The Odyssey.

"This is beautiful," Simon says we walk inside. "You've recently renovated."

"Right after I took over," Callie says with a nod, looking over her handiwork. "Everything is new except the bar. It was in good shape, and quite old even when my dad bought it."

"This is my kind of pub," Simon replies and he and I take a seat at the bar while Declan goes to get ready for his set. Callie walks behind the bar and begins helping her partner, Adam.

"Simon, this is Adam. He co-owns the place with me."

"Pleasure," Simon says and reaches over the bar to shake Adam's hand.

"Good to meet you," Adam says and waves hello to me. "And this gorgeous woman is my girlfriend, Sarah."

"Oh good! I finally get to meet you! I've heard all about you," I say and lean over to hug the pretty woman to my right. I was so excited, and surprised, to hear that Adam found someone.

"It's great to meet you, too. Hi, Simon."

"You're meeting a lot of people tonight," Callie says with a laugh to Simon. "How are you holding up?"

"I'm perfectly fine," he says and takes my hand in his. He kisses my knuckles and Callie's eyes find mine. She winks at me and nods, and I know that I have her approval.

For reasons I'm not entirely sure of, that makes me very happy.

"Well, slap my ass and call me Sally! Here come some more," Callie says with a laugh. I spin around and find Gabby and Savannah walking to us, all decked out in sexy dresses and heels.

"Hey!" I stand and hug them both, then proceed to make introductions.

"So this is the famous Savannah," Simon says and leans in to kiss her cheek. "It's truly a pleasure to finally meet you."

"Oh God, what did you tell him?" she asks me, making us all laugh.

"Only great things," Simon replies and then frowns and pulls his phone out of his pocket. The frown doesn't leave his face when he returns it to his pocket and takes my hand in his.

"Is everything okay?"

"Fine. It's just my mother."

"It's awfully late. Are you sure nothing is wrong?"

"No, darling. She's fine. And it's early morning there. I'll call her later."

I nod and turn back to my sisters. "What are you guys doing here?"

"Beau kicked us out of my house," Gabby says and orders an extra dirty martini from Callie.

"Why?" I ask.

"Because she really needed a night away," Van replies for her. "I've received at least twenty texts from her today. She was having a shitty week."

"Do tell," Simon says as Adam pulls a bar-height table over for us, along with extra chairs. This way, we can stay close to the bar so he and Callie can still be part of the fun while they work.

"Well," Gabby begins with a sigh and takes a sip of her drink. "Rhys has been gone back to Chicago for less than a week, right?"

We nod.

"And I'm pretty sure my kids are already trying to kill me."

"Come on, it can't be that bad," I say, but Van is already shaking her head and giving me the warning *look*.

"It's that bad," Van says. "Go ahead and tell them. Let it all out, honey."

"On Tuesday, Sam informed me that he needed cupcakes for the last day of school, which was the next day, and he decided to wait until bedtime to tell me. Of course. Then Ailish came down sick the evening after we saw you and Simon. The dog decided to poop all over the freaking house while I took Sam to a birthday party on Thursday, and then later that afternoon, Sam broke another damn window."

"How many does this make now?" I ask, trying to hold my laughter in.

"Nine," she replies between gritted teeth.

"Sam wants to be a baseball player, like his daddy," Van informs us all, earning a glare from Gabby.

"Rhys doesn't break windows. Rhys doesn't need me to actually assemble every single snack he has." She turns to us, her eyes a little manic now. "I swear, the kids never want something simple to snack on like an apple, or some little fish crackers. No. They want a sandwich with cheese and meat and mayo. Or better yet, mac and cheese."

She lays her head on her arm on the table and whimpers.

"All I wanted was a bubble bath."

"Shh, it's okay, ladybug," Declan says as he approaches the table and strokes his hand down Gabby's hair while the rest of us laugh with hilarity. Even Simon is chuckling, his eyes dancing with humor.

I lean in to him. "I know this is a lot. We can go whenever you want."

"Are you kidding? I'm having a great time. I'm about to start asking questions about you as a child."

Gabby's head comes up. "Oh, this is a better subject by far. We have lots of stories."

"Great." Simon rubs his hands together eagerly and I shake my head.

"No one wants to hear this."

"Oh, but they do," Van says with a gleeful smile. "What do you want to know?"

"Was Charly always so confident?" he asks.

"Oh yeah," Gabby says with a nod. "She was always the most headstrong and put together."

"I was not. That was Eli."

"Of the sisters," Van clarifies. "Charly was the most organized. Even if we were playing, it had to be in a certain order."

"No one likes chaos," I mutter, and Simon tightens his hand on mine.

"But she has the best sense of humor of all of us, and she loves so *big*, you know?"

"I do," Simon replies and lifts my hand to his lips. "She has a big heart."

"She wears that heart on her sleeve," Van says but I shake my head.

"No way."

"For the most part," Gabby says, agreeing with Van. "But there are times that she pulls in, and guards herself fiercely. I hate it when she does that because she's hard to read."

"So did she ever do something scandalous in school, that may have gotten her in trouble? Come on, girls, I want the dirt."

"Hmm…dirt." They look at each other, as if they're trying to come up with something, and then shrug.

"Honestly, Charly never really got into much trouble," Gabby says. "I was the one that got pregnant right out of high school. Van got married right away. Charly was always just career minded."

"Yeah, I don't think she got into much trouble," Van says, but Declan is just smiling at me, keeping his mouth shut, but he couldn't be more obvious.

"Clearly, Declan knows something you don't," Simon says. "Spill it, mate."

"I was sworn to secrecy," Declan says and shakes his head. "Sorry."

"Wait, you know something we don't?" Gabby demands. "I want to know."

"Me too," Van says.

"Me three," Sarah adds, who has been watching the conversation with rapture, "and it's completely none of my business."

"I will pull every hair from your body with tweezers," I say calmly and take a sip of water, my eyes on Declan. "And you know that's not a threat."

"I do like my hair," he replies. "But it was a long time ago, Char. Who cares if I tell them now? Even Dad isn't here to punish you."

"It deserved punishment?" Simon asks and leans over to whisper in my ear. "I can spank you later."

And cue the wet panties. Again.

"I heard that," Declan says and scowls at Simon.

"I don't care," I say with a shrug, and everyone leans toward Declan in excitement.

"Charly was about sixteen," he begins, then looks at me for confirmation to continue. I just sigh and nod.

What the hell?

"It was summertime," he continues, "so we were all staying out in the Bayou, at the house Gabby lives in now. The nearest neighbor is about a half a mile away, and at the time it was owned by this really mean old lady with her teenage grandson."

"She wasn't *that* old," I remind them all, "but to us back then, she was ancient."

"Was this that guy, oh what was his name?" Van asks and taps her nails on the table. "Jerry? Larry? Terry?"

"His name was Eddie," I reply.

"Eddie!" she snaps her fingers. "That's right."

"And we were just friends."

"Sure," Gabby says with a nod. "Of course you were."

"Anyway, Charly told Mom that she was going to a friend's house for a sleepover and instead she snuck out with Eddie to go camping."

"In the swamp?" Sarah asks.

"No, just in his backyard. I wasn't that adventurous,

but he had a really cool telescope, and you could see the planets and stuff."

"Sure, he was going to show you his *telescope*," Gabby says with a snort.

"Do you like looking at the stars, darling?" Simon asks and kisses my cheek.

"Yeah, it's kind of fun." I shrug and prepare myself for the rest of the story.

"Well, all I know is, in the middle of the night, I can't sleep, and I'm sitting up, looking out my window, and I see Charly running over the grass, under the trees, to the house. And I mean she's *running*. I don't think she's ever run that fast.

"So I go downstairs, and she is sneaking in the front door, trying not to make any noise, but then she turns around and sees me and lets out a scream."

"You snuck up on me!"

"So I put my hand over her mouth and she fucking bites me."

"Again, you snuck up on me."

"And when she finally calms down and stops being so freaking dramatic, she tells me that Eddie's yard is haunted and it scared her so she ran home."

"Yep, that's what I told you."

"But I don't believe that was true."

Now all of the eyes swing toward me and I'm left squirming in my seat.

"Not really, no."

"What really happened?" Simon asks.

"It's dumb."

"You have to tell us now," Van says with a grin.

"Well, we had already looked at the stars and the planets and stuff, and I could tell that Eddie didn't just ask me out there to look through his telescope."

"Shocker," Gabby says with a snort.

"But I wasn't going to let him into my pants. I was only sixteen. So, I challenged him to a throwing competition. It was lame, even to me, but I bet him that he couldn't throw as far as me. His yard had tons of rocks in it.

"It actually got kind of fun. We would find different targets to challenge the other to hit, like a tree or a bush and stuff like that. I had a good arm. But then, it was my turn to throw, and I tripped and the rock went flying in the wrong direction, right through his grandmother's bedroom window.

"I panicked and ran away."

"You left him to take the blame?" Sarah asks incredulously while the rest of my family is wiping tears from laughing so hard.

"I didn't want to get into trouble. His grandmother was a mean old thing." I glance up at Simon to find him also laughing. "It's dumb, but I thought for sure I was going to get my ass whooped for that. I lied to Mama, I broke someone else's property, *and* I was out with a boy. Alone."

"Yeah, you would have gotten into trouble for sure," Van says when she could breathe again. "I'm just happy to hear that you made *some* mistakes."

"Oh, I've made my share, sugar. Trust me."

"Okay, now let's talk about all the trouble Declan used to get into."

"Good idea," I reply and prepare to pay my baby brother back.

CHAPTER TWELVE

~Charly~

"It's beautiful here," Simon says quietly from the passenger seat next to me as we drive out to my sister's inn. "It's hard to believe we're only a few minutes from the city."

"We go from city to boonies very quickly," I agree and smile when he takes my free hand in his and gives it a squeeze. I've quickly become comfortable with Simon's affection. "Thank you for last night."

"I didn't do anything," he replies, surprised.

"You hung out with most of my family for the evening, listened to old stories, and you were a good sport about it."

"I genuinely had a good time. Your siblings are fun." He kisses my fingers, then places my hand back on the wheel. "I found out last night that you're quite the rebel, but let's keep both hands on the wheel."

"I was not a rebel," I say with a giggle.

"Apparently, sixteen was a rebellious year for you."

"I'm going to kill Declan," I mutter and turn off the freeway. "Let's face it, if that's all my parents had to deal with out of me, they were doing well."

"Were there other little mischievous acts that no one knows about?"

"No." I shake my head. "I was always convinced that I'd get caught, so I didn't try to get away with much. I'm boring, I guess."

"You're anything but boring, love," he replies and tucks a strand of my hair behind my ear, sending shivers down my spine. This man doesn't just make my knees weak. He makes me forget that I even have knees. Or anything else for that matter, aside from the perpetually wet and throbbing spot between my legs. All he has to do is look at me with those hot, sky-blue eyes and I'm a pile of mushy goo.

Damn him.

"Our property line used to begin here," I say, trying to get my mind out of the damn gutter. "It was a few thousand acres in the beginning."

"When was the beginning?" he asks.

"A couple of hundred years ago," I reply with a shrug. "My family has owned this since the mid-nineteenth century."

"That's a long time," he says with a raised brow.

"Not by European standards." I look over at him and smile. "We're a baby compared to stuff over there."

"True, but for the same family to own a piece of land for several hundred years is impressive. Where does the property line begin now?"

"Not far from the house. My great-grandfather began to sell pieces of the land, and my grandfather continued. We were building ships, not farming anymore, so the farmland was sold to families who wanted it to support themselves. We just didn't need it."

"That makes sense."

"By the time my father inherited, the house was used for summers and holidays. We spent the majority of our time in the city. But I loved coming out here for the summer. We ran all over the place."

He nods and looks out the window, watching the plantation houses go by, along with tall trees and swamp land.

Finally, we turn a corner, and Inn Boudreaux comes into view, flanked by ancient oak trees and green grass.

"There she is," I say quietly and slow the car so he can take it in. The house is white, with tall columns and a red front door. The wrap-around porch is deep, perfect for sitting in the evening and watching lightning bugs.

"Wow," Simon says with wide eyes. "These trees are magnificent."

"They're ancient," I reply, looking at the familiar landscape. "Probably around six hundred years old."

"You're kidding."

"I never kid about trees," I reply with a straight face, then bust up laughing. "We don't really know how old they are because they've been here much longer than this land was inhabited, but they're perfect because they create a wind-tunnel of sorts to the house. It's the first air conditioning system. When the house was built two hundred years ago, there was no air conditioning. The trees keep the house cool."

"You're intelligent," he says out of the blue and drags a finger down my arm. "It's fucking sexy."

"Don't start," I reply and pull into the driveway. "We're about to pick up my eleven year old nephew to take him to see the gators. No getting me all hot and bothered."

"My apologies." His smile is wide and smug, and I know that he's not sorry at all.

And really, neither am I.

"Come on, let's see if Sam is ready."

I lead Simon up the steps of the front porch and inside without knocking.

"Gabby?"

"In the kitchen," she calls out.

"So, Gabby runs the inn, as you know," I say and point out the different rooms as we walk to the back of the house. "She makes breakfast for the guests every day."

"Does she do this all by herself?"

"No, she has housekeepers who come in daily, and she hired someone to cover her days off after Rhys badgered her into it. Before that, yes, she did."

"So you're a family of workaholics," Simon says.

"I suppose we are."

"Hey, sugar," Gabby says, her hands buried elbow-deep in a bowl of bread dough. "I'd hug you but I'm a mess."

"It's okay. Is Sam ready to go?"

"Almost," she says and blows a strand of hair out of her face. "He's helping the housekeeper clean the last couple of rooms."

"Is he working off that window he broke?" I ask with a grin.

"He is," she confirms and rolls her eyes. "Before I know it, I'll have Sarah here from social services telling me I'm violating child labor laws."

"He broke the window," I reply and open the fridge, scan the contents, then snoop in a cupboard, hoping there are some pastries left over from this morning. "He should have to earn the money to replace it."

"Agreed," Simon says with a kind smile. God, he's so damn *nice.*

Well, most of the time. In bed, I've learned he's bossy and aggressive. He's just what I need in that area.

"Why are you smiling like that?" Sam asks as he bounds into the kitchen.

"I'm not smiling," I reply and tug him against me for a hug as I take a bite out of a croissant. "Why are *you* smiling?"

"Because we get to go see *gators*!"

"Are you done with Miss Rosie?" Gabby asks.

"Almost. Just one room left. Do we have time, Aunt Charly?"

I check my phone, my mouth full of the delicious pastry. "Yep. Lots of time."

"Yes!" He pumps his fist in the air and runs back out of the kitchen and clomps up the stairs.

"You're so classy, Char," Gabby says. "You'll teach Sam bad manners."

"Nah," I reply and grin. "You've taught him well."

"I think you're rather adorable," Simon says and kisses me on the nose.

"See?" I smile at Gabby. "I'm adorable."

"Why don't you take your adorable self outside and show Simon around? Sam will be done when you get back."

"Are you trying to get rid of me?"

"No, I'm trying to save my pastries from you," she says with a grin.

"I'd love to see more," Simon replies and takes my hand. "Take me on a tour."

"Yes, sir." I lead him out back and we set off down a paved path between more massive oak trees. I take a deep breath and sigh happily. "I love the way it smells out here."

"The fresh air is nice."

"So, these small buildings out here were once slave quarters," I begin and point to the simple wood buildings not far down the path. "Gabby had them moved from out in the fields and renovated so guests could see them. We used to play in them as kids."

"Are these lists of slaves who lived here?" Simon asks, pointing to a placard in front of the quarters.

"They are. These journals were found in the attic when Gabby dug in to renovate for the inn. My great-great-great grandfather was good at keeping records. These have their name, age, who he bought them from, and for how much."

"Incredible," Simon murmurs, reading the pages. "I'm assuming these are copies."

"Yes. The originals are in a safety deposit box."

He nods. "It looks like, despite being a slave owner, he was a fair man."

"From what I understand, ours was not a cruel plantation. The hours were long, and it was hard work, but they were given homes, food, clothes. And they were never separated from their families while they lived here. Meaning, one or two members weren't sold while the others stayed here."

"Amazing."

"As kids, we would play in the slave quarters, but as I got older, and could read well, I found the carvings inside to be fascinating. Of course, we understood what slavery meant, and that it wasn't something to take lightly, and we didn't. I just found it interesting."

"Show me."

I grin and take his hand, leading him inside. "There are carvings in here, of names and dates. Some couldn't read or write, but others could."

"Your history is a rich one," Simon says and pulls me in for a big hug. "And I don't mean money."

"I know," I reply and bury my face in his chest, breathing him in. He smells even better than the bayou. "There's more to show you, but Sam is probably ready by now, and we don't want to be late."

"Another time then." He tips my chin up and lays his lips gently on mine, sweeping back and forth, then sinks in and kisses me long and deep. "We'd better go before I take you against the wall here."

"Another time then," I reply, echoing his words and grin when lust flashes in his blue eyes. "Come on. We have a date with a gator."

***

"We haven't seen any gators yet," Sam says with a frown as he scours the swamp. "Where are they, mister?"

"We'll see some," the guide replies with a wink. He's an older guy, probably running tours through the swamp in his retirement. His voice is as rough as his skin, but he's gentle and good with the kids.

"I hope so," Sam says and glances up at me. "I promised to show you some."

"Well, we've already seen a few snakes," Simon says, not at all helpfully and grins at me when I wince.

"Thanks for the reminder," I mumble and glare at the sexy man who simply laughs.

"That was pretty cool," Sam says. "But I don't think they were poisonous."

"Oh darn."

"Look what I found," the old guide says as he leans

over the side of the boat and pulls up a small gator, making me grab onto Simon. "This little fella is just a baby."

"Oh God." I swallow hard as Sam stands up excitedly. "Sam, don't get too close."

"You can hold 'em!" Sam says. "Ain't that right, mister?"

"*Isn't* that right," I correct him, still clinging to Simon. "Why did I agree to come again?"

"Because you love him," Simon says simply and kisses my forehead. "And you're an excellent aunt."

"I'm okay," I reply with a shrug, then cringe again when Sam turns to me. "You can hold him too!"

"Oh, that's okay."

But the guide comes at me with the little gator, holding him out to me.

"I'm really fine."

"Come on, Aunt Charly, you're not scared of a *baby*."

"Yeah, Aunt Charly," Simon says. He loves to tease me. "It's just a baby."

"Oh." I look between all three men, and feel trapped. Sam has such hope in his eyes, I can't let him down. So, I reach out, and just before the guide puts it in my hands, I squeeze my eyes shut.

Hard.

Suddenly, something scaly and wet is in my hands. It's lighter than I expected, but I just keep reciting to myself: *I'm not holding a reptile. I'm not holding a reptile.*

Almost as soon as it's in my hands, I say, "Okay, that's enough. Take it. Take it. Please, for the love of Moses take it."

To my relief, it's taken away and placed in Simon's hands.

"Look how cute it is," Sam says and pets its little head. "I want one."

"I don't think that's a good idea," the guide says gruffly. "He'll grow up to look like that." He points to the side of the boat, and there on the shore, not twenty feet from us, is a gator the size of our boat.

"Holy crap!" Sam exclaims. I've lost my voice. I'm pretty sure I'm going to die here in the swamp.

"I don't think your aunt is as excited," Simon says with a laugh. "And here you were so outdoorsy in Montana."

"Montana isn't a swamp land with snakes and gators and other poisonous things that can kill you."

"Right." Simon nods. "It's just full of bears and mountain lions and rattlesnakes, all of which can kill you."

"Thanks." I swallow hard and mentally pray that we make it back to civilization alive.

"Isn't this *so fun*, Aunt Charly?" Sam asks excitedly as the guide puts the baby back in the water.

"Absolutely." I smile and nod, careful not to touch anything. "Do you have anything we can wash our hands with?"

"Nah. You'll have to wait until we get back."

"Great."

Simon tucks me into his side and kisses my head.

"Don't touch me," I say. "You touched a gator."

"Don't worry, darling. The gator germs won't hurt you."

"Do you know that for sure, Marlin Perkins?"

He laughs and kisses my head again.

"You delight me every day, love."

"I'm so happy I delight you. I'd rather delight you

without gators nearby."

"You like it," Sam says smugly. "You just can't admit it because you're a girl."

"You got me," I say and kiss his cheek. He sticks his tongue out like it's gross, but then he smiles.

"Thanks for bringing me."

"You're welcome."

***

"I didn't realize we'd get back so late," Simon says quietly as we pull into the inn. Sam fell asleep long ago in the backseat.

"Ours was the last tour of the day. But I agree, I didn't realize how long they ran."

Longer than I would have liked.

"Your face got a little red in the sun."

I grin over at him. "So did yours."

"Next time, we take sunscreen. Sam didn't get red at all."

"He lives in the sun," I reply and look at the sweet boy in the rear view mirror. "And I don't think there will be a next time. I've seen all the gators I need to for my lifetime."

"You were a good sport," Simon says and cups my cheek in his palm.

"Are you sure you washed your hands?"

"Twice." He glances up. "Looks like Rhys is home."

I smile as I park and climb out of the car, caught up in a bear hug from my brother in law. "It's about time you came home."

"I'm a working man, you know." He kisses my cheek and sets me on my feet, his face sobering as Simon rounds the car to shake his hand. "You must be Simon."

"I am. It's a pleasure to meet you, Mr.

O'Shaughnessy."

"You can call me Rhys," he says and glances down at me. "Are you happy?"

I tilt my head, not used to the overprotective brother routine from Rhys and grin. "You're sweet, sugar."

"That doesn't answer my question."

"I'm always happy."

"Hmm." He nods once and looks in the backseat of the car. "I hate to wake him, but I'm dying to see him."

"He'll be upset if you don't wake him," Gabby says from behind him. "Thanks for taking him. Was he good?"

Before I can say anything, Simon steps forward. "Sam is a joy, Gabby. He's a sweet boy, and he loves his Aunt Charly. You've done a wonderful job with him."

Gabby's face softens as she watches her husband wake her son. "Thank you. He is a sweetheart."

"Daddy!" Sam exclaims when he opens his eyes and sees Rhys leaning over him. "You're home!" He wraps his arms around Rhys's neck tightly and looks at his mother over Rhys's shoulder. "You didn't tell me he was coming home today. I wasn't here."

"Hey, it was a surprise," Rhys says when he pulls Sam from the car, holding him in his arms. Sam isn't a small boy anymore, but Rhys is a big guy. "I asked your mom not to tell you."

"I'm so glad you're here." Sam's eyes fill with tears, which he quickly brushes away. "It's been two whole weeks."

"I know. Baseball season is rough, kiddo. But now that you're out of school, you and your sister and mom will be coming with me more."

"Good." Sam sighs in relief and grins at Simon. "Did you meet my dad?"

"I did, and he seems like a great guy."

"Yeah, he's awesome. He plays baseball."

"I've seen him play," Simon replies. "Thank you for taking us to see the gators today. I had a great time."

"You're welcome. You did good. You didn't even flinch when you held the baby."

"Did Aunt Charly flinch?" Gabby asks with a smile.

"Yeah, she didn't like it," Sam says when Rhys sets him on the ground and we make our way inside. "But she covered it up good."

"I did?"

Simon shakes his head no, making everyone laugh.

"Well, you tried," Sam amends and then yawns. "I don't want to go to bed."

"No bedtime shenanigans tonight," Gabby says with her stern mom voice. "Your sister is asleep, and you're going to bed. We have lots to do tomorrow to get ready to travel with your dad for a week."

"Okay," Sam says and wraps his arms around my waist, squeezing me tight. "Thanks again, Aunt Charly."

"You're welcome, buddy."

"And thanks, Mr. Simon," he says, offering his hand for a fist bump.

"My pleasure."

"I'll get him settled," Rhys says and kisses his wife on the cheek. "Good night, y'all."

"We should go," I say and yawn. "It's not that late, but it's been a long day."

"Why don't you stay?" Gabby asks. "I had a cancelation, so I have a room available, and it *is* late. I'd feel better if you slept here."

"I'd love that. Rumor has it you make a delicious breakfast," Simon says with a smile. "What do you think?"

"Are you sure? I don't want to make more work for you."

"Oh please." Gabby rolls her eyes and gestures for us to follow her up the stairs. "It's the same amount of work. Adding two is nothing, trust me." She leads us to the Penelope room and grins. "And you get the prettiest room in the inn."

"Why is it called the Penelope room?" Simon asks.

"Each room is named after a different woman from our family," she says with a smile. "Penelope was our great grandmother. From what I hear, she was funny, hardworking, and the life of the party."

"It's a lovely room," Simon says, checking out the four-poster bed covered in an antique quilt. "Thank you."

"Sleep well," Gabby says with a wink and closes the door behind her.

I turn to Simon and sigh, happy to finally be alone with him.

"Come here," he says quietly. I comply, walking to him and stopping just before we touch. "How do you feel?"

"Tired. Happy. Ready for a shower."

His lips twitch as he drags a finger down my cheek. "Let's take that shower. Then I want to curl up in that bed with you and hold you while you sleep."

I blink at him. "No sex?"

He smiles now. "Are you disappointed?"

Yes. "It's no big deal." I shrug and turn away, but he catches my arm at the elbow and spins me back to face him, kissing me deeply.

"Trust me, when I'm inside you tonight, it will be a *big deal*."

"Promises, promises."

"I love your sassy side."

"Is that all?"

He laughs and turns to the bathroom, pulling me behind him. "Come on, sassy, let's get cleaned up so I can remind you what a big deal I am."

CHAPTER THIRTEEN

~Simon~

"This *is* the best breakfast I've ever had," I say the next morning. We're seated at the breakfast bar, watching Gabby bustle about.

"Thank you," Gabby says with a grin.

"She's always been a good cook," Charly says as she munches on fruit and sips her coffee. She's fresh faced this morning, her hair brushed and up in a tail. She looks young and carefree, and because I know her, well-fucked.

It was the first time we made love without making much noise. I do prefer to have privacy so she can be uninhibited, but last night was just as much fun. We smiled and covered our moans with kisses, as if we were young and trying to hide from our parents.

Charly delights me at every turn.

"What are your plans for the day?" Gabby asks as Rhys walks in the room. He snatches a slice of bacon, shoves most of it in his mouth, then swoops his wife into his arms and bends her back into a dramatic kiss, making her laugh.

"Yuck," Sam says, rubbing the sleep from his eyes. "Do you have to do that in front of *people*?" he asks.

"Well, I'm married to her, so I can do it whenever I please."

"You did it before you were married to her too," Sam points out and takes a piece of bacon. "It's pretty gross."

"It's not gross," Gabby says and passes Sam a plate of pancakes with blueberries and syrup. "Ailish is sleeping late today."

Just then, the baby whimpers through the baby monitor.

"Oh, let me go get her!" Charly says and jumps up. "I never get to get her when she wakes up."

"Go ahead. She'll need a diaper change."

"I got this." Charly winks at me and disappears up the stairs.

"So what's next?" Gabby asks me when Charly is out of earshot.

"Excuse me?"

"What are your plans," she says and pulls more pastries out of the oven. "And if you say that this is just a casual thing for you, I will stab you with this knife."

"She'll do it," Sam says while shoving pancake in his mouth.

Rhys leans his hips against the countertop, crosses his arms, and simply listens.

"Good morning, sweet baby girl," Charly croons through the monitor. Ailish giggles. "Oh, aren't you just the sweetest little thing in the world?"

"She's adorable with the kids," I say.

"You're not getting out of my question."

"Honestly, we don't have a plan. And I'm not saying

that because I think it's casual; it's the truth. I can tell you that I'm pursuing your sister. She's an amazing woman, and I enjoy her very much."

"I don't know how I feel about that answer," Gabby says after a moment. "But I can see that you're nice to her, and I don't think you would intentionally hurt her."

"Of course not."

"Because if you did…well, let's just say there are plenty of places to hide a body in the swamp." She smiles brightly, and for the first time, I think I might be truly afraid of a woman.

"Stop bullying him," Rhys says with a laugh and kisses her on the head. "Although, it is impressive."

"I'm tougher than I look."

"I believe that."

"I have some work to do out back, why don't you come with me?" Rhys says to me and gestures for me to follow him. "Gabby's not subtle about being protective over her siblings. Then again, none of them are. Have you met all of the brothers yet?"

"Just Declan," I reply.

"He's the laid-back one," Rhys says with a grin. "I'd like to be there when you meet Eli and Beau, but I think I'll miss it. Maybe Kate will film it for me."

"Should I be worried?"

"Depends." He leads me across the field to an older barn. Inside is workout equipment. "Do you love her?"

I stop cold and watch Rhys as he sits at a machine and begins lifting weights. But I don't really see him. I see Charly. Her smile, her laugh, the way she feels when I'm inside her.

"I'm learning her," I reply and frown when Rhys busts up laughing. "What's so bloody funny?"

"That's what I said about Gabby when Beau asked me the same question." He shakes his head and stands. "I knew the minute I saw Gabby that she was the one for me. I never believed in all that love at first sight crap, but I knew that she was *mine*. Being away from her was torture."

"I don't like being away from Charly either," I say quietly, remembering how horrible it was when I was in London after the retreat. "But it's still early—"

"You should know by now if it's a sex thing, or if she's someone you can see yourself with for the long term."

"It's not just a sex thing." It was never just a sex thing, I was just too bloody stubborn to admit it.

"How much longer are you in town for?"

"Only a couple more days." And that stabs me in the heart. I don't want to leave.

Maybe I don't have to.

"If you break her heart, you'll have to worry about her family. They're as tight as they come. Did Gabby tell you that Kate is my cousin?"

"No," I reply, surprised.

"I met Gabby through Kate. I needed a place to disappear to so I could rehab my shoulder, and Kate suggested I come here. It was the best fucking thing I ever did."

"You are beautiful together."

"She's everything, man. It's because of her that I have my kids, and they are my life."

"You're a lucky man."

"I just want you to know that Charly is an amazing woman. I don't know much about her relationship history, but then, none of her family does. She's pretty tight-lipped. So, if she's bringing you around, it's because she has feelings for you."

This is not news to me. I can see by the way she looks at me that she has feelings for me.

"They all look out for each other," he continues. "The girls as much as the guys, and if they think something isn't right, they'll tell you."

"As they should," I reply. "I think Charly is extraordinary. She makes me feel things that I don't think I ever have before, and I was married, Rhys. She's special. Do I love her?"

Fuck, I don't want to contemplate that yet.

"I don't know. I care about her, and I want her to be happy."

"You're scared," he says and holds his hands up in surrender when I glare at him. "I'm not trying to piss you off. I get it. The Boudreaux women can be scary. Good luck to you, man, if you stick around long enough to get *the talk* from the brothers."

"Isn't she a little old for that?"

He laughs. "Didn't you hear a word I said? It doesn't matter how old she is. She's their sister."

I nod.

"Are you sure you need to leave in a couple of days?"

"I'm going to make a call," I reply, juggling things in my head. "I'd like to stay."

"Then I think you should stay. I'll let you make that call." He pats me on the shoulder and leaves the barn, and I immediately dial Todd's number.

"Hey, mate."

"I need to stay a while longer. Let's take a look at the schedule."

"You got it."

***

"Are you sure you can stay?" Charly asks as we drive through the Quarter later that afternoon. She's grinning, but her eyes look a bit guarded, as though she'll get her hopes up and then I'll crush them later.

"I'm going to stay for another two weeks," I reply and smile when she shimmies in her seat. "And I take it that's okay with you."

"I was sad at the thought of you leaving," she replies softly. "But I also don't want to be greedy or needy and ask you to stay. I know you have a business and a life that isn't here."

A big part of my life is here.

"If you're needy then so am I," I reply honestly. "I enjoy you, Charlotte. I'm not ready to be away from you, and there's no need to be. I can continue to work remotely. I also need to write my book, and I can do that anywhere."

"Okay. As long as you're sure."

"You're stuck with me, love."

She smiles, and then looks over my shoulder and her eyes go wide. "Oh! I want to check this place out!" She pulls over and cuts the engine. "Kate has been in this shop and loved it. The owner came in my store a few weeks ago, and she's just the sweetest thing. Do you mind if we go in?"

"Of course not. Let's go."

"Beau lives above this place, and Eli and Kate live next door."

"Do they own the block?" I ask.

"Actually, they do," she says with a smile and leads me in the shop. It smells like…well, all kinds of things. There are frilly soaps and lotions, herbs and oils.

A petite blonde is standing behind the counter, unpacking a box. She's wearing a flowy sundress, humming to herself. She looks up with happy blue eyes when she hears the bell above the door.

"Charly," she says with a smile. "What a pleasant surprise."

"Hi, Mallory," Charly says. "I have been meaning to stop in, and we were just driving by. This is Simon."

"Hello," Mallory says and nods.

"Pleasure."

"What are you in the market for?" Mallory asks and sets the box aside. There's suddenly a loud thump from upstairs.

"What is Beau doing up there?" Charly asks with a frown. "Wait, he's usually at work right now."

"He's not up there," Mallory confirms. "It's Miss Louisa."

Charly stops cold. "He has a *woman* living with him?"

"No. Well, not a living woman, anyway. Miss Louisa has been here for about a hundred years."

I wrap my arm around Charly's shoulders. "So it's haunted then," I reply.

"Oh, yes," Mallory says with a nod. "It's hard to find a place around here that isn't. This is New Orleans, after all."

"Have you seen her?" Charly asks, looking up to the ceiling. She shivers and leans into me.

"Several times, but she doesn't show herself often. I'm sure your family hasn't seen her, but they may have heard her. I know Beau has because he's constantly accusing me of making the noise."

"What does he say when you explain that it isn't

you?"

"Charly, I've never met your brother in person, but he doesn't seem like the type to believe in ghosts."

Charly laughs beside me and shakes her head. "You'd be right. Is he giving you a hard time?"

"He's just difficult now and then. He's nothing I can't handle."

She pushes her blonde hair over her shoulder and winks, and I believe she can handle just about anything thrown at her. There's an air about her that's just a little…different.

"Ah, but you believe in ghosts, don't you, Mr. Simon?"

"I'm from England, darling. Of course I do."

She nods.

"Do you see ghosts often?" Charly asks, shivering again at the word. Mallory smiles, but her eyes are sober.

"I like you, Charly. I don't want to scare you off with paranormal talk."

"You won't scare me off. I like you too," Charly says.

"Well, I do see things quite often that can't really be explained by science. I see Miss Louisa about once a month, and there's plenty to see in the Quarter in general."

"Does Miss Louisa talk to you?"

Charly shivers again.

"No, she just looks sad. I don't ask her questions, I just smile and let her know that she's safe here." Mallory takes Charly's hand and frowns suddenly. "You're terrified, honey."

"No, I'm not."

"You've seen some things," Mallory says, surprising me. She knows things, all right. Her eyes look like she's seen more than she'd like to share. "You don't have to be scared. The spirits around you are kind."

"I have spirits around me?" Charly squeals, her eyes wide.

"We all do," Mallory replies with a chuckle. "You have problems sleeping. I have just the thing for that."

She turns to the wall with essential oils and pulls down a small brown vial. "This is vetiver. Just put one or two drops on the soles of your feet and rub them together at bedtime. It'll help you sleep like a baby."

"Really?" Charly uncaps it and sniffs, then scowls. "It doesn't smell good."

"No, but it works. Here, take some lavender as well, and that'll cover the smell of the vetiver."

"How much do I owe you?" Charly asks.

"This is on me," Mallory replies. "Those shoes you sold me are divine, and I was the talk of the wedding."

"It's not nice to outshine the bride," Charly says.

"Well, then I guess the bride should have bought her shoes from you." Mallory bags up the oils and passes them to Charly.

"I think we're going to be good friends, Mallory."

"I hope so," Mallory replies. "It was a pleasure to meet you, Simon."

I nod and guide Charly back out to her car. "Are you okay?"

"Of course. Why wouldn't I be okay?" Her hands shake as she starts the car.

"She spooked you."

"I'm a grown woman who lives in the ghost story capital of the world," she says with a roll of the eyes, but she's not fooling me. "I'm just fine."

"If you say so."

***

"Did you hear that?" Charly asks that night as we lie in bed. This is the third time she's asked me in ten minutes.

"No," I reply and hug her close. "Go to sleep."

"The vetiver isn't working."

"Because you're too busy listening for ghosts," I reply and kiss her forehead. "How long have you lived in this house?"

"About five years."

"And have you ever heard anything before?"

"I don't think so."

"Well, there you go. Your imagination is working overtime. Now go to sleep."

She settles against me, and just as I'm about to drift off, her head jerks up. "Don't tell me you didn't hear *that*."

"Okay, that's it." I roll on top of her and pin her to the bed, my face buried in her neck.

"What are you doing?"

"Refocusing your attention, since you won't let me go to sleep."

"You can sleep. I'm sorry." She gasps when I pull her nipple between my teeth. "Oh, that's nice."

I grin and pay the same attention to the other breast, then slide down her body. I push her knees up beside her ears and lick her, from anus to clit, twice, and then I push inside her in one fast thrust.

"Oh my god!" she exclaims and wraps her legs around my hips, holding on tight.

"Maybe this will help empty your mind." I plant my thumb on her clit and watch her go wild as I fuck her hard, pressing the base of my cock on my thumb.

"Jesus, Simon."

"That's right. Just me, Charlotte. Just me and what we have together."

She's clutching onto my shoulders, and arches her neck back as she comes apart, moaning my name.

I pull out and flip her over, pinning her hips to the mattress. I spread her cheeks apart enough to see her glistening pussy, straddle her legs, and push inside her again.

"Fucking love this angle," I growl and bite her shoulder. She's white-knuckling the sheets, biting her pillow. I fist her hair and pull back slightly, just so I can see her gorgeous, flushed face. "Your pussy is so bloody tight."

"Your cock is just big," she replies between gasps. "God, you're hitting my spot in just the perfect way."

"Like this?" I ask and push harder, making her moan.

"Fuck me," she moans.

"Oh, I am, love." God, she brings me to my knees. Whether it's hard and fast or soft and sweet, I'm lost in her. I can't get enough of her.

Her pussy clenches down on me as she comes again, and I follow her over this time, the orgasm shooting along my spine, sending electricity through every part of me.

"Damn, you're amazing."

"You were doing all the work," she says, still catching her breath. Finally, I roll off of her and she manages to roll onto her back. "I think I'm going to pretend to be afraid more often. The benefits are spectacular."

"You weren't pretending, darling," I reply and suck her nipple into my mouth, loving the way she gasps. "You taste delicious."

"I bet you taste delicious right now."

With a wicked look in her hazel eyes, she takes my semi-hard cock in her mouth and sucks me gently.

"Fucking hell." My hips jerk, and I'm already at full attention again. God, she's sucking herself off of my cock.

It's the sexiest fucking thing I've ever seen in my life.

"We taste good," she says with a satisfied smile. "And look at that. You're hard again."

"What are you going to do about it?"

She tilts her head to the side as she rises over me, as though she's considering my question. She takes me easily inside her and begins rocking back and forth, milking me with those strong as hell muscles of hers.

"I think I'll do this."

"I won't complain." I grip her hips and guide her up and down, but suddenly she takes my hands in hers and pins them over my head, kissing me lightly. She licks my lips, down my jaw and to my neck where she nibbles leisurely, all the while riding me at a slow, even pace.

"I like this," she breathes. "I love feeling you inside me, against me." She bites my shoulder. "But do you know what I like the most?"

"Tell me."

"I like the look on your face while you fuck me."

"What look is that?"

"Surprise. Happiness. Lust."

I sit up, easily breaking out of her hold and wrap my arms around her waist, picking up the pace. "I never stop wanting you, Charlotte."

"You're the only one who uses my full name, you know."

"I'd better be the only one to do a lot of things." Her eyes find mine in surprise. I fist her thick dark hair in my hand and tilt her head back, giving me access to her smooth neck. "I'm the only one."

"Yes."

I push up hard, making her gasp.

"The *only fucking one*."

"Yes, Simon."

She comes around me, then collapses against me, breathing hard, eyes closed. I lie back, cradling her on my chest, and smile when she simply drifts off to sleep, unaware of the creaks and groans in the house around us.

CHAPTER
FOURTEEN

~Charly~

I feel dumb this morning. My house is *not* haunted. I was just all worked up because of what Mallory said yesterday, and well, because that shit does freak me out. I'm quite sure Gabby's inn is haunted, and probably every other building in Louisiana.

But not my house.

I'll have plenty of time today at work to lose myself in other thoughts and by tonight, I'll be back to normal.

Although, maybe I should pretend to still be scared because apparently, that gets me some good sex.

"What are you grinning about?" Simon asks as he walks into the bedroom. I'm getting ready for work, and he's pulled the clothes he's been wearing for a couple of days back on.

"Nothing important."

"You look like you're cooking up some sort of scheme," he says.

"Maybe I'm just happy," I suggest.

"Perhaps," he concedes and kisses my neck. "Or maybe you were thinking about last night."

"Are you a mind reader?" I ask and playfully elbow him in the ribs.

"You wound me," he says, rubbing his ribs as though I've broken them and makes me laugh. "I really need to go back to my hotel room to change clothes. These are starting to stand on their own."

"Why don't you just bring everything back here," I suggest calmly, as if it's no big deal at all, but my stomach is turning. "If you're going to stay longer, there's really no need to keep two places."

"Are you sure?" His eyes narrow as he watches me closely, and I nod. This is a big step for me. I've never suggested that anyone come stay with me for any length of time.

But I don't like the idea of Simon keeping his things somewhere else. He should be here, with me.

"Here's a key."

He accepts it, then takes my hand and kisses it tenderly.

"You'll hardly know I'm here," he says, his eyes dancing with mirth.

"Right." I laugh and shake my head. "You're kind of hard to miss, Simon."

"I blend quite well."

I laugh now and cup his cheek in my hand. "Given that I can't seem to stay away from you, I doubt that I'll forget you're here. But I want you here. So please make yourself at home."

"Thank you."

"You're welcome." We're grinning foolishly at each other when his phone rings.

"Sorry, I have to take this." He frowns and accepts the call. "Hello, Mum."

He walks out of the room, not bothering to lower his voice, and I can't help but listen.

"No, I won't be calling her."

I sit on the edge of my bed.

"Because I don't want anything to do with her. I'm sorry that she's going through that, but it's no longer my problem."

There's a pause and I hear him sigh.

"Yes, I know how you feel. You've made it quite clear. I'll make myself clear. I would rather you didn't speak to her, but I can't control who you choose to talk to."

His voice has gone hard and cold. I've never heard him like this.

"Mother, I didn't tell you everything that happened because it was none of your business. But I will say this, please consider the source when she's crying on your shoulder. Well, then I guess I'm heartless."

What the hell? Simon is the least heartless man I know!

"Listen to me. I'm not going to bloody call her. Ever. That part of my life is closed. Have a good evening, Mother."

He ends the call, and I wait for what seems forever for him to come back. When he doesn't, I walk into the sitting room to find him sitting with his head in his hands. He looks...*defeated*.

I cross to him and rub circles on his back.

"Are you okay?"

"I don't like arguing with my mother," he says softly. "And it seems that we argue more than anything lately."

"What do you argue about?" I ask, not at all ashamed to pry.

He lets out a humorless laugh and stands, pacing away from me, then back again. He rubs his neck and I sit, waiting for him to work out whatever is torturing him.

"I told you about Amy, my ex-wife, and how our marriage ended."

"Yes, that you'd found her cheating on you."

He nods and paces the room.

"The thing is, her cheating on me was the least of it. She did me a favor by fucking around because she gave me a valid reason to leave her."

"What did she do to you?" I ask, and clench my shaking hands in my lap.

"Physically? Just the scratches on my arm. But she was manipulative and emotionally abusive from the moment we got married. I was an idiot. I would give in every time she threatened to kill herself if she didn't get her way or like the way things were going."

"She threatened to *kill herself?*"

"Not often in the beginning, but as time went on, it became more frequent. I don't know how many times I'd come home to find that she'd swallowed pills and I had to call an ambulance. She could cue tears at the drop of a hat.

"I had her in therapy over and over again. She would claim that the therapist came on to her, or tried to have sex with her, and would refuse to go back." He turns to me, his deep blue eyes radiating pain. "Those poor men, and one woman, did nothing wrong but tell her that she's a sociopath.

"I couldn't help her, and it tore me apart. I thought I loved her, and I did. Otherwise I never would have asked her to marry me."

"But she was abusive, Simon."

"She was ill."

"Bullshit." I stand and prop my hands on my hips. "She was a mean, manipulative woman. She knew exactly what she was doing. She was playing head games with you for her own enjoyment."

He swallows hard.

"I'm sorry, I don't know her, but I can see what she did to you."

"I've made it my life's work to empower women. To help them believe that they are worthy of everything wonderful in this world. I've helped women leave their abusive husbands, end careers that were toxic, and even stand up to parents and family members who were nothing but bullies. And here I am, a man who couldn't help his wife. You were right in Montana, I am a hypocrite."

"Oh for fuck's sake, you are no such thing." Now I'm just angry. At him for believing this bullshit and at her for, well, for being her. "I was mad at you and I shouldn't have said that. She didn't *want* to be helped, Simon. That's what you need to realize. I hate this saying, but it's true: you can lead a horse to water, but you can't make it drink. You did what you could for her, but she didn't think anything was wrong. She was manipulating you, and she was pretending to be sick. In reality, she loved the attention you gave her, and she loved getting her own way."

He's watching me with so much hope in his eyes that I want to cry. My God, has he been clinging to this false sense of responsibility for all this time?

"I'm proud of you for walking away and washing

your hands of her. And I understand not wanting to air all your dirty laundry to your family, but they should know some of it, Simon. Especially if your mother is choosing to keep Amy in her life."

"I don't think she's choosing it, I think Amy is just pressing all the right buttons to keep herself there. You're right, I should tell Mum more of it, so she knows what she's dealing with. I just didn't want her to be disappointed in me. And that may be the first time I've ever admitted that. I sound like a coward."

"You sound like someone who was abused," I reply gently and wrap my arms around him. "I've never been there, but Savannah has, and she had many of the same feelings. You do so many great things for people. You should be proud of that, and if it was your relationship with Amy that circled you around to it, well, then maybe it was worth it. But you have to reconcile it for what it was and move on, Simon."

"You're an amazing woman, Charlotte Boudreaux."

"I think I'm just the voice of reason right now."

He catches my chin with his finger and tilts my face up to look at him. "Thank you."

"You can pay me back later." I press my lips to his chin, then check the time. "I'm about to be amazingly late. Feel free to unpack and just put your things wherever you want. I'll see you tonight."

"Are you okay, love?"

"Of course." I send him a bright smile. "Just call me if you need me."

"Have a good day."

I blow him a kiss and leave, my mind reeling. When he was telling me what Amy did to him, I wanted to sit and weep for him. What a grade-A bitch. I'd like just five minutes alone with her.

And given that I'd like five minutes alone with her, I'm just fucking angry. How could anyone treat another human being like that? What kind of sick joy does that bring them?

I've never felt this overwhelming need to protect a man before. Not that he needs it; she can't hurt him now. But I feel fiercely territorial.

And this is new.

I don't know what to do about it. I still don't see how a relationship with Simon can make it long-term. He can't stay in New Orleans forever, and I don't plan to leave.

But I do know that I'm going to enjoy him for every minute he's here.

***

I flip the sign to *closed* at exactly six o'clock. It's the first time I haven't stayed open later in…I can't even remember. I usually take my time, visit with straggling customers, count the till, organize credit card receipts, and I even sit and pore through shoes online, deciding what to buy next.

But not tonight. I'm excited to go home. Not because there's someone to go home to, but because it's Simon.

I'm ready to see Simon.

Even the evening traffic doesn't bother me a bit. I whistle along with the radio, and patiently make my way through town. Butterflies set up residence in my belly as I pull into the driveway. Simon's rental is parked at the curb.

I walk in and grin when I see him at my dining table chatting on the phone. He glances up and smiles at me, that smile that makes me forget that I have knees, and finishes his call.

"How was your day?" he asks.

"Busy, so it was a good day," I reply and set my handbag and keys on the table. "How about you?"

"The same." He kisses me gently, sending a shiver down my arms. "I brought all of my things over."

"Great."

"There are a few things that I couldn't find a home for, so you can just tell me where you want to put them."

"That's fine." I look up at him and realize that he looks nervous. "What's wrong?"

"Nothing's wrong." He grips my shoulders, then rubs his hands up and down my arms. "But I need a favor."

"Okay."

"I have to record my weekly video today. I missed last week, and I can't miss two in a row."

"Of course not. You have quite a following."

He grins. "I usually have a camera guy, but I obviously didn't bring him with me from London. I can record the whole thing here, then send it to him and he'll cut it together and make it look nice to go live."

"Sounds good. What do you need me for?"

"I need you to run the camera. I'll just use my phone, which is fine, but I'll need you to make sure I'm centered in the shot, hit record, and end it as well."

"This sounds like a very easy job. I can handle it." I give him a mock salute. "Why do you look nervous? You've recorded hundreds of these."

"Today's topic is going to be a bit more personal."

He doesn't say anything more. He sits at the table, and I realize he's already set up his phone across from him.

He looks amazing. He's in jeans and a casual polo shirt, showing off the tattoos on his arm. His hair is combed back, and he's clean-shaven.

He looks professional and comfortable, which is perfect for pulling a viewer in. It worked for me, anyway, when Van and I sat and watched just about every video he had available. Of course, this is the first time he's recorded a video without long sleeves.

And now he's sitting in my house, recording his video.

And I'm sleeping with him.

Crazy.

"Everyone will see your tats."

He glances down and then shrugs. "I've decided I don't care."

"Any special reason?"

"I didn't bring a long-sleeved shirt." He grins and I shake my head.

"Are you ready?" I ask, looking at the camera. "You're in frame."

"Yes, ready when you are. If I mess up, I'll start at the beginning of my thought, and Perry will fix it later."

"Okay. One, two, three." I press record, and Simon's whole demeanor immediately changes. He's the confident, in control life coach that his fans can't get enough of, and I'm excited to see what he's going to speak about.

"Hello, everyone, and thank you for joining me this week. As you may have noticed, I missed last week's video, but I'm back this week with something that I think many of you will identify with. This week's topic is *How to know when your partner is manipulating you.*

"I try to keep my personal life very separate from my professional life, but I'm also a human being, and I've experienced many of the same things that you have. This topic is one that I've been hesitant to talk about because it is so deeply personal, but someone whom I care about very much reminded me today that there is no shame in being human."

He's not looking into the lens now, but rather in my eyes. I'm stunned. I sit quietly and listen intently as he describes what it is to be in an intimate relationship with someone who betrays your trust by manipulating and hurting you. His face is passive, but his eyes are passionate.

"I know what it is to feel responsible for making a partner happy, and how defeating it is when nothing you ever do is good enough. To have your significant other threaten personal harm if they don't get their way. It's a helpless, horrible position to be in.

"And I'm here to tell you that it's not normal, and it's not okay. If you are being treated this way, by anyone in your life, whether it be a colleague, a boyfriend or girlfriend, a family member or friend, it is imperative that you draw the line in the sand and make it very clear that while you care about them, they may *not* manipulate you. Offer to help them find a counselor, and if they insist they don't need help, perhaps it's time to step away from the relationship, no matter how scary that may be.

"I want you to remember that no matter what, your physical and mental health are the most important thing. That is not being selfish; that is protecting yourself, so you can participate in healthy relationships. Cutting toxic people from your life is necessary for your own personal health and growth.

"I personally think a lot of us feel ashamed when we try so hard to help someone, only to have that help thrown back in our face or ignored altogether, and we are doing ourselves such a disservice in feeling that way. It's important to speak up, and to talk to those closest to you so they can help you. No one who loves you will stand for you being manipulated or hurt, and you should not be ashamed to talk about it."

He smiles kindly at the camera and I can feel tears in my eyes. Something tells me this is a *huge* step for Simon.

"Thank you for joining me this week."

He nods and I stop the recording, and then take a long, deep breath. I don't quite know what to say.

Simon scrubs his hands over his face.

"Please tell me that was okay because I don't think I have it in me to do it again."

"You did great," I reply and clear my throat. "I think it was a beautiful message, and you were eloquent in your delivery."

"I rehearsed it all day. I've never done that before." He looks up at me, still across the table. "I still don't know if I should air it."

"Can I be brutally honest?"

"Always."

"I think you'd be doing yourself and your fans a disservice by *not* airing it. If even one person sees that and recognizes herself and pulls out of an abusive situation, it will have been worth it. And I think that fans like it when they can see that you're a human being. That you may know a lot of things, but you don't know *everything*. We are all a work in progress."

Without a word, he stands and walks around the table, then pulls me to my feet and into his arms. He hugs me tightly, rocking back and forth, his face buried in my hair.

"Thank you, Charly. You have no idea what you did for me today."

"Simon, you already had all of this in you. I just talked you through it. I imagine I'm not the first to try."

"No, but it was the first time I was willing to hear it," he says, his voice muffled against my head. "You are a brilliant, gorgeous woman, and I'm so thankful that I found you."

I cling onto him, enjoying the way he's rocking us, settled against him. "I think I found you, remember?"

"Either way," he says, a smile in his voice. "Thank you."

CHAPTER FIFTEEN

~Charly~

"They're here already," I say to Simon as we walk into a restaurant just a few blocks away from my shop the next day. "Now you'll have met everyone."

"Rumor has it, Beau and Eli are the hardest to win over."

"That rumor is probably true," I reply and smile sweetly. "Don't worry."

"I'm not," he says and kisses my forehead, just as we approach the table, earning glares from both of my brothers.

"Hi, guys, sorry we're late."

"You're not," Kate says. "We were early because your brothers wanted to have home court advantage."

"You're not supposed to tell them that," Eli says to his wife with a scowl. "I'm Eli."

"Simon," Simon says, shaking Eli's hand. "You must be Beau."

"That's right. I'm the oldest brother," Beau says, and Kate and I both roll our eyes at the way my brothers puff out their chests and give Simon stern looks.

"I'm thirty," I remind them all. "And this isn't some sort of weird approval thing. This is just lunch."

"I don't know what you're talking about," Eli replies and holds Kate's hand.

"Neither do I," Beau says. "We're just here to enjoy a meal with our sister and her...*friend*."

"Men," I mumble and smile apologetically at Simon, who just squeezes my thigh reassuringly.

"I've seen you on television," Beau says, breaking the ice after the waitress takes our orders. "You seem to know what you're talking about."

"I hope so," Simon replies. "People pay a lot of money to learn my techniques. I'd better know what I'm talking about."

"Do you actually have a degree in psychology, or are you self taught?" Eli asks.

I try to kick him under the table.

"It's good to hear you have your own money and aren't after Charly for hers," Beau says, earning a kick from me, which connects because I'm sitting right next to him. "Ouch."

"Stop being an ass."

"No, I'm not with Charly for her money. She has a successful business here in New Orleans, and I have a successful business as well. But frankly, that you would imply that her business is the only thing that a man would find attractive about her says a lot about your opinion of her."

"I like him," Kate says, grinning at me.

"Head Over Heels is not all she has," Eli begins, but I cut him off.

"It's all that matters," I say sternly. I realize that I've never really gotten into my family money with Simon, and I'd rather talk to him about it alone.

"God, you're stubborn." Beau scowls at me.

"And yet, you love me anyway."

"Sometimes," Beau says with a half smile. "How long are you in town, Simon?"

"A couple more weeks. I decided to extend my stay," Simon replies.

"How can you run a business from half way across the world?" Eli asks.

"The internet is a beautiful thing," Simon says. "Video conferencing. Phone calls. I can really work from anywhere, unless I need to be somewhere for an appearance."

"I see," Eli says. "And what are your intentions with my sister?"

"Eli!" I exclaim. "Simon, you do not have to answer that."

"Oh, I think he does," Beau says, pissing me off.

"We didn't come here for this."

"You guys are being ridiculous," Kate adds.

"It's okay, ladies." Simon holds up a hand and never flinches under the scrutiny of my overbearing brothers. "My intention is to continue pursuing a consensual, mutually respectful, and affectionate relationship with Charly. Where it goes from there is our business."

Eli's eyebrows climb into his hairline.

"I don't think you understand the dynamic of this family."

"I understand it just fine. I can respect and admire your need to protect Charly. But as she already told you, she's an adult, and what we have between us is healthy. To be frank, it may be the healthiest relationship I've ever been in."

Beau and Eli both sit back in their chairs, studying Simon silently.

"For Godsake," Kate mutters.

"If you try to make her move to London, I will beat you to a pulp." Eli's face is hard.

"And if you hurt her, I'll also beat you to a pulp," Beau adds.

"So noted," Simon replies. "And likewise."

Everyone looks up at Simon in surprise.

"Do you think it's only non-family members who can hurt each other?" Simon asks seriously.

"No," Beau says, looking at Simon with a new respect in his eyes.

"Charly," Eli says, turning his attention to me. "I have papers at the office for you to sign."

"Which papers?" I ask and take a drink of my sweet tea.

"Your new lease is in. I don't know why you insist on it, but it's ready for you."

"Because it's the right thing to do." I shrug and glance at Simon. "Do you mind going over to my brother's office after lunch? It'll only take a moment."

"That's fine with me," he says and smiles. "So you lease your building from Eli?"

"No, she leases it from the company," Beau replies as he takes a bite of bread. "Boudreaux Enterprises owns the building, and Charly is a part of Boudreaux Enterprises, but she insists on paying rent."

"We've discussed this," I say.

"You're so fucking stubborn," Beau says.

"Gee," Kate adds with a roll of the eyes. "I have no idea where she might have come by that. It's not like it's a family trait or anything."

"Watch yourself," Eli says and kisses Kate's hand. "Punishments happen."

"Excuse me?" Simon chokes out over his own sweet tea.

"He's kidding," Kate says, waving Simon off. "Honestly, Eli would never really hurt me. Been there, done that, had the hospital stay to prove it. Eli saved me from a lot."

Eli kisses Kate's hand again as she blushes. "I'm not sure why I told you that."

"He has this weird thing about him," I say, nodding. "He's like a priest. You just want to tell him stuff. Except, he's no priest, let me tell you." I wink at Kate, then bust out laughing when Eli and Beau both scowl at me. "Oh, lighten up."

"We really should get back to the office," Kate says after Eli pays for lunch. "You can ride with us, if you want."

"We have a car," I reply. "We'll be right behind you."

We all gather our things and leave, and when we're in Simon's rental, he pulls me in for a long, hot kiss before I have the chance to buckle my seat belt.

"What was that for?" I ask breathlessly.

"I just needed to get my hands on you," he says, still looking at me with lust-filled eyes.

"And your lips, apparently." I swallow hard. "I'm sorry for the third degree from my idiot brothers."

"They're not idiots," he replies and starts the car. "Do you know how lucky you are to have the family you do? I've never seen anything quite like it."

"I know."

"You are down to earth, and loyal and fun, all rolled into one. They wanted to make sure I wasn't just fucking around with you, and like I told them, I respect that."

"Thanks for being so open minded about them," I reply and point out a parking space in front of the building. "This is where we're going."

"The office is in this building?"

I take a deep breath and turn to him, ready to share more about my family with him. "No, this building is Boudreaux Enterprises."

His jaw drops for a moment, but then he shakes himself out of it and climbs out of the car. He follows me inside the posh, ornate foyer where I say hello to the receptionist. She immediately buzzes us up.

The building is expensively decorated and recently renovated. Savannah and Kate led that project last year.

"Eli and Beau's offices are on the top floor," I inform him. He's suddenly grown quiet, but before I can ask him about it, we reach our destination.

The doors open up to another opulent lobby, in grey, yellow, and hints of red. Eli's assistant smiles at me as we walk past her to Eli's office.

"You guys got here fast," I say as we walk inside and find all three of them gathered around Eli's desk.

"Kate drives too fast," Eli replies with a frown. "Here are the forms that need your signature."

"Great." I sit and look through each one, but nothing has changed. I sign and pass them back to Eli. "There you go. I get to stay another year."

"You get to stay forever," Beau replies. "Unless you kick yourself out."

"So tell me more about Boudreaux Enterprises," Simon says, interrupting us. "I was under the impression that it was a small family business."

"It is a family business," Eli replies. "But it's not

small. Well, not anymore."

"We are the fifth generation to lead Boudreaux Enterprises," Beau says. "When our father passed away, all six of us inherited it evenly, but only Savannah, Eli and myself were interested in working here day to day. Eli is the CEO, Savannah is the CFO, and I'm the COO. We have about five hundred employees here in this building and another three hundred that actually build the ships in the harbor."

"I see," Simon says. "I'm not much of a sailor, but now that I see your logo, I realize that I've seen it before."

Simon won't look me in the eyes. Is he mad at me? And if so, what in the world for?

"Would you like a tour? I can show you around up here," I offer, relieved when he smiles and nods. "Do you need anything else from me?"

"We're good," Eli says and stands, offering to shake Simon's hand. "It was nice to meet you."

"Likewise."

I wave as I lead Simon out of Eli's office and down the hall. "This is Savannah's office. It looks like she's out somewhere. And on the other side there is Beau's office." We continue along, and I point out different offices and what happens in each one.

Suddenly, George comes around a corner and smiles in surprise when he sees me.

"Charly. What a pleasure." He hugs me and then pulls back. "We should get together soon for lunch or drinks."

"Absolutely," I reply and turn to Simon, who has completely stiffened up and is glaring at poor George. "George, this is Simon. I'm just showing him around before we head out."

"Nice to meet you," George says. "Seriously, call me. I'd like to catch up."

I nod and lead Simon further down the hall, but he stops me.

"I'd like to go."

"Oh, okay. Are you feeling okay?"

"Fine."

He's so not okay.

I don't say anything as we walk out to his car, and continue to sit in silence while he drives back to my house rather than the store.

I have someone working for me today, so it's no big deal. I'd rather have this conversation in private anyway.

Without a word, we walk into the house, set down our keys and my bag, and then he turns to me.

"So, let me get this straight. You're wealthy."

Is this a trick question?

"My family is wealthy."

"That's not what I said," he replies and paces away from me.

"Why are you angry?" I ask, getting angry myself.

"Because you weren't honest with me."

"When?"

"When you told me what your family business was."

"I was honest." I plant my fists on my hips and look at him like he's stupid. "I told you my family builds ships."

"You failed to mention that it's a huge conglomerate, or that you're a freaking heir to an empire."

"Hold up." I hold my hand up and have to take a deep breath so I don't slap him across his handsome face. "You're mad because I have a trust fund you didn't know about? When was I supposed to say that? When I met you? *Hi, my name is Charly, and I have a sizeable trust fund.*"

"That's not—"

"I'm not done. I haven't touched that trust fund since college. My business, my home, my car…it's all *mine.* I work my ass off for what I have. It made sense to put the building that Head Over Heels is in in the company name for tax purposes, but because it's not in my name, I pay fucking rent. Because it's technically not *mine.*

"And yes, that pisses my family off, but they can just deal with it. So if you're pissed because I didn't tell you that my family is wealthy, well, that's your problem, Simon. Because it's not even something that I think about on a daily basis. And let's not forget that *you*, my friend, are fucking rich."

"Which you knew from the minute you met me," he says. "It's not like I can hide that. I'm a public figure, for bugger sake."

"I refuse to apologize for not telling you that my family has money. Especially when I wasn't being deliberately dishonest. I told you all about my business, and you've been freaking living in my home. Everything you know about me is real."

He shakes his head.

"You don't believe me?"

"I do believe you, and I'm still fucking pissed."

"Well, so am I."

"I should have known the scope of your family's business before I walked into that lunch today. I was thrown off guard. Now I know why they wanted to know if I'm with you for your money."

"I'm successful *on my own,* damn it, and I will continue to be."

"I know you will. But come on, Charly, at some point you could have elaborated on what your family does and what they have."

"I showed you the inn. My family owns that, and I told you that it had been in the family for generations. I was never hiding anything from you."

He takes a deep breath and shoves his hands through his hair. "It never occurred to me."

"And it never occurred to me to spell it all out for you." I cross my arms over my chest. "And while I'm mad, why were you rude to George?"

"Because he wants to fuck you," he replies immediately. I feel my mouth fall open.

"No, he doesn't."

"Trust me, darling, I'm a man. He wants you."

"I went out with him," I reply and feel like a bitch when Simon's eyes ice over. "Eli set us up on a date after I got home from Montana."

"So you've already fucked him, then."

I stop moving, stop breathing as I stare at Simon in shock.

"Who the fuck do you think you are?" He closes his eyes and drops his head to his chest.

"I'm sorry."

"No. You assume that if I've gone out on one motherfucking date with a man that I must have fucked him? Why, because I let you in my pants so easily?"

"Charly—"

"Not that I need to explain myself to you, given that I didn't think I was ever going to see you again, I went on one damn date with George. He was kind and funny and a perfect gentleman. But I couldn't stop comparing him to *you*. There was no chemistry there, and we decided that we would be friends.

"How *dare* you assume that I'd slept with him. I'm not a whore."

"Of course not."

"And if that's what you think of me, you can just go get on a fucking plane back to London."

"Charly."

"I will *not* be treated like a piece of trash!" I can't stop talking. I can't stop pacing and railing and throwing this fit. All I know is, he's fucking pissed me off in a way that I haven't been since I was a child.

Suddenly, I'm wrapped in Simon's arms and held close to his chest.

"I'm sorry, Charly." I fight him at first, but then I collapse against him, and I'm even angrier to discover tears rolling down my cheeks.

"You don't get to judge me like that."

"I'm so sorry, darling. It was a heartless, horrible thing to say and I didn't mean it." He kisses my head and rubs his hand down my back. "I was already reeling from the information about your family's business, and then George was there, and whether I was right or wrong, it looked like he wanted you.

"I don't like feeling jealous. This is new to me, and I clearly don't handle it very well."

"No. You don't." I pull away, not willing to look him in the eyes. "All you ever have to do is *ask*, Simon. I'll answer any questions you have. Now, if you'll excuse me, I want to be alone for a while."

I turn and leave the room, jogging up to my bedroom. If I stay in the house, I'll have to talk to him, and I just don't want to do that right now. But I can't go to the shop looking like this. And if I go to any of the family, they'll immediately hate Simon.

Which he deserves.

It's begun to rain outside, cooling the warm afternoon air. So I pull on my running outfit and shoes and leave the house.

I need to run and think and clear my head. Simon is still standing in the living room when I pass by.

"Where are you going?" His voice isn't angry anymore.

"For a run. I won't be long."

Before he can answer, I set off jogging down the street and through my neighborhood. It feels good to be outside, and the rain is nice.

God, he hurt me. I realize now that it wasn't just anger that drove me close to hysteria. It was the hurt.

Simon can hurt me, and I've never let a man get close enough to do that before. Is this all a mistake? Have I let myself get too close to him?

I guess that most couples have spats. I never saw my parents fight, but it must happen. Kate and Gabby have both told me that they've wanted to stab their husbands in their sleep.

And the stories Callie tells us about Declan have us rolling on the ground with laughter.

But this isn't funny, and I don't know how to handle it. I'm not equipped with the tools to deal with it.

I turn the corner toward the house, still not sure what I'm going to say when I go inside when suddenly, out of the haze of rain, are squealing tires.

CHAPTER SIXTEEN

~Charly~

Strong arms wrap around me and pull me roughly onto the sidewalk as the car screeches to a stop where I was just standing.

"Are you okay?"

I look up into Simon's ocean blue eyes, full of fear now. His hold on me is tight, and he's not letting go.

"I'm fine. It didn't touch me."

"Oh my God!" the driver cries out as she hurries out of the car and around to where Simon has me in a death grip on the sidewalk. "I'm so sorry. I didn't see you in this rain until it was too late. Are you okay?"

"I'm fine," I reply and pull away from Simon, but he won't let go of my hand. "You didn't hit me."

"But I would have, if he hadn't pulled you out of the way. My husband has been badgering me to get new tires, and now I know why. I'm so sorry."

Drivers lined up behind the woman's car begin to honk, their patience running out.

"I'm fine," I repeat. "You can go. Really."

"Here's my card," she says as she walks away. "Call

me if you need anything."

I nod, and before I know it, Simon is leading me back to my house and inside.

"Thanks for dragging me down the block." I'm still a little angry at him, but he just looks…*terrified.*

"Are you sure you weren't hurt?" he asks as he pulls me against him, hugging me tightly. He buries his face in my neck. "You're soaked to the bone."

"So are you," I reply and rest my shaking hands on his hips. "I'm fine, Simon. Thank you for pulling me out of the way. But what were you doing there?"

"I was going out to look for you," he says, not pulling away. If anything, his grip tightens. "You were gone a long while, and I needed to see you."

"I can't breathe, Simon." He loosens his hold, but still doesn't let me go completely. "I'm not going anywhere."

"I'm sorry," he says immediately. He's not desperate. He's not sarcastic. He's just honest, and it softens me a little more. "I was a dick earlier, and I'm sorry for it."

"You were a dick," I reply, agreeing wholeheartedly.

"I regretted the words as soon as they left my mouth. And then when I decided to go find you, and I saw that car almost hit you, bloody hell, Charly, I lost ten years off of my life."

"Hey." I reach up and cup his cheek gently. "I'm fine."

"I can't lose you," he says, his voice low and maybe a little tentative, as if he's wary of voicing it aloud. I've never seen him quite this vulnerable, even the other day when he was telling me about his ex-wife. He drags his fingertips down my face and steps closer again. We're both dripping on the floor, and neither of us seems to care. "You mean more to me than I can put into words, and I just can't lose you now."

He swallows hard and keeps talking, which is good because I'm not sure what to say.

"But what I said earlier was rude and inexcusable, and if you want me to go, I understand."

I bite my lip and watch his handsome face as emotions I can't put a name to cross his face.

"Why did you assume that I was deliberately withholding information?"

He closes his eyes and shakes his head.

"Because betrayal is more common in my life than I like to admit. Because the man my ex-wife fucked around with was my business partner, who happened to hide a *lot* of money from me. The business struggled needlessly for a long time because he wasn't honest about his financial situation, and frankly, I'm not accustomed to honesty.

"I'm used to having to figure out the puzzle, and it pisses me off."

"It pisses me off too," I reply, still not touching him back. His shoulders slump in defeat.

"I know that you are not any of the people from my past, and it's ridiculous that I would compare you to them, or allow those experiences to trigger my reactions to you."

"Yes, but that's called being a human being," I reply, the mad gone from me now. "At least now you know I'm not a gold digger."

His lips twitch.

"But, I wonder if it would make you more comfortable if I was?"

He tips his head to the side and he pushes his fingers in my dripping hair.

"No. I wouldn't be more comfortable. I'm quite taken with you, just as you are. I'm deeply sorry for what I said earlier, Charlotte. I can't promise that my baggage won't make me screw up in the future, but I can promise that I'm learning from it. I won't jump to conclusions again."

"Good," I reply and wrap my arms around his waist now. "Just talk to me, Simon."

"I can do that."

***

It's been four days since my fight with Simon. He's been true to his word, asking me questions when he has a concern, and he's been even more open with me about his family. The fight sucked alligator balls, but I think it brought us to a closer place with each other.

I've never felt so comfortable, or more connected to, another human being the way I do Simon Danbury.

Who would have thought?

And, just like every single day since he's been here, I close my shop on time. Just as I'm flipping the sign over to *closed*, Simon walks through the door, with his sexy smile all over his face.

"Hi there, handsome."

"Well, hello, love."

"You know," I say as I lock the door behind him, then walk to my counter to close out the till and get ready to leave. "I've discovered that since you've been here, you're very bad for my productivity."

"How is that?" He leans on the counter and braces his chin on his fist, watching me.

"I'm closing the shop early, for one."

"I do believe the sign in the window says you close at six." He checks his watch. "And look at that, it's six."

"I haven't actually closed at six since…well, I don't remember. I usually chat with customers, redesign displays, shop for new stock. But most of that has been set aside because I seem to be spending most of my time with a certain sexy Brit. It's a good thing you're cute."

He raises a brow and stands to full height, taking my breath away. His ink is on display again in a simple black T-shirt, stretched over wide, muscular shoulders.

Where did my knees go again?

"Cute, am I?"

His accent gets even thicker when he's turned on, and it's on full blast now.

"Adorable."

He slowly circles around the counter and leans into me, pinning my hips against it. His lips are inches from mine.

"I don't think a man is supposed to be *cute*."

"No?" Oh, God, I can't breathe right when he's this close to me. His hands are on my hips now, his fingers under the hem of my blouse, and then gliding up my skin and over my bra to cup my breasts.

"We shouldn't do this here." Is that my voice? I sound breathy and turned on, which is pretty accurate.

"No one is here," he says and brushes feather-soft kisses over my cheek to my ear. My body is one giant shiver. Thank God for the giant display I built today that blocks us from outside traffic.

As if by their own volition, my hands make their way down the back of his jeans to cup his very fine ass just as he nips my neck, making me gasp.

"How *cute* am I now?" he whispers, never taking his lips from my skin.

"You're just precious," I reply, hearing my own

accent thicken along with his cock pressed to my belly.

"You make me laugh," he says, smiling against my neck. "You make me so hard it hurts. And I'm grateful that you're wearing a skirt."

"Why is that?"

He reaches down and balls the material in his fists, raising it above my waist.

"You're not wearing panties," he says with surprise, his blue eyes pinned to mine.

"Not today."

"Fucking hell, Charly." He boosts me up on the edge of the counter and grinds his hard, jean-clad cock against my core, setting me on fire. "You're already wet."

"I look at you and get wet," I reply. I'm breathless. On fire. "If you're not inside me in two seconds, we're going to have an issue."

"We don't want to have an issue," he replies and unzips his jeans, frees his cock, and pushes inside me immediately, stealing what breath I have left.

"God, you feel good," I moan, clutching his shoulders. "I've been thinking about this all day."

"Good because there will be more later." He grips my hips and picks up the pace, fucking me hard and furiously here in the middle of my shop.

Sex in the middle of gorgeous shoes? Am I in heaven?

Because I'm pretty sure this is what heaven looks like.

"If you're able to laugh, I'm doing this wrong. You're not good on the ego, love."

"No, I was—oh, God—just thinking that this must be what heaven looks like."

He cocks a brow.

"Amazing sex surrounded by shoes."

His lips twitch into a satisfied smile. He rips my shirt

open, not giving one shit about the buttons popping off, and sucks my already hard nipples into his mouth.

"How cute am I now?" he asks, his eyes serious and narrowed as he fucks me relentlessly against the countertop.

"You're not cute," I reply, holding on for dear life. He presses his thumb to my clit, tearing me apart inside out. "You're everything."

I cry out, clinging to him.

Everything.

Fucking baby Moses, I've fallen in love with him.

***

Why is there a baby chick in my bed?

Okay, so I can't actually *see* it, but it's nestled up against my cheek, all warm and fuzzy. I might not kill whoever put it here.

"Darling, I need you to wake up," Simon says, patting my ass. I'm on my stomach, which is my usual way to sleep. I reach my arm out and come up with cold sheets.

Simon's up already?

"Why are you awake?" I ask, not opening my eyes.

"Because I had work to do," he replies. "And I brought you this."

"A baby chick?"

"What?" He bursts out laughing. "No, love. Open your eyes."

"Can't."

"Yes, you can."

"No, you killed me last night."

I smirk and stretch my arms over my head, frowning when I feel the baby chick leave my cheek. Our sexual relationship has been out of control over the past few days since the quickie in my shop.

And by out of control, I mean non-stop and *wow*.

"Do I smell bacon?"

I immediately sit up and spin around to find Simon sitting, shirtless mind you, with a tray of food.

"Happy Breakfast," he says with a sheepish smile. "I'm not a great cook, but I can make a plate of bacon and eggs."

"God love you," I reply and reach for a slice of bacon. "Mmm."

"Good?"

"Mmm." I nod and search the bed. "I feel bad eating eggs in front of the chick, though. It might have been his sibling."

"There's no chick," he says, laughing again. "It was your own hair. I brushed it out of your face."

"No way."

He nods slowly. "Yes way. I had no idea that you have been pining away for a baby chick all this time. I would have gotten you one."

"I don't want one," I reply. "I must have been dreaming about them."

"About farm animals?"

"Maybe I was a farmer in my dream," I reply and then smile when Simon laughs again. "It could happen."

"Not in this life," he replies and holds a forkful of eggs up for me to eat. "Here, no chicken siblings around to witness this."

"You're pretty good at this breakfast thing," I say as I chew and hold a piece of bacon up for him to bite. "And I like you well enough to share my bacon."

"How kind of you," he says and takes a bite, then the whole piece, practically biting my fingers.

"Hey, you took all of it."

"There's more."

My landline begins to ring, but I shake my head. "Ignore that."

"Happily." He smears strawberry jam on toast and holds it to my lips. "Here's something sweet."

I take a bite, sure to get the sugary jam on my lips, then lean in and kiss him, grinning when he licks my lips clean.

"You taste delicious," he murmurs.

"It's the jam."

"That's good too."

My cell phone pings with several incoming texts.

"Seriously, ignore it. It's my day off. If the shop is on fire, it's just going to burn."

His brows climb into his hairline.

"Really?"

"No, please pass me my phone."

He chuckles and reaches behind him to fetch it for me. To my surprise, it's not my employee, but several of my siblings.

Fear clutches my heart. What if it's Mama?

"Is everything okay?" Simon asks, but I don't answer until I open the text from Gabby.

You're bringing Simon to Mom's for dinner tomorrow.

"No," I reply in relief. "I'm being told that you're coming to Sunday dinner with the family tomorrow."

I scowl at him.

"Hey, it's not my fault," he says with a laugh.

"You really don't have to go if you don't want to." I toss my phone on the end of the bed and take another bite of toast, already dreading the fiasco that's sure to happen at my mother's.

"What's the big deal? I've already met them all."

"But not all at once," I reply and flop back on the bed, covering my face with the pillow. "When we all get together, we can just be...*horrible*."

"I doubt that." He takes the pillow from my face and smiles down at me. "You're adorable in the morning."

"I'm serious, Simon. This isn't funny. Do you know how many people we've run off in the past?"

"How many?"

"Lots. I lost count." I take the pillow back and slam it on my face. "Mmph mpfff nrffft."

"What?" he asks with a laugh and peeks under the pillow.

"This can't end well."

"I'm a tough guy," he reminds me and sneaks his face under the pillow to kiss my cheek. "I can handle some questions."

I stare at him for a moment and then break out in giggles, laughing until my stomach hurts and tears are rolling down my face.

"Oh my gosh," I gasp. "You're so cute."

"I think you know how I feel about that word, love, but if you need a reminder, I'm happy to give you one."

I laugh again and then sober, wipe my face clean, and cup his cheek in my hand.

"It was so nice knowing you."

He raises a brow.

"*Was?*"

"After tomorrow, you may be running back to the airport."

"Stop it. Your family is lovely, and like I said, I've already met them. Everything is going to be just fine."

"Yeah." I chew my lip and stare at the last piece of

bacon, which is calling my name with evil glee. So I snatch it. "Just know that I warned you. And if you decide that you don't want to go, I totally understand. We could go somewhere else like Iceland. Or Alaska."

"Only cold places?" He peels the covers off of me and kisses my naked chest, just between my breasts. "What about Brazil?"

"Too many bugs," I reply, then gasp when he nibbles my navel. "I've heard Montana is nice."

He looks up at me and grins. "Those rumors are true. It's even better when a certain beautiful woman is there as well."

"Oh?" I bury my fingers in his hair as he kisses his way down to the promise land. "Tell me more."

"Words are overrated, love. I'll show you."

***

"Is it just me, or is the way Simon says *billiards* the sexiest thing ever?" Callie asks later that night.

I'm sitting with Callie at her rooftop bar in The Odyssey enjoying a glass of wine while Declan and Simon are downstairs playing pool. We decided it would be good for us to get out of the house for the evening, and I'm glad we did. I love Callie, and this bar.

"Oh, just about everything he says is the sexiest thing ever," I reply and lean my elbow on the back of the red couch, looking into the gas fire in the middle of the table in front of us. "And the sex might be the end of me."

"Really?" Callie grins and holds her glass out to clink mine. "Do tell."

"We can't keep our hands off of each other," I reply and then laugh. "This, of course, is not a bad problem to have. But we came out tonight to hang with you guys just to take a break."

"How do you find the time to do anything else?" Callie asks and crosses her long legs. She's in a short denim skirt with fishnet stockings, a black tank, and sleeveless denim jacket. Her blonde hair is hanging in curls. Her ink is bright and bold, just like her makeup and deep red lipstick.

Callie is a fucking knockout.

"Don't tell me you and Declan didn't fuck like rabbits when you were first together."

"Of course we did," she replies with a satisfied smile. "We still do. That better never change."

"I'm sure it ebbs and flows, right? I mean, how in the world can people have this much sex for their whole lives?"

"Your parents didn't have six kids just because they enjoyed conversation," Callie reminds me. I wrinkle my nose.

"Ew."

"So, the sex is good. And I'm glad. But is that all it is?" Her voice is casual as she takes a sip of her martini.

"I don't think so," I reply softly. "I thought so in the beginning, but now, I think there's more to it."

"That's great." Callie squeezes my shoulder.

"I don't know if it's great," I reply. "I mean, how in the world do we make this work?"

"One day at a time, friend. That's how we all make it work."

I nod and sip my drink, thinking that Callie might be one of the smartest people I know.

CHAPTER SEVENTEEN

~Charly~

When Simon and I pull up to Mama's house the next day, I can tell that we're the last to arrive.

"Sure, they all choose *today* to be early," I mutter and stay in my seat when Simon cuts the engine. "We really should have driven separately so you can make a break for it when it all gets to be too much."

"Stop fretting, love," Simon says and kisses the back of my hand. "I'm not worried about this in the least."

"That's because you haven't seen this shit show in action." I turn my gaze to his, memorizing his face. "Remember me fondly."

"Oh good lord." He rolls his eyes and opens his door. "Come on, drama queen."

"He calls me a drama queen now," I mutter to myself, "but I give it twenty minutes before he's high-tailing it down the road."

"I can hear you, you know," he says when he joins me on the sidewalk.

"I won't hold it against you if you turn to me at any point in the next two hours and say, *you're so not worth this.*"

He cups my face, and right here in front of God and everyone, lays a kiss on me that would make the gods weep. "Yes, you are. Let's go."

He takes my hand as we walk up to the front door. Before I can reach for the knob, Sam flings the door open.

"We all saw that," he informs us, and tosses his baseball up in the air, catching it easily in his mitt. "Just sayin'."

"Thanks." I ruffle his hair. "If Maman catches you throwing that ball in the house, you'll be dead meat."

"She won't."

"I saw it," Mama says and gives Sam the stink eye. "You know what happens to little boys who throw their ball in my house?"

"They don't get dessert," Sam says, hanging his head. "It was an accident."

"Right." Mama kisses his head and smiles at us. "Go throw that ball around outside. And take your uncles with you."

Sam runs back toward the kitchen as Mama enfolds me in a big hug. She's petite. My sisters and I all got our frames from our mom. And I notice that as she gets older, she's more fragile, which makes me a little sad.

"I'm so glad you're here," she says and then kisses my cheek.

"And you, young man, need to come down here. You're too tall for me." Simon leans down to kiss her cheek. "Welcome."

"Thank you, Mrs. Boudreaux."

"Come on back, you two. As soon as you came to the door, everyone ran back to the kitchen. They were spying on you, of course. Not me, I was busy slaving over the stove."

My parents' house is large, but no mansion. Daddy always taught us that just because we were wealthy, didn't mean we lived lavishly. Mama usually had a housekeeper because with a family our size, it would have been difficult for her to keep up with all of us. But she's always enjoyed cooking herself.

"And so it begins," I say, smiling sweetly at Simon.

"I hope you have a thick skin, Simon," Mama says just before we reach the kitchen.

"Hi, everyone," I say and wave. "You've all met Simon."

I'm surprised to find that not only are all my siblings here, but Rhys has flown in with Gabby, and even Ben is here as well.

The whole gang is accounted for.

Great.

"Hey, Simon," Eli says, "we were just about to go out and toss the ball with Sam. Why don't you join us?"

I start to interject, wanting to keep Simon close by so I can defend him against my overprotective brothers, but Simon just squeezes my hand and replies with, "Sounds great. I'm in."

"Good. All of you boys out of my kitchen."

"You always make the boys help," I remind her with a frown, but she just shrugs and returns to stirring the collard greens on the stove.

"I want to chat with my girls this afternoon."

I see Callie and Kate exchange a grin, and I'm

immediately suspicious. When the boys have all filed out to the backyard, I turn to Van.

"What's going on?"

"Nothing," she replies with wide eyes.

"You don't lie well."

"We just want to talk to you," Gabby says and shoves a carrot in her mouth. She wanders over to the back door and grins. "Simon is already throwing the ball with Sam."

"So, we hear the sex is out of control," Kate says. I whip around and stare at Callie.

"You *told* them?"

"What?" She holds her hands out to her side. "You didn't say it was a secret."

"There was alcohol involved," I hiss. "Anything said when alcohol is involved is not to be shared. You own a bar; you should know that."

"Oh please," Van says and rolls her eyes. "Like you wouldn't have told *me* that if the roles were reversed."

"Don't waste time," Gabby says, waving at us and staring out the window. "Oh my gosh, Eli just got real close to Simon's face and he looks serious. Go on, tell us about the sex."

"My mother is right there," I point out, desperate for this conversation to *not* happen.

"I've had sex, darlin'," she replies with a smile. "A lot of it, actually. I have plenty of children to show for it."

"Let's not talk about Mom's sex life," Van says. "Ever."

"Agreed," I reply. "Let's not talk about sex at all."

"Now Beau pushed Rhys," Gabby says, pressing her face against the glass. "What the hell did he do?"

"I wonder if they'll get into it and take their shirts off," Callie says.

"My brothers have to keep their clothes on," Van says.

"No, they don't," Callie counters. "I'm not related to any of them. They can all get naked."

I just lean on the breakfast bar and pinch the bridge of my nose, willing the headache starting to go away.

"Awww, Simon is giving Sam a piggyback ride," Gabby says and looks back at us with heart eyes. "He's really good with kids. Does he want kids, Char?"

"I hope so," Mama says. "I need more grandbabies."

"We haven't talked about it," I reply, feeling slightly sick. "Why would we talk about it?"

"Oh, don't be a pain in the ass," Van replies with a roll of the eyes. "You're crazy about each other, and the sex is amazing."

"Oh God, Ben just took his shirt off."

We all stop talking, look at each other, and rush to the door to press our noses to the glass.

"Holy sweet merciful Jesus," Mama mutters to all of our surprise. "Don't look at me like that, I may be old but I'm not dead and that boy is fine looking."

Boy, is she right. Except, he's no boy. He's one fine man.

I haven't seen Ben shirtless since high school. I had no idea he had so much ink now. I glance over at Van, whose eyes have glassed over.

"Did you know he had that many tattoos now?" I ask her.

She shakes her head wordlessly and swallows hard just as Ben glances over and a slow smile spreads over his handsome face. He winks, aimed right at Van.

"He has a thing for you," Kate says to Van. "It's painfully obvious."

"It's been obvious since he was sixteen," Gabby replies, earning a jab in the ribs by Van.

"Whatever," she says and walks back to the breakfast bar. "Mom, your pot is going to boil over."

"Oh! Thank you." We all peel ourselves from the door. Well, everyone except Gabby.

"What are you, the lookout?" I ask.

"Something like that. We don't want Simon to walk in when we're in the middle of talking about your sex life."

"For Godsake, I'm not discussing our sex life with you." I prop my hands on my hips and glare at my sisters and sisters-in-law.

"Callie gets to have all the fun because she has liquor," Kate says with a pout. "Will you at least tell us if you've said the *L* word yet?"

NO. No. No. No.

But I just casually shake my head. "It hasn't come up."

"That's not what I hear," Gabby says and then giggles at her own joke. "Holy shit, Beau just took a swing at Declan, and he rolled away, dodging it. That martial arts crap really works. And if they weren't my brothers, I'd say it's hot."

"I'll say it," Callie says with a smirk. "It's hot. Almost as hot as Charly's sex life."

"You know, I thought it was Simon that was going to get the third degree today. Not me." I glare at them all. "You've betrayed me."

They simply laugh their pretty little heads off.

"No, this is just new, Char," Van says and pats me on the shoulder. "You've never introduced us to anyone before. You've told us stories about men you've met or been with, but this is more, and we're so happy for you."

Shit, now they're going to make me cry.

"We just want to know more," Gabby says, nodding and watching whatever is happening outside.

"All I know for sure is, he's not like anyone I've ever known before. He's thoughtful, and affectionate, and yes, we're compatible in bed. But you know what's even better?"

They're riveted to me now, listening with wide eyes.

"The conversation. He's so fucking smart—sorry, Mama—and he makes me think. He listens to me. When he messes up, he apologizes, rather than pinning the blame on me and making me feel guilty. He can admit when he's wrong, and he does his best to make it up to me." I bite my lip and twist my fingers together, thinking about the man who's come to own my heart.

"I don't know where it's going to go, or if it'll go anywhere at all, but I like him. I respect him. I love that it's his life's work to help others, and it's not just for the money. He genuinely wants to make a difference in women's lives."

"He's already made a difference in yours," Kate says with a watery smile. "I'm so happy for you, Charly."

"Me too," Callie says. "I'm sorry I told them about our conversation, but I was so happy for you, I was ready to burst. And this room of people is who we all trust the most."

I nod and offer Callie a soft smile. She's only been in our family for a short time, but I don't remember what we did without her. She fits. And she loves Declan to distraction.

"It's okay." I shrug and look around the room. "I'm scared to trust him."

"That's the hardest part," Mama replies gently. "It's easy to fall in love. But to trust? That takes time. You'll get there."

I nod and wipe one tear off my cheek. "What are they doing now?"

Gabby looks outside and gasps. "They're coming this way!"

"Some lookout you are," Van says just as Ben walks inside and catches Van's eye. He grins and pulls his shirt over his head, catching all of our attention. Van clears her throat and turns away to help Mama at the stove.

"Dinner's just about ready," Mama says as all the guys file in. "You have good timing."

"Did anyone get hurt?" I ask as Simon smiles at me.

"No one threw even one punch," Sam says, totally deflated.

"Hey, I threw a punch at Declan," Beau says.

"It isn't the same," Sam replies. "You didn't give him a bloody lip or a black eye. My friend Logan at school got a bloody lip."

"You didn't throw the punch, did you?" Gabby asks in horror.

"Not that time," Sam says and ducks his head.

"But you threw a punch *another* time?" Gabby asks.

"Maybe."

Gabby looks at Rhys in horror. "Say something."

"We'll have a talk tonight, buddy," Rhys says and puts his son in a headlock. "No throwing punches."

Simon sidles up behind me and wraps his arms around my waist. "You look magnificent," he whispers in my ear. I lean back and smile up at him.

"Thanks."

"Didn't we just talk about this outside?" Beau asks

and reaches for a cherry tomato in the salad bowl, only to be slapped by Mama.

"You talked," Simon replies with a smile. "And I listened."

Eli sighs. "He makes it hard for me to not like him."

***

"It wasn't so bad," I say later that evening when we return to my house. "Once the girls finished asking me about our sex life, and my brothers were done intimidating you in the backyard—"

"They tried."

"—it went pretty well, actually."

"Your mother is an excellent cook."

"She was pleased that you thought so. She likes you."

"The feeling is mutual," he says and reaches for his phone when it pings with a text. "It's good that I'm going home next week."

My stomach sinks at the thought of him leaving. I don't want him to go.

"I'm sorry. I know I'm keeping you here away from work."

"You're not forcing me to be here," he says as he types out a response. "I am not complaining. But I do have some work that needs my personal attention."

"I completely understand."

I open the dishwasher and begin unloading it, trying to keep my hands busy. I've never been the girl who pined away for a guy, wanting to spend every minute of every day with him. Then again, I've never known anyone like Simon.

And that scares me a little.

Or a lot.

A lottle?

I smirk and rinse out a wine glass, then place it in the dishwasher.

"What's so funny?" Simon asks as he joins me, hugging me from behind the way he did at my mom's. He tucks his face in my neck and gives it a bite, making me squirm.

"I'm just thinking silly things," I reply and set the glass aside. I turn and hug him tightly. "These past few weeks have gone by so quickly."

"I know." He kisses my head. "Come with me to London."

I pull back and stare up at him in surprise. "What?"

"I know it's asking a lot, and if you can't, or won't, I understand. But I'd love for you to come back with me."

My mouth opens and closes but no noise comes out. He's flummoxed me.

"Maybe I shouldn't have asked."

"No." I shake my head and hug him again, then pace the kitchen. "That's not it. Thank you for inviting me. I guess I'm just surprised."

"I can't see why, love. In case you haven't noticed, I don't like being away from you. I would love to show you around London, to take you to my favorite restaurants, show you where I grew up."

I would *love* that. I am dying to see the house he grew up in, to meet his parents, to see where he lives now. I'm curious about all of it, and I want to jump at his offer.

"I have a business," I say, biting my lip.

"You were gone for a few weeks not long ago," he reminds me gently. "Nothing fell apart then, did it?"

"No, they did well, actually." I stop pacing and turn to him with a wide smile.

"I hope that means yes because I'm not ready to be

apart from you, Charlotte. I don't like being away from you."

How in the hell can I say no to that?

He folds me in his arms and hugs me close. "Yes?"

"Yes."

CHAPTER EIGHTEEN

~Charly~

We're leaving for London tomorrow. The past week has flown by as I prepared to be away from the shop for two whole weeks and Simon worked more and more remotely. I know he's ready to be home, and I couldn't be happier to have the opportunity to see him in his own space.

I'm still reeling a bit that he asked me to go.

"Did you sleep at all?" he asks as he rolls over and wraps an arm around my waist, tugging me closer to him.

"No," I admit with a smile and push my fingers through his hair. His face is soft from sleep, stubble sprinkled over his cheeks. I kiss his forehead. "I kept going over all of my lists."

"You can sleep on the plane," he says and kisses the ball of my shoulder. He scoots even closer to me, turning me on my side and tucking my ass against his hard cock. "I love waking up to you."

"Mm." I can't say anything else. My mouth won't

work. He cups my breast, pinching my nipple into a hard bud.

"You're the sexiest woman I've ever seen," he whispers into my ear. "I want you to close your eyes, and just feel, Charlotte."

I'm a step ahead of you. I can't do anything *but* feel him. His hands, his hardness, the rasp of light hair on his thighs against mine. His stubble rubbing against my shoulder as he places wet kisses all over my back.

And then he's inside me, and I'm lost in the rhythm of his hips and touch. I don't know where I end and he begins.

Every nerve ending is on fire, every hair follicle standing on end. His breath is on my neck as he moves slowly, all the way in and then out again, taking his time with every stroke.

But even more than that, I can feel myself fall further in love with him. He's tender and sweet. He's solid and sure, taking charge without being an overbearing ass.

He's mine.

Oh yes, I feel. I feel everything, and it's new and wonderful and I don't ever want this feeling to end.

"So sexy," he mutters. "I can't get enough of you." He kisses my neck, making me clench around him. "You're the closest to heaven I'll ever be, Charlotte."

I love you.

Tell him! Swallow your fucking pride and tell him how you feel!

But I can't. Not now, in the middle of the best sex we've ever had. I need the first time I tell him to be when we're not mindless with lust.

Instead, I cover his hand with mine where he's gripping my hip and link our fingers as I bite my lip and ride out the sweetest orgasm of my life.

"You're going to bloody kill me," he says and rolls me onto my back so he can kiss me deeply. "But fucking hell, what a way to go."

I smile and cup his face, the words on the tip of my tongue.

"I'll come fetch you for lunch today," he says.

"I can't join you," I reply, disappointed. "I have too much to do today to get ready to leave tomorrow. There's a lot to see to since I'll be gone for two whole weeks again."

"I suppose I can survive one day without you," he replies. "I see you're mostly packed already."

"Of course. We leave *tomorrow*."

"I usually pack at the last minute."

I stare at him, horrified. "Don't you make lists of what you'll need? I have spreadsheets."

He laughs and tugs a piece of my hair. "Now I know what your sisters were talking about in the bar. You're incredibly organized."

"Of course I am." I bite my lip. "So you're just going to throw everything in your bag in the morning, just all willy-nilly?"

"I rarely do anything willy-nilly, darling," he says with a laugh. "But yes, I'll throw it in the bag."

I cringe. "I can do it for you if you like."

"You're busy enough. Trust me, I've been packing this way for years. I won't forget anything."

"If you say so." I kiss him, then climb out of the bed, satisfied when his eyes dilate as the bedsheet falls away from my naked body. "Don't give me that look. I *have* to go to work today."

"You're the one walking around naked, all willy-nilly."

I laugh and shake my head, finger combing my hair. "I'm taking a shower."

"Excellent idea." He bounds out of the bed and jogs toward me, making me run ahead of him into the bathroom, both of us giggling like kids.

Jesus, he's fun. I couldn't love him more than I do right now.

***

I glance at the time on my phone and frown. How is it possible that it's barely one in the afternoon? This day is dragging.

Painfully.

"Charly, someone is here to see you," Linda says as she pops her head through the stockroom door. I've been spending all morning placing orders and drawing up plans for displays for the girls when I'm gone.

My hopes are immediately boosted, certain that it'll be Simon who comes walking through the door, but instead I'm shocked to see Ryan saunter in.

"Thanks, Linda," he says and winks at my assistant, then tosses me his most charming smile. "Boy, you're a sight for sore eyes, darlin'."

Ugh.

"Ryan—"

"I know, it's been a while, but hear me out." Linda disappears into the store, and I'm left alone with the one man on this earth that I'd rather not see. Not because I hate him, or even feel anything for him, really. I've moved on from him.

"I really don't have time."

"All I need is five minutes." He drags his knuckles down my cheek and leans on the counter next to me, caging me in. "You're beautiful, Charly."

"Thanks. Now, if that's all you came for—"

"You know better," he replies and smiles, and all I can think is, *what in the hell did I ever see in him*? He's kind of... smarmy. And he hasn't grown up even one bit since college.

"What can I do for you, Ryan?"

"I want to see you. Later."

"Not possible."

"Come on, don't be stubborn, baby. I'm telling you, what you heard Pam say was all a misunderstanding."

I snort. "Right. And I'm the tooth fairy."

"I'm not seeing her," he insists. "And I miss you. I miss what we had together."

"What did we have together, Ryan?"

"Are you going to deny that the sex was fantastic?"

I sigh and rub my fingertips over my forehead. "No. I'll give you that. The sex was pretty great. But at the end of the day, that's all it ever was, Ryan."

"And we both knew the score, Charly. You never complained about that."

"You're right." I nod. "I didn't. And maybe I should have."

"Are you saying you want more?" he asks, and seems to be genuinely intrigued at the idea, and I simply chuckle.

"I don't think so. Look, Ryan, you're not a bad guy."

"I'm a great guy," he says, all full of ego and arrogance, only turning me off more. I want to roll my eyes, but it's almost funny now. "And you like me."

"I always liked you," I concede. "I'm not positive that was ever returned."

"I like you." He leans in closer and rubs his hand over

my hip. "I want you. I miss you, baby."

I sigh, looking up in his green eyes, and realize for the second time today just how much I love Simon. Ryan touches me and I feel *nothing*.

When Simon touches me, I'm on fire.

But if I start this conversation with Ryan now, I'll never get him out of here, and I *really* don't have time to argue with him.

"Ryan, I have a lot of work to get through, and I'm leaving town in the morning."

"Don't send me away with nothing," he says, almost pleading.

"I'll call you when I get back to town."

I will so not call you when I get back to town.

"Excellent," he replies and kisses my cheek. "I can't wait."

He winks and leaves, a spring in his step, and I can only shake my head. I guess I should be thankful for Ryan and the lessons I learned from him.

But it's completely over between him and me. I have closed that chapter in my life, and I'm happy with the chapter that Simon and I are writing together.

I smile at the romantic path my thoughts have taken and turn back to the computer, just as Linda walks back into the storeroom carrying a brown paper bag.

"You just missed Simon. He brought you lunch, but said he couldn't stay."

"Oh, how sweet." I smile, but I'm disappointed that I missed him. "Thank you. Is everything okay out there?"

"I'm fine," she says and pats me on the shoulder. "I'm glad you hired Abby. She's great with the customers and that girl *loves* shoes."

"That's the first priority," I reply with a smile. "If you

love the shoes, selling them is easy."

"I like her."

"Good. Because I need to know that everything will be handled here while I'm out of the country."

"Don't worry, boss. We got this." Linda winks and leaves me alone with the delicious smells coming from the bag Simon delivered. I grab my phone and type out a quick text to him.

I'm so sorry that I missed you! I was dealing with some needless drama, but all is well. Excited to see you tonight! And thank you for the food. <3

I hit send, dig into some gumbo and get back to work, hoping to wrap things up early so I can get home, see my man, and finish packing.

***

"I'm going to London, uh huh, uh huh," I sing, changing the words of the song on the radio as I turn down my street. I'm dancing in my seat, jamming out, on top of the world.

"Now I'm just cheesy," I mutter as I kill the engine and dance my way toward the door. "And I don't even care."

I giggle as I open the front door. Simon's car is parked at the curb, so he's home already.

"'Ello, Govnah," I say in the worst imitation of a British accent ever. "I'm home! Are you ready to—"

My voice dies and I stop cold when I see Simon standing in the living room. His suitcase is sitting next to him. He's wearing jeans and a polo; his hair is still wet from a shower.

"What's going on?"

"I've decided to leave tonight," he says. His voice is cold, and I'm completely thrown off balance.

"Oh, okay. Well, I'm mostly packed, just give me fifteen minutes to finish up and I'll be ready to go."

"No."

My gaze flies to his. He's not looking me directly in the eyes.

"I'm going alone," he says. I don't know who this stranger is.

"What's going on, Simon?"

He shakes his head once. "This isn't going to work out, Charly. I think we both know that."

"We do?"

He nods and shoves his hands in his pockets.

"And you're leaving."

"I was always going to leave," he replies. "I just changed my mind about you coming with me."

"Why?"

"Because I did." His jaw ticks as he clenches it; his blue eyes are ice cold. Every muscle in his body is tight.

He's pissed.

And by God, so am I.

"You were never going to take me with you."

He simply shrugs, and I see red.

"So, when I bought a four-thousand dollar airline ticket last week, you didn't think *that* would have been a good time to tell me that you'd changed your mind?"

"You can afford it," he replies. "Don't pretend like it was a hit on your trust fund."

Direct hit.

My fists clench, but I make myself keep my face passive.

"You're a dick," I say.

He shrugs again.

"And you're a motherfucking hypocrite. You spew all

these ideals about communication and knowing your worth and then you play me like this? Was this always a game for you?"

"It doesn't matter what it was for me," he replies and grabs the handle of his suitcase. "I stayed to say goodbye."

"Well, thanks for small favors," I reply. "I don't have to take this from you."

I walk to the front door and open it, holding it open for him.

"Someone taught me to stand up for myself and to not settle for less than what I want. You should meet him sometime. He's a hell of a man."

He sighs and walks to me, pausing before he walks out. He reaches up to drag his hand down my face and I jerk back before he can touch me.

"No. You don't get to manipulate me and then touch me. You don't have any right to be anywhere near me.

"I don't know who the fuck you think you are, but you need to get the hell out of my house. Now."

"I didn't manipulate you."

"Wrong." I lean in until my nose is inches from him. "You're no better than your ex-wife. You deserve each other. Thank God I found out now, before I fell in love with you."

He steps onto the porch and I slam the door shut, standing in the middle of the room, stunned.

Am I in an alternate universe? Am I asleep? Is this some stupid episode of Punk'd?

No, that show went off the air years ago.

I hear Simon's car start and pull away, and I'm numb with pure anger.

"Serves me right," I say as I march upstairs to my bedroom and begin unpacking my bags. "I knew from the beginning that he wasn't forever. I *knew* it. And I let myself fall in love with him anyway."

I shake my head, disappointed in myself, as I carry my underwear into the closet. "It's better to find out that he's a lying, manipulative piece of shit now. Who needs him? I don't. I don't need anything from him."

My phone buzzes with an incoming text. If it's Simon, I'll smash my phone against the wall.

What a prick.

But it's not Simon. It's Van.

Have a blast in London! Take lots of pictures.

I smirk and reply, *I'm not going. He dumped me and left.*

I toss the phone on the bed and set to work unpacking the rest of my things and wiping him away from my life. I need him gone. Now.

If I let the anger pass without using it to fuel my need to wipe any trace of him out of my house, I'm afraid that I'll crumple and not get back up.

That asshole.

"Don't let him do this to you, Charly." I stow my empty suitcase under my bed and strip the sheets off it, shoving them in the washing machine with jerky, angry movements. "He's got the problem. Not you."

I'm leaning over the bathtub, giving it a good scrubbing when I hear footsteps behind me.

"What the hell is going on?" Van asks.

"I'm cleaning."

"I see that."

Suddenly, Kate calls out from downstairs. "Where are you?"

"Upstairs," Van yells back.

"You called *Kate*?" I ask and sit back on my heels,

glaring at my sister.

"Of course. Callie's with her."

Both women come running into my bathroom and frown when they see me kneeling at the tub.

"What's happening?" Callie asks.

"I'm having a Mardi Gras party in my bathroom," I reply, my voice clipped. "Why are you all in my house?"

"We're here for the party," Kate says. "Gabby won't be here for a couple of hours. That's what sucks about living so far out of town."

"I don't need any of you to be here," I reply, angry all over again. "I'm not a child. I can handle this."

"What, exactly, are you handling?" Van asks. "And would you please stop cleaning the tub? I'm sick of talking to your ass."

"It *is* a nice ass," Kate says.

"He's gone." I stand and throw my rag in the sink, then tear off my gloves. "Simon went to London."

"Without you," Callie adds.

"Without me. He said he changed his mind, and that this wasn't ever going to work out between us."

"What the hell?" Callie demands and props her hands on her hips. "That makes absolutely no sense."

"He's a man. They rarely make sense," I reply with a shrug and march out of the bathroom, through my bedroom, and downstairs to the living room. The girls follow me down like baby chicks following their mama.

Baby chicks.

I shake off the memory and wrap the anger around me like a warm blanket.

"It doesn't matter," I say finally. "He's right. I knew he wasn't the one for me, and I let myself get attached. That's my fault."

"You're pinning this on yourself," Van says in surprise and I shrug.

"Well, it *is* my fault. I trusted him, and I let him in. I shouldn't have. It's on me."

"I want to deck her," Kate says to Callie, who nods. "But I'm not a violent person."

"I can be," Callie replies. "This is *not* your fault."

I stop pacing and let my hands fall to my sides, staring at Van. Her eyes are sad, and that just tears me apart.

"I want to stay mad. If I don't stay mad, I'll fall apart, and I refuse to shed even one tear over that British pain in the ass."

"Okay." Van nods with encouragement. "Being mad is good. But at *him*. Not you."

"I didn't do anything wrong," I say at last. "I'm confused. How can he go from being the sweetest, most loving man this morning to a stranger this evening?"

"You didn't fight?" Callie asks.

"No. We made love this morning. And then he attacked me in the shower. And then I went to work. *Nothing* happened. I haven't even seen him all day."

"This is on him," Kate says, shaking her head. "Something might have happened with him, and it scared him off."

"Or he's a piece of shit who was manipulating you," Callie adds.

"I like that one better."

I sit on my ass in the middle of my living room and look up at these amazing women who I love more than anything and feel my eyes fill.

And that pisses me off all over again.

But I'm all out of energy.

"I don't understand."

"I know, sugar," Van says and sits next to me. She wraps her arms around me and hugs me close, letting me cry a little. "I'm sorry."

"I'm only going to cry for a minute, and then I'm going to forget him." I wipe my face and look up at Kate and Callie, who both have tears of their own. "He's not worth this."

Except, I thought he was. I thought he was *everything*. And now I know it was nothing.

CHAPTER NINETEEN

~Simon~

"Can I get you anything before we take off, sir?"

What in the bloody fuck just happened?

"Sir? Mr. Danbury?"

I glance up at my name and realize that the flight attendant has been trying to get my attention.

I don't fucking care.

"What?"

"Can I get you anything before we take off?" She offers me a wide smile and glances down at the ink on my arm, and all I can think is, *get the fuck away from me.*

"No." I wave her off and scowl at my phone when it rings. "Mother."

"Hello, Simon. I'm glad I caught you. It's not too late, is it? I can't keep track of these time differences."

"It's fine, Mum. What's up?"

"Well, I just got off the phone with Amy, and I really think—"

"Listen to me very carefully," I say, interrupting her mid-sentence, which would have gotten me slapped when I was a boy. "I want you to stop speaking to that woman. Now."

"Simon Daniel Danbury, you do not speak to your mother that way."

"Yes, apparently I do. I'm not going to say it again."

"Sir, we're about to take off. You'll have to turn your phone off."

I wave at the attendant again and sigh.

"Are you on a plane?" Mother asks.

"Yes, I'll be home tonight." I take a deep breath and realize that it's time my mum and I had a long heart-to-heart conversation, no matter how much I hate the idea. "I'm going to come to your place on my way home from the airport. Will you please make sure Dad is there too?"

"Of course, darling. Have a safe flight. I'm so happy that you're coming home. I'll see you soon."

We click off and I check my messages, not expecting to see anything from Charly, certainly not *wanting* to see anything from her, and yet I'm disappointed when there's nothing. I open the last message from her and read it for the fifth time since she sent it earlier this afternoon. She thanks me for bringing her lunch, sorry that she missed me.

She should be thankful that she missed me. I wish I'd never gone to surprise her. Then again, I wouldn't have seen her get cozy in the storeroom with her ex, telling him that she'd see him when she returned from London, showing me exactly what I was getting myself into.

Today was a long series of events that led to me seeing the truth: I can't trust her. I can't trust *me*.

We're better off without each other.

And thank God I saw it before I took her to London and fell even further in love with her. Which is exactly what I've been doing: falling completely in love with her.

First, I got an email this morning from Jack, my former partner and friend, the man I caught in bed with my fucking *wife*. It was full of spite and hate and such rambling drivel that I was on edge, every cell in me screaming for Charly.

So I went to her, needing to see her, to talk to her, to hear her soft voice giving me words of wisdom, putting everything in perspective in that sexy as fuck accent of hers.

And instead I found her in the arms of another man.

That seems to be the story of my fucking life.

Was this all just some elaborate mind fuck for her?

It's time I get home, back to work, back to my responsibilities, and remember what's important.

That doesn't include dishonest women disguised in a sexy package.

***

"Simon," Mother says, staring at me with tear-soaked eyes. "Why didn't you tell us before?"

"A lot of reasons," I reply and stare at my father as he paces their living room, his hands linked behind his back. When he's this quiet, it means that he's angry.

"No reason you might have," he says with controlled anger, "is ever good enough to not tell us that your ex-wife was emotionally abusive."

"I know," I reply. "At the time, I was just focused on trying to help her. And when it was all over, I told you the truth, that I caught her being unfaithful, and I thought that was a valid enough reason to leave. I just didn't think it was necessary to bring up the rest of it."

"But I wouldn't stop speaking with her," Mother adds and hangs her head in her hands. "You told me to stop, but I wouldn't listen. I just wanted everything to be okay, and I knew that she'd made a mistake, but I'd hoped that you could work it out, especially when she told me over and over how lost she was without you, and how very sorry she was."

"She's excellent at manipulation." I sigh and wrap my arm around my mother's shoulders. "It's not your fault, Mum. I should have told you more."

"I can promise that I won't be speaking to her again, except to give her a piece of my mind."

"She's not worth it," I reply, shaking my head.

"I gave her money," Dad says. "She was pathetic and sad, saying that you wouldn't help her."

"You gave her *money*?" I ask, appalled. "Jesus, Dad, I didn't even know that she'd come to you with that bullshit."

"You clam up whenever we mention her name, and I felt sorry for her," he says. "Obviously, not so much now."

"I could just slap her," Mum says, clenching her fists. "I should have known better. She told me once that she didn't know how she was going to go on without you, and thought about ending her life."

"That's typical," I mutter and rub my eyes. "That was her M.O."

"Thank you for telling us," Mum says. "I'll back off, and I'm so proud of you for being strong enough to see her for what she is."

I'm not terribly strong. I fell for it again.

I simply kiss her cheek and stand to leave. "I'm heading home. I'll call in a few days."

I pull away from their house, toward my loft which

isn't too far away and the heaviness of exhaustion hits me. I'm so fucking tired.

My loft is quiet, everything exactly as I left it, and yet it feels like nothing is the same.

I'm not the same.

I shoot Todd a text.

Got home early. Meet me at the office tomorrow morning at 9:00.

He replies immediately. *Got it.*

I thought I would sleep on the plane, but I didn't. Instead I tortured myself over and over again with the vision of Charly and the fucker with his hands on her, and then my focus would shift to how she looked naked, writhing beneath me. Laughing. Sleeping. Eating. Her touch.

Fucking hell, how did I fall in love with something that wasn't real?

***

"You look like shit," Todd says as he walks into the office and sets a cup of coffee under my nose.

"Fuck you," I reply and sniff the coffee, then decide *fuck it* and take a drink, then scowl. "This is black."

"You're the one that turned into a pussy and decided to drink coffee rather than tea, mate. I have no idea how you take it."

"Fuck you again," I reply and set the cup aside. "Let's get to work."

"Okay. But first, what's going on? I thought you were bringing Charly."

"Don't want to discuss it. Let's work."

"Great." He nods and sighs in frustration. "Speaking of work, we had all of the slots filled for the retreat this fall, but we had one back out last night. Savannah

Boudreaux sent me an email and said that she wouldn't be attending because she refuses to give her time or money to a hypocrite."

I sigh and push my hands through my hair, frustrated.

"Fine. Grab someone from the waiting list."

"So, you're not going to tell me what happened."

I stand and stomp across the office, staring out the window. Todd's the only one who has known everything as it happened in my life. He's my closest mate, and I trust him implicitly.

But talking about it cuts deep.

"Yesterday was a bloody disaster." I pull my phone out of my pocket, bring up Alex's email, and hand it to Todd, then turn back to the window.

He reads silently behind me for a moment. "What the fuck?"

"Keep reading."

"'*You know that I never would have been able to have an affair with Amy if you'd been keeping her happy. You were too obsessed with work.*' Fuck him. I always hated Alex."

"I know."

"'*But speaking of the company, you wouldn't be where you are now without my contribution in the beginning. My lawyer agrees that I'm owed compensation.*'"

I turn around to see Todd stare at me in horror. "Is he on motherfucking medication? He thinks he's going to get *money*?"

"He won't," I reply, much more calmly than I feel. My blood is still boiling over that email. "I forwarded it to my lawyer, and they're on it. He doesn't have a case. He's just broke and grasping at straws."

"He's an arsehole," Todd says and finishes reading the email, then passes it back to me. "Not a great way to start any day."

"No." I shake my head and sit at our conference table. I can't get comfortable, no matter what I do. I spent all night pacing my flat.

"So now you should tell me why Savannah sent that email and Charly isn't here."

"Charly is no longer a part of my life," I reply shortly. "That's all there is to it."

"I don't think that's true," Todd says. "What happened?"

"The same thing that always happens. I went to surprise her at work and walked in on her with another man."

I glance up and Todd is scowling, shaking his head. "I don't buy it."

"Saw it with my own bloody eyes."

"Charly Boudreaux was fucking another man. You saw it."

I shake my head and decide bugger it and take a sip of the horrible coffee. "They hadn't gotten that far yet, and I wasn't about to stick around and watch."

"So you didn't actually *see* it." Todd sits across from me and fiddles with his wedding ring.

"I saw enough."

"Sounds like you were having a shit day and saw what you wanted to see."

"Fuck you," I reply and throw the coffee against the wall. "I made the mistake of trusting her. Of trusting *me* with her. And it didn't work. I may give good advice, but my own love life has been one big fuck up."

"Well, that's true enough," he says, unfazed by the

coffee dripping down the wall. "But Charly isn't Amy, Simon."

"Seems they're not that different."

"But *you're* different. You didn't love Amy, mate. You cared for her, sure, but you were with her out of some misguided sense of responsibility. You thought you could save her, but she didn't want to be saved. Amy is a bitch, plain and simple, and you can't fix bitch.

"Are you saying Charly is a bitch too?" Todd asks and I clench my fists, ready to come out swinging. "Guess that pissed you off."

"You don't know shit. You aren't walking around in my shoes."

"Because you have horrible taste in shoes," he replies. "But this time around, you didn't have horrible taste in women. You don't know for sure what you saw yesterday because I bet you didn't stick around to ask many questions."

I bloody hate it that he knows me so well.

"It doesn't matter," I reply and hang my head in my hands. "I'm not going down this road again. Even if it wasn't what I think, it just goes to show that I can't trust, her or me. And without trust, we have nothing anyway."

"That's a sad way to live, Simon."

"I'm not discussing this anymore. We have work to do." I open my agenda and look at Todd expectantly. "What do we have this week?"

***

"I've wanted to attend one of your workshops for *ever*," a blonde in her mid-thirties raves as I sign her book and pose for a photo. "Thank you so much."

"My pleasure, darling," I reply and smile as she walks away. That was the last one in line and I'm bloody exhausted. I just spent six hours coaching a room of six hundred women on dating techniques. The last hour was open to questions, followed by another hour of signing books and meeting the attendees, and my energy is now gone.

Todd walks back to the makeshift greenroom that the hotel provided.

"This was a great workshop," he says. "The attendees were riveted. Of course, they always are when it comes to you."

"It went well," I agree. Since I returned from New Orleans three weeks ago, everything has been in a fog. I'm not numb, but nothing excites me. Today went well simply because I know my material inside and out and I know how to charm a room from years of experience.

But my heart isn't in it anymore.

Because despite my better judgement, I left my heart in New Orleans. With it being several weeks since I last saw Charly, I can admit that I miss her, but it doesn't change what happened. It doesn't change that I can't trust her, and I can't control the jealousy I feel when another man even *looks* in her direction.

"Do you want me to stick around?" Todd asks as he stows away my mic and readies the equipment to be picked up by the crew later.

"No, I'm fine. I'll be leaving right behind you."

I turn around as he walks away.

"This is going to be interesting," I hear Todd say from the doorway and I spin around to find Amy standing there next to him. "I'll be outside," Todd says.

I nod and watch wordlessly as Amy steps inside, closing the door behind her. She's changed her hair since the last time I saw her in the restaurant several months ago, but otherwise, she's the same.

She'll never change. It took me too long to figure that out.

"Amy."

"Hello, Simon," she says and sends me a soft smile. "I sat in on your little class today. It was wonderful."

My teeth clench. *Little class.*

I simply cross my arms over my chest and wait for her to continue.

"Violet was right, you've really done very well for yourself over the past year or so, and I wanted to stop by to say congratulations."

"Thanks. There's the door."

"Simon, I know I was horrible." She rushes forward and lays a hand on my arm, which I flick off. "I'm so sorry for what happened with Alex. I was just lonely, and you were working all the time and—"

"Are you telling me that it's *my* fault that you had an affair with my business partner?" I ask, interrupting her.

"No, of course not," she says. Her eyes are shrewd. She knows this tactic isn't going to win me over. "It was all my fault, and I'm so sorry. I've been in therapy again, and I really think it's working this time."

"Good for you."

"It *is* good, isn't it?" She smiles hopefully. "I feel so much better already. And I am really so happy for you. I hear you have a beautiful new flat."

And here it is.

"I'd love to see it sometime. How can I make all of this up to you, Simon?"

"By walking out that door and never coming back," I reply, my resolve not slipping a bit as tears fill her eyes as if on cue.

"I deserve for you to be cruel," she says and wipes a single tear from the corner of her eye. She really is a very good actress. She could be a professional. "I never should have left."

I shove my hands in my pockets and regard her silently. How in the hell could I have ever compared Charly to *her*? Charly is nothing like Amy. She's kind, loving, giving. She's not self-serving in the least.

I don't know what I saw at her shop that day, but maybe Todd was right when he said I should have stuck around to actually ask questions like I promised her in the first place.

"I never should have given up on you," she says when the silence stretches between us.

"I gave up on you," I reply simply. "And I'm glad I did, Amy."

Her whole demeanor changes now; her eyes narrow, her shoulders stiffen. She's not getting what she wants, and now she's going to fire back.

"Do you think I don't know all about your little American girlfriend?" she asks and circles the room, watching me. "I know everything."

"Charly wasn't a secret," I reply with a shrug.

"Do you think she's with you because of your sparkling personality?" she asks with a laugh. "Hardly. You're handsome, rich, famous. She's with you so you can pay for her precious little shoe store."

I cock a brow.

"That's right, I've been there. I wasn't about to let you go fuck some gold digger in Louisiana without seeing what she was all about for myself. She's nothing. Her little store is nothing."

I want to slap her, and I've never wanted to slap a

woman once in my life.

"You deserve so much better than that. Aren't you the one out there on a stage, spouting all kinds of advice about going after what you're worth? Why would you downgrade to such a pathetic little money-grubbing whore?"

"That's enough." My voice is steel. She stops pacing and stares at me with wide eyes.

"What did you say?"

"You heard me. You know what, Amy? I don't know if she's a money-grubbing whore." I shrug one shoulder, as if it's of no consequence to me. "I really don't. She might be. But I do know that *you* are. Now, you want to know how you can make everything up to me? Get the fuck out of this room and don't ever look back. If I so much as suspect that you're fucking with my family, friends, or Charly, I will make you regret it for the rest of your life."

"You're bloody threatening me!"

"No. I'm telling you how it's going to be."

"I should just kill myself." She stomps her foot like a child and I can't help but laugh. "This is not funny!"

"You're right. It's ridiculous. Goodbye, Amy." I turn away from her and ignore her completely until she finally stomps away and slams the door behind her.

Seconds later, the door opens again and I spin, ready to threaten to call the cops, but it's Todd standing there instead of Amy.

"Are you okay?" he asks.

"No." I shake my head and rub my hand over my mouth. Todd nods and looks toward the door.

"She's such a bitch, Simon. Don't let her into your head."

"I don't give two shits about Amy," I reply. "She no longer lives in my head. But I fucked up, mate."

"Yeah, I've been telling you that for weeks."

I'm pacing the room in agitation. God, how do I fix this?

"So, go after her, Simon. Get on a bloody plane."

"I can't." I shake my head and push my fingers through my hair. "I'm a jealous moron with her, Todd. I'm a complete jerk and I want to tear off every man's head who even looks in her direction. I overreact to even an innocent interaction, and I promised her that I would talk to her before jumping to conclusions, but I didn't. I *couldn't.* I've had a lot of time to go over everything in my head, and I handled it so badly."

"Simon, there's a difference between being jealous and being territorial," Todd says calmly. "It's okay to stake a claim on the woman you love."

"I didn't say love."

"Jesus, you're stubborn," he mutters. "Come on, mate. I've never seen you like this before. You've been in love with her since you met her. And that's why you get so jealous, because she's amazing and anyone would love to be with her. But she loves you too, you know. No way a woman lets a guy stay with her for weeks if she's in *like* with him."

"I can't go after her," I repeat and hold my hand up when Todd begins to disagree. "I need to figure out a few things first. I need to get my head on straight because I can't go back into it with her in the same space. She needs more. She deserves more, and damn it, so do I."

"Then get your head on straight and go get your girl. But don't wait too long. You've already buggered it all up. If you wait too long, she'll tell you to go fuck yourself."

"She might do that anyway."

"But you won't know unless you try," he says. "And you have to try, Simon. You deserve this too. It's long overdue."

CHAPTER TWENTY

~Charly~

It's been a month since I last saw Simon, and the mad is still hanging on like a bad rash. But I prefer it that way because when I'm not angry, I'm sad, and I'm much more comfortable with being pissed off.

I refuse to miss him.

I refuse to *anything* him.

But that doesn't mean that I don't, and that makes me mad too.

After closing up my shop late one evening, I walk the few blocks over to Beau's condo and let myself in like I've been doing for the past few weeks. I don't like being home alone, especially at night. That's when I miss him the most.

I must be desperate if I'm willing to stay on my brother's couch in a haunted apartment rather than sleep in my perfectly comfortable bed.

"You're later tonight," Beau says casually as I walk through the door, winded from the steps. I really need to start running again. I'm out of shape.

"I had a lot to do," I reply, not meeting his gaze. All

of my siblings have taken turns lecturing me about working too hard, but I don't care. I need to focus my energy on something constructive.

"How are you?" he asks, just as he does every night. Beau has had the patience of Job over the past few weeks. He hasn't said a word about me staying here, he's simply made sure I had a pillow and blanket. He offered me his bed, but I didn't have the heart to throw him out of it.

Not when I have a perfectly good one at home. I'm just too much of a weenie to go there.

"I'm fine."

"You may be okay," he counters, watching me with sober hazel eyes, "but you're not *fine*."

I stare back at him and finally sigh, my shoulders sagging, and sink onto the couch. "I'm not fine."

"What do you need?" he asks. Leave it to my brothers to always want to fix everything.

"I don't think there's anything I need except time," I reply. "There's nothing else to do."

"Have you heard from him at all?"

I shake my head. "No. And I won't. Not only did he make his decision, but I made it pretty clear that I didn't want to see him again."

"Are you sure about that?"

My head whips up so I can stare at him in surprise. "Of course I'm sure about that, Beau. He just *left*. I didn't do anything wrong."

"I'm not saying you did." He holds his hands up in surrender. "I'm just making sure that with a little time passed you haven't changed your mind on wanting to see him again."

"No. And I won't." I twist my hair on top of my head and lean back on the couch. "I do have something to run by you, though."

"Oh?" He stands to pour us each a finger of brandy, passes me one, and sits in his chair again. "Shoot."

"Head Over Heels is doing amazing. In fact, I have customers who call me after they've gone home from visiting New Orleans on vacation and ask me to send them photos of my current stock."

"Are you thinking about an internet store?" He asks, rubbing his fingertip over his lip.

"No, I was thinking of expanding," I reply, suddenly excited all over again at the thought. "I want to open a second store in Miami."

"Why Miami?" he asks.

"It's a hip, fun vacation destination, and I think my shoes would go over well in that demographic."

"True." He nods.

"I want to buy my building from Boudreaux Enterprises as well."

That has his attention. He cocks a brow, then frowns. "Why the fuck would you do that?"

"Because I *can*. I've built this business on my own, and I want to keep doing that. I can buy the building, and have enough money left to lease a shop in Miami and get it going."

"Hold on." Beau leans forward now and rubs his hands together. "Charly, are you under the impression that using your trust fund, or any of the moneys available to you through the family company, makes you weak in some way?"

"I want to do it on my own," I repeat.

"You *are* doing it on your own, with money that belongs to you, just as much as the money that Eli, Van, me, hell, all of use is ours. Dad left it to all of us and he was specific that we split it evenly."

"But I don't work for it—"

"Bullshit," he replies. "You work your ass off, more hours than any of us. Your office may not be in the same building, but you're working, Charly. If you want the building to be in your name, we'll have the title changed, but for all intents and purposes, it's yours, 100%."

I shake my head, but he interrupts before I can speak.

"There are billions of dollars at your disposal and you don't use it. Do you know how frustrating that is? I know that this family isn't frivolous or flashy—we weren't raised that way—but it's there for you. And if you want to expand your business, use it and do it. Open a dozen stores if you want to. Dad was a businessman, Char. Do you know how fucking proud of you he'd be?"

Tears prick my eyes as I realize that he's right. Dad would want this. I've been too stubborn trying to do everything on my own to realize it.

"Will you go with me to speak to Eli and Van about it tomorrow?" I ask.

"You don't need our permission."

"That's not it. I want all of your advice. I want to talk it out with other businesspeople that I respect and trust."

"In that case, yes. I think it's an amazing idea. You're going to kick shoe ass."

I grin. "I am. I can't wait."

Just then there's a loud crash that sounds like it's coming from downstairs.

"That damn woman," Beau mutters. "I don't care about the noise during the day, but doesn't she ever sleep?"

"It's not Mallory," I reply, chills running down my spine. "It's a ghost."

"Oh for fuck's sake," He says and pinches the bridge of his nose. "Now you sound like her."

"Like who?"

"The woman downstairs."

"Her name is Mallory," I reply. "And she seems to know about this stuff."

"She sounds like a whackjob," he says with a sigh. "And I don't believe in ghosts."

"You live in New Orleans," I point out. "How do you *not* believe in ghosts?"

"It's for books and movies," he replies. "I wish my house was finished being built."

Beau used to live on the plantation property before Gabby and Rhys got married. Now that Rhys is there to look after things, Beau has moved into town, and has a beautiful home being built in an exclusive neighborhood.

We may not be a frivolous family, but Beau appreciates the finer things in life.

"When will it be finished?" I ask.

"It's another year away. We're waiting for supplies from Italy."

I cock a brow, but I don't say anything.

"What? Some of us aren't afraid to use our trust funds, darlin'. You can't take it with you when you go, we can all attest to that."

He has a valid point.

"I honestly haven't needed it, Beau. Some of it is pride, but I've managed just fine on my own. My business is thriving. But you're right, it makes sense to use what's available to me for the expansion."

"Say it again," he says with a smile.

"Which part?"

"The *you're right* part."

I stick my tongue out at him, then jump when the lights flicker.

"She's here," I whisper.

"Who?"

"Miss Louisa."

"Who the hell is that?"

"*The ghost*," I whisper loudly. Beau just shakes his head and laughs.

"It's an old building, Charly. The electrical probably needs to be replaced."

"You should talk to Mallory. She'd convince you."

"As long as she stays out of my way and pays her rent on time, I don't need to see Mallory."

I shrug. "Suit yourself."

"I always do."

***

I've been talking to Van, Eli, and Beau for an hour about the expansion. Eli hasn't said one word, and I can't read his face.

Frankly, it's starting to piss me off.

"Eli, it's a great opportunity. If I can do so great with this store in my small shop in the Quarter, just think what I can do in an even busier storefront. Eventually, I might expand to New York, LA, Seattle, and then I'd have a store in every corner of the country." He nods, but doesn't say much. "Are you having issues with me using the family money?"

His head jerks up and he stares at me like I just asked him if I could get naked.

"No. Why would you think that?"

"Because you're not *saying anything*."

"I think it's a brilliant idea," Savannah says with an excited smile. "You've clearly thought this through and done your homework, Charly."

"Beau and I were up late last night talking about it," I reply.

"I was surprised when she suggested it, but the more she talked about it, the more it makes sense." He looks at Eli. "Whatever she decides to do with her money isn't our concern."

"I don't give a fuck about the money," Eli replies and shoves his hand through his hair. "You're right. You should do it."

"But?"

"But it'll take you away," he replies and looks at me with soft whiskey eyes. Eli and I have always been close. "You'll be gone, starting these new stores, and we won't see you often."

"God, you sound like a girl," Beau says, disgusted.

"Fuck you," Eli replies, still holding my gaze. "But you should do this. I'll help you in any way I can."

I grin and clap my hands. "I'm doing this!"

"You're *so* doing this," Van says just as Eli's phone beeps with an incoming call from his assistant.

"Mr. Boudreaux, your one o'clock is here."

"Thank you."

"I should go anyway." I stand and settle my handbag on my shoulder. "Thanks, guys. Your support means the world to me."

"Let's go to lunch," Van says. "We can talk about making a trip to Miami soon. I'd love to come with you to scout out possible locations."

"Oh, I would love that! Let's do it."

We wave goodbye to our brothers and walk out of Eli's office, and I'm suddenly face to face with Simon Danbury.

At first I think my eyes are playing tricks on me, but Van says, "Simon." She nods her head and continues to walk, but I pause. Simon is in New Orleans.

At my brother's office.

His amazing blue eyes blaze as his gaze rakes over me, as if he's been starving for me, and when they meet mine again, I simply smirk and follow Van to the elevator where she's holding it for me.

***

"Simon's in town," I mutter for the fiftieth time as we walk down to The Odyssey. "I don't need food. I need to drink my lunch."

"Agreed," Van says as she holds the door for me and follows me into the dark bar. Callie and Adam are standing at the end of the bar, looking at an iPad.

"Hi, Callie," I say with a wave. "I have a thousand dollars and I need to get drunk."

Callie's lips purse as she watches us belly up to the bar.

"Well, your money's no good here, but I can get you good and drunk."

"Fantastic."

She pours us all, including herself, a shot of tequila. We clink glasses and swig them back.

"Another," I say.

"So what are we celebrating?" Callie asks as she pours more liquor.

"Simon's in town," Van says.

"Are we happy about that?" Callie asks before chugging back another shot.

"Fuck no," I reply, wrinkling my nose. "I don't know why he's here. He's at Eli's office."

Callie laughs long and hard. "Well, he's in for a fun

afternoon because Declan was just headed that way for their Krav Maga session."

"Oh God, they're going to kill Simon," I say. "I wanna watch."

"Easy, tiger," Van says.

"What? Maybe they'll let me help."

"They're not going to kill him," Callie says, but her voice isn't completely certain.

"Some brothers they are," I mutter. The alcohol is already clouding my head, and I don't feel the knot of despair in my stomach anymore. Which is good because the knot of despair sucks.

"Oh! Declan just texted me and asked if you're with me," Callie says, staring at her phone. "What should I tell him?"

"Here." I motion for her to hand me the phone and then I dial Declan's number with it. "Don't you *dare* tell Simon where I am."

"I don't know where you are," he replies. I can hear the others in the background.

"I'm obviously with your wife, Einstein, I'm on her phone." I roll my eyes and shake my head.

"Look, Simon wants to see you."

"No."

"He has some things to say."

"He should have said them a month ago," I reply and close one eye while I stare in the bottom of my empty shot glass. "I don't want to hear his smarmy, sexy, dumb British voice."

"Are you drunk?" Declan asks and then laughs. "That was fast."

"I didn't eat today. I mean it, Declan Boudreaux, don't you tell him where I am. Or I'll beat you up."

"Right."

"Tell him I won't have sex with him," Callie says, but then shakes her head and says, "No. Scratch that. Sex is too good."

"Ew." I wrinkle my nose at her. "Declan, I don't want to know about your sex life."

"I wasn't telling you about my sex life. Is Callie drinking too?"

"My sisters are loyal! Of course they're drinking with me. Callie is my sister by marriage," I inform him, as if he didn't know.

"I was there," he reminds me. "Say goodbye, Charly."

"Goodbye Charly." I hand the phone back to Callie. "He won't tell."

"He's so going to tell," Van says. "Maybe he realizes how badly he screwed up."

"Declan screwed up?" I ask in surprise.

"No, Simon," Callie says with a laugh. "No more tequila for you."

"I don't want to see him," I say and lay my head on my crossed arms on the bar. "I was just starting to not hurt all the time. Why is he here?"

Callie and Van talk, sharing theories and thoughts, and I just listen, enjoying this hazy place between fall-down drunk and sober. It's a good place to be when you don't want to feel.

"Uh oh," Callie says, catching my attention. I look up at her and she nods toward the doorway. I turn on my stool and there they are: Eli, Declan, Beau, and Simon.

"Who gave him the black eye?" I ask, holding Simon's gaze.

"We're not sure," Declan says.

"I want to give them a high five because I also want

to give him a black eye." I turn back to the bar and stare at Callie. "I need another drink."

"You'll pass out," Van hisses in my ear.

"I should be so lucky." I glare at Callie, but she just shakes her head and suddenly Simon is standing next to me.

"Stop smelling good," I snap at him. Just look at him, standing there smelling all good and stuff like he owns the place.

"Charlotte, I'd like to speak to you," he says and his voice is like a balm to my wounded soul.

And that pisses me off too.

"Look, I don't want to talk to you," I reply and point my finger in his face. "You're mean and sexy and... *mean*." I nod once and turn to Van. "I told him off."

"You did great," she says with a smile.

"Also," I say and turn back to him. "I think you should have *two* black eyes."

"You're probably right," Simon says, making me scowl.

"You're not supposed to agree with me."

"My apologies."

"Do his manners annoy anyone else?" I ask the room at large. My brothers are just hanging back, watching us. They're not kicking anyone's ass, and that just irritates the hell out of me. "Aren't you supposed to beat him up?"

"They already did. Charly," he begins, but I cut him off.

"Good. I'm glad they beat you up. I told Declan not to tell me where you are, so he's in deep shit with me."

"You mean tell me where you are?"

"Are you trying to confuse me?"

He simply laughs and reaches up to brush my hair off

my face, but I flinch away from his touch, and then the room starts to spin.

"Shit."

"What's wrong?" Eli asks.

"Gonna pass out."

CHAPTER TWENTY-ONE

~Simon~

True to her word, Charly passes out, right into my arms.

"She always passes out when she drinks too much," Van informs me. She and Callie are both glaring at me, which I completely deserve.

It's almost worse than Charly's brothers all taking a round with me in their martial arts studio.

Almost.

But having her in my arms, feeling her against me, smelling her hair, makes it all worth it. Now I just have to convince her to take me back.

As soon as she sobers up.

"I'm going to take her home," I say and lift her into my arms. She's so damn small, she fits perfectly.

"Like hell you are," Van says and stands, pulling herself up to full height, which is no taller than Charly. "She would have my ass if she found out I let you take her home. She doesn't want to see you."

"I know." And God, it bloody hurts. "I'm hoping to change her mind about that."

"Are you really going to let him walk out of here with her?" Van demands, pointing at her brothers.

"It's okay, Van," Beau says. "He may be an idiot, but he loves her."

"Thanks, mate," I reply and smile at Savannah. "I won't hurt her again, darling."

Charly whimpers and buries her face in my neck. I want to hold her all night. I want to comfort her and protect her and love her.

"I don't know," Van says, shaking her head.

"I respect your opinion, but frankly, you're not going to stop me. I'm going to take her home, let her sleep this off, and then I'm going to make things right with her."

"Oh, trust me," Savannah says, her eyes almost green. "I can stop you. I may be small, but I can kick your ass."

I grin and nod, charmed by her loyalty and determination.

"I'll remember that."

I nod at Callie, then turn to walk out of the bar. Eli steps out of my way, but lays a hand on my shoulder, stopping me.

"Hurt her, and it'll be a hell of a lot worse than a black eye," he warns.

"Understood."

The drive to her house is quiet, the silence broken only by her sweet little snores. It's the middle of the afternoon, and my girl is passed out stinking drunk.

She's bloody adorable.

I manage to get her inside and up the stairs to bed. Once her shoes are off, I contemplate changing her clothes, but decide that I'd rather survive long enough to actually talk with her, so I leave her yellow dress on her and tuck her into bed.

I spend the rest of the afternoon and evening working, talking to Todd, and waiting.

But she doesn't wake up.

Her makeup is a mess. She has dark circles under her eyes, leading me to believe that she hasn't been sleeping well.

She's exhausted.

I want to be nearby, but again, climbing in bed with her isn't a wise choice, so I pull up a chair and sit next to her. I didn't think I would ever see her again, and here I am, just inches away.

I need her to wake up, and yet it terrifies me. What if she turns me away?

I take her hand in mine and lay my head on the bed next to her shoulder, listening to her breathing, and let sleep come.

***

The phone is ringing.

Charly shifts on the bed, reaching for it, as I sit up and scowl at the stiffness in my body. God, everything hurts. I'm pretty sure I'll never be able to turn my head to the left again.

"Hello?" she says and shoves her hand through her hair. She hasn't looked back at me yet. "No, I'm fine." She yawns. "I'm not hung over, which is good, I guess. Yeah."

Now she turns to stretch and sees me, and immediately scowls.

"Who the fuck let Simon in my house? You let him bring me home?"

"I'm sitting right here," I remind her with a smile.

"Of course I slept all night. I was drunk, and I haven't slept much in weeks. But you and I are going to talk about this later." She hangs up and glares at me. "Why are you here?"

"Charly—"

"Wait." She climbs out of the bed. "I'm not doing this in my bedroom. You go downstairs and I'll be there in a minute."

I'm not going to argue. The bedroom isn't the place for this. I make my way gingerly down the stairs, rubbing my neck and wishing for coffee with everything in my being.

But I sit on the couch, my elbows resting on my knees, and wait.

After what feels like an hour, she comes downstairs. She's taken a shower, and is in clean clothes. Her face is washed clean.

"You're so beautiful, you take my breath away."

"Right." She nods once and sits on a chair opposite me. "I'm not interested in hearing that you think I'm beautiful. I'd like for you to tell me why you're here."

Because I've missed you so much it feels like my heart has been ripped from my body.

"First, I'd like to apologize, Charlotte. I'm truly sorry for the way I left things last month. You didn't deserve that."

"No," she says. Her voice is calm, her face emotionless. I wish she'd throw something at me. "I didn't deserve it."

"I guess I didn't realize how many unresolved issues I had to resolve. I almost equate it to a bit of post-traumatic stress." I shrug and shake my head. "I walked into your shop that day and saw you with the man in your storeroom."

She cocks a brow. "And rather than interrupt, or ask me about it later, you jumped to conclusions. Again."

"I did." I link my fingers and lower my head. "I'm a fucking idiot."

"I won't argue there," she says. "Okay, you've apologized. There's the door."

She stands to leave the room, and I jump up, rushing after her.

No.

"Charly—"

"What?" she yells and turns back me, her eyes blazing now. *This* is what I need. Emotion. "What do you want from me?"

"I just want *you*."

"Well, you had me, and you fucked it up, Simon. I was ready to tell you all about Ryan that evening. I didn't have any fucking secrets from you."

"You're magnificent when you're angry," I murmur.

"You'd be angry too if the person you'd fallen in love with left you without an explanation. If the person you love threw all of your insecurities in your face on his way out the fucking door."

I reach for her, but she ducks out of my way.

She loves me.

"You'd be exhausted too if you couldn't sleep in your own bed because of the memories there, and instead you crash on your brother's lumpy couch every night."

"Baby—"

"I had just learned to trust you, to trust what I was feeling for you, Simon. I opened myself up to you."

"I know."

"And now you think that you can show up here, get a

black eye, apologize, and everything would be okay? You can't just fix this with that smile of yours."

"I know that too." I sigh, wanting to pull her into my arms so badly that it hurts. She stomps over to the door and pulls it open, and it's exactly like the day I left.

"I want you to leave."

"No." I stay where I am, staring at the woman I love. "Not until you hear me out. And then, if you want to throw me out, I'll go and not come back. But I came a long way to see you and to say a few things."

She closes the door, not slamming it, which gives me a bit of hope, then turns around and crosses her arms over her chest, waiting.

"You have five minutes. I have to work today."

God, she's tough.

"First, you should know that I am completely and irreversibly in love with you."

She blinks, but her expression doesn't change, and the pit in my stomach grows.

"Amy fucked me up. I didn't know just how much until I'd fallen in love with you and the baggage kept rearing its ugly head. I know that leaving, especially the way I did, was absolutely wrong, but to be honest, Charly, I'm glad it happened that way. I needed to go home and set some things right before I could make them right with you."

I swallow and pace the room.

"I don't mean that I had to make anything right with Amy, or my parents. I needed to make it right with *me*. I was convinced that I'd never be able to shake the blinding jealousy I had every time another man *looked* at you." I turn to her now in time to see her frown. But she doesn't interrupt. "I'd never been jealous in my life. I didn't like it. And when I saw you with Ryan, my first instinct was to run because I convinced myself that I would never live through another repeat of what happened with Amy."

"I'm *not* Amy," she says.

"No. You're not. And it took some time and some soul searching for me to realize that I was, well, intensely fucked up." I sigh and shove my hands through my hair. "Amy came to see me."

She cocks a brow.

"She was her usual, manipulative self, and not only did I not give a fuck about what she had to say, but it drove home for me that you are *nothing* like Amy. You are so kind and sweet and loving. You're everything she isn't, and I knew that I'd not only screwed up, but that I needed to come make it right.

"But first, I spent about a week in intense therapy, coming to terms with a lot of what happened in my life before you."

"I'm glad," she says softly. "I'm very happy for you, Simon, that you worked on yourself and that you're in a better place."

Just when my hopes rise, she turns to me and crushes them down again.

"But I just don't know if I can trust you again."

I nod, and feel my heart sink to my knees. I'm too late. I hurt her too badly.

I cross to her and drag my knuckles down her cheek. She doesn't pull away this time. The feel of her soft skin is a balm to my wounded soul.

"I understand," I say, my voice gruff. "I'm sorry for everything, Charlotte. I love you."

Just as I'm about to pull away, she lays a hand on my chest.

"Wait." She squeezes her eyes shut for a brief moment, then looks up at me. "I didn't say no. I said I don't know."

I wait, watching her lovely face as she struggles with herself, and that makes me hurt almost as much as the idea of losing her completely. I've hurt her so badly.

"I want the chance to make this all up to you, love."

"I need some time to think about all of this," she says at last. "I can't just jump back into this with you."

"It's a trust thing," I reply with a smile and tuck her hair behind her ear. "I'll be here for as long as you need. I'm staying at the same hotel I was at last time. You can come to me, or call, anytime, day or night."

She nods and steps back as I open the door.

"Simon?"

"Yes, love."

"Thank you."

I nod and leave before I pull her into my arms and carry her upstairs to her bed.

***

"You and I need to talk," Savannah Boudreaux says when I open the door to her knock.

"Hello to you too," I reply and gesture for her to come inside. "Can I get you anything? I have some hot tea here."

"No," she replies and walks into my suite. "I love this place. I've always wanted to see the inside."

"Is that why you came by?" I ask and gesture for her to have a seat on the sofa by the window.

"I'll stand," she replies. "I have too much energy to sit."

"I understand."

"No, I didn't come here to check out the inside of

this inn," she begins. "I came to see you when I'm sober."

"Do you girls drink a lot when you're pissed?"

"Sometimes." She shrugs and wanders into the bathroom. "Look at this tub!"

I grin and wait for her to return.

"So, Charly's at work and you're here, so I'm assuming she didn't just jump into your waiting arms this morning."

"You haven't spoken to her?" I'm surprised. I figured Charly would call her sisters first thing. I know that they're her closest friends.

"No." She shakes her head and sits on the sofa now. Her eyes, so much like Charly's, are worried. "That's usual for her too. When she needs to think, or if she's sad, she stays mostly to herself. Especially since our father died."

She looks at me now. "I want to hear where your head is, but I also want to give you some insight into Charly. I don't see this as speaking out of turn because she loves you, and I think you love her too."

"More than anything."

She smiles softly. "That's lovely. Charly was the closest to our father. Don't get me wrong, we all thought we were the closest one, but in hindsight, I can see that Charly and Dad had a very special relationship. They had many of the same interests. She idolized him. Losing him was hard on all of us, but I think that a piece of Charly died that day too."

She wipes a tear away, and I sink into a squat next to her, listening to her intently.

"Our parents were married for the better part of forty years, and for all we kids knew, it was a wonderful marriage. I still believe it was good, but having been married once myself, I know that no marriage is perfect.

They made sure they never fought in front of us, and Dad took care of things; the business, us kids, and our mama. He loved her so much. And he used to tell us girls that we deserved nothing less than the fairy tale of love at first sight and happily ever after."

She smirks and some of the pieces begin to fit together in my head.

"Love at first sight and happily ever after are for fairy tales," she says softly, "but I think Charly believed in them. That's why she'd never been in a serious relationship. She was waiting for that instant burst of passion, that immediate recognition that she'd met the man of her dreams, all in the first five minutes. And it wasn't until she met you that she realized that love can be a slow burn, starting low and building into something wild and passionate.

"She had that with you. She was...*careful*. I don't think she understood what was happening with you at first, but once she did, well, she fell hard."

"And I was a broken prick who broke her heart."

"Well, those are strong words, but I'll take them," she says with a laugh. "I don't think you're a prick, Simon. I think you fell truly in love for the first time too, and maybe you didn't know exactly what to do with it."

"That's a simple, and accurate, way to phrase it."

She nods, and the pain in her eyes is blinding.

"What happened to you, love?"

She just shrugs and smiles through the tears. I have a feeling she's been doing that for a very long time.

"I've had my own hurt. And Charly watched that, too." She looks up at me now and swallows hard. "Sometimes love is disguised as something evil. Something horrible."

"Yes. It is."

"So when you find true love, that makes your heart swell and comforts you, that makes you feel safe and protected, you fight for it, Simon. You fight."

"She said she needs time to think."

"Give it to her, but then you go after her and you fight for her. Nothing in this world will be more worth it."

"I know." I lean in and kiss her cheek and pull her in for a tight hug. "Thank you, Savannah."

She nods, wipes her eyes, and stands to leave. When she reaches the door, she looks back at me. "Daddy would have liked you."

And with that, she walks out.

CHAPTER TWENTY-TWO

~Charly~

It's been a long day. Maybe the longest day of my life. I've finally just got home from work, and it's almost midnight. I didn't go to Beau's because I need to think this all through on my own. The one person I would normally go to about these things is gone.

My dad would know what to say. God, how I wish I could talk to him, just one more time.

But I can't.

I'm exhausted. I spent all day deep in thought. I was so preoccupied that I finally had to call Linda in to help me because I had to ask customers to repeat themselves two, sometimes three times. So I went into the back and spent the day placing new orders, balancing the books, and looking at real estate in Miami to keep my mind occupied.

I undress and flop into bed. I wonder if Simon is asleep, and then shake my head. What does it matter? I'm not going to call him over, and I'm not going to show up at his place. I wanted to ask him to stay so badly this morning. Seeing him, feeling his touch, almost made the last month of agony disappear.

Almost.

I thought about him all day today, and I still don't know what to do. I want to be with him, but I knew from the beginning that he wasn't my forever, even though I'd started to hope that I was wrong. He was much more than a Mr. Right Now. And then the way he ended things just hurt so badly, how do I trust that he won't do it again? He says he won't, but I don't trust words. I barely trust actions. But I always believe in patterns, and he jumped to conclusions before.

I don't know what to do. I yawn again and turn onto my side, enjoying my soft bed after so many nights on Beau's couch. I don't want to think anymore. I just want to sleep.

"The fish sure don't seem to want to bite today."

"We're even using the good bait," I reply and grin at my dad. I really don't care if the fish bite, I just like being out on the river with him. This is our alone time, when the other kids don't get to come along. He does this with all of us.

"I guess we won't have any fish for dinner," he replies and winks at me. "But that's okay. It's a nice day to be on the boat."

"Yep," I reply and set my pole in the holder thingie, then stretch my legs out so they can get some sun while I sip on a Coke.

"How are you doing, baby girl?"

"I'm doing just fine," I reply. "School is hard, but it's almost summer."

"Time sure flies," he says and sets his pole aside as well so

he can turn and look at me. He takes a package of peanut butter cups out of the cooler and hands me one, then munches on his. My dad is a big man. Super tall. I think my brothers will probably be tall like him. "Tell me about your Simon."

And suddenly, I'm not a child anymore. I'm a woman, and the poles are gone. But my dad still looks young and full of life, and my heart bursts with love for him.

"He's not the one for me," I reply with a shrug. "I should have known better from the beginning."

"Why do you say that?"

"Because it wasn't love at first sight."

"So?"

"What do you mean so?" I ask. "You're the one who always told me to wait for the love at first sight and happily ever after."

"You were a child, Charlotte," he replies with a soft smile. "Of course I would say that to a little girl."

"I was waiting for a love like yours and Mama's. I wanted the perfect love."

"Love is never perfect," he replies and narrows his eyes on me. "Your mother and I loved each other to distraction. I still love her, and while I'm anxious to have her with me again, I'm content to sit in this boat and wait for her to finish what she needs to do with you and the others. But Charly, there was many a day that your mama wanted to beat me over the head with her cast iron pan."

"You were wonderful together. You never fought."

He tips his head back and laughs. "Oh, darlin', of course we did. But we tried not to in front of you kids. Maybe that was a disservice to you." He rubs his hand over his mouth. "There were some hard years in there, especially when the babies were small and I had to work, or chose to work, more than I should have. We fought a lot, and she threatened to leave me."

"She what?" I'm shocked.

"She said I either needed to be a father and help her with you kids, or I could go be married to my empire. And you know, she was right. Scared the shit out of me, though."

"Which was probably her goal," I mutter, utterly shocked that my parents had issues that I didn't know about.

"We're all human, darlin'. We make mistakes. I guess you have to decide if what your Simon did was so bad that you can't forgive him."

"I can forgive him. He explained why it happened, and I believe him. But what if it happens again? And again? I don't think I could survive it, Daddy."

"Seems to me, Simon might be the kind of man who learns lessons after the first time. Otherwise, you wouldn't have fallen in love with him."

I blink at him and nod slowly. "He's a good man."

"And he loves you back."

"He says he does."

"Do you trust that too?"

I think about the look in his eyes when he told me he was in love with me, and when he apologized for hurting me. He looked tortured inside.

"I do."

"Well, then I don't see where the problem is. It's important to forgive, darlin'. Doesn't mean you have to forget. If you forget, you didn't learn anything."

"I've missed you so much," I say and climb over the seat to settle next to my dad and lay my head on his shoulder. "I've needed this with you."

"I've missed you too, baby girl. I'm so proud of you and what you've done with your business."

"You can see it?" I smile up at him, so happy that he

knows about Head Over Heels.

"I can see everything y'all are doing. Expanding is a good idea, and I'm glad you finally realized that I left that money for you to use rather than resent."

"I don't resent it, Daddy. I just... I want to do this on my own."

"And you are. But it's okay to let your old man help you now and again."

"Will I see you again?" I ask, afraid that he'll say no.

"If you need me," he says. "I'm always right here, for all of you. But you're going to be just fine, baby girl. I'm proud of you."

I smile and kiss his cheek. "He's going to be good for me."

"You're good for each other. There will be more good than bad; you just have to adjust your sails and ride through the rough waters to get to the smooth ones."

"We've all been adjusting our sails since you've been gone."

"Me too, baby girl. Me too."

"I don't want to go yet."

"I'm always right here."

***

It's four in the morning and I don't care. I need to see him right now.

The woman at the front desk didn't love the thought of letting me up, but I assured her that he'd want to see me.

And she seemed like a bit of a romantic, and finally agreed to let me up, as long as I was quiet and didn't wake the other customers.

I knock on Simon's door and wait. He's usually a

light sleeper, but what if he doesn't hear me? I should have called. I should have waited until morning rather than rushing over here like a crazy woman.

I turn to slink away and hear the door open behind me.

"Charlotte?"

I bite my lip and spin around and stare at his sleepy, messy haired hotness.

"Hi."

"Come in." He backs up and I get a good look at him in the glow from the lamp beside the bed. He pulled on shorts, but he's shirtless. He's tousled and sexy and his blue eyes are bright, not sleepy at all. "Are you okay?"

"Yes," I reply, surprised that it's the truth. "I know it's late, or early, but I didn't want to wait—"

"You're fine. I told you to come anytime. Let's sit."

"Okay." I nod and follow him into the suite and sit where he gestures on the sofa. He sits across from me on the coffee table and takes my hands in his.

"You're cold." He rubs my hands vigorously.

"I'm nervous," I say with a chuckle.

"Why?"

"Because this is a big deal." His gaze whips up to mine.

"Go on."

"I love you, Simon. I think I fell in love with you in Montana, and then when you were here, well, I just… I felt things I never had before. And it scared me. It still scares me."

"We're in agreement there," he says with a soft smile. His eyes are full of hope and love.

"I think I had some misguided notions about love," I continue, thinking of my dream about my dad. "And I think I expected a lot."

"You should expect a lot," he says and squeezes my hand. "When you love someone you should expect *everything.*"

"But I can't expect you to be a mind reader, or to be perfect. Because none of us are perfect."

"I'm far from it," he says. "I'm just a man, Charly. I'm a man who loves you fiercely, and I'm going to fuck up. I can't promise that I won't."

"But we'll learn from it when we do," I interject and revel at the feel of his stubble on my palm as I cup his cheek. "There's a learning curve involved here."

"Are you saying that you're willing to give this a try?"

"No," I reply and lean closer when he frowns. "I'm saying that I want to commit myself to you. I'm not a tryer, I'm a doer. We can't pick it up where we left off, Simon, but we can grow from it and move forward."

"That's more than I deserve and everything that I'd hoped for," he replies and pulls me into his arms, rocking us back and forth. "God, I missed you, love."

"I missed you, too." He kisses my temple.

"What made you decide to come here now?" he asks softly.

I swallow hard. "My dad. I had a great conversation with him."

He pulls back to look in my face. "Did you now?"

I nod. "He likes you."

"Savannah thought he might," he replies and brushes a piece of hair off my cheek.

"You saw Savannah?"

He nods.

"What did she say?"

"To fight for you." He grins and kisses me, softly at

first, and then more passionately, waking up parts of me that have been asleep for more than a month. "And if you hadn't shown up here when you did, I was going to come to you in about four hours."

"I beat you to it." I stand and take his hand in mine, leading him toward the bed. "I don't want to sleep alone anymore."

"I don't have any sleep in mind," he replies with a wicked smile.

"Thank goodness."

***

"You have done an amazing job with this," Simon says six months later. He's standing in the middle of *Head Over Heels Miami*, taking in everything. It's the night before our grand opening.

My stomach won't settle down.

"I'm nervous," I admit.

"Trust me, it's going to be fantastic. And I'm going to insist that we go back to the condo now." He takes my hand and kisses my fingers. "It's almost midnight, you're exhausted, and I haven't seen you in days."

"That's an exaggeration." I roll my eyes, but stand on my tiptoes and kiss his cheek. I have absolutely nothing to complain about. Simon has been in Miami with me for the past month while I put the store together. He helped me when he could, and we bought a condo on the beach to use when we're in town.

"Okay, I haven't seen you *much*."

"After grand opening week, things will slow down a bit. I hired a great team to take the reins." I smile up at him as we walk through the displays and racks of gorgeous shoes. I decided early on that I didn't want to live in Miami full time. New Orleans is where my heart is, but we will come often to check in on things. "When do we leave for London?"

"In about ten days," he replies. "My parents are anxious to meet you."

"Your mom is sweet." I've spoken to her on the phone a few times, and I'm looking forward to meeting her too.

"She already likes you very much."

He leads me outside. The shop is on the boardwalk, nestled amongst designer shops, looking out on the water. Our condo is only a few blocks away.

But rather than lead me toward home, he pulls me out onto the pier and leans on the railing, looking out into the night. He wraps his arm around me, tucking me against him.

"Are you okay?" I ask.

He doesn't say anything at first, and finally after a long, silent moment, he turns to me and hugs me close, then pulls back so he can look into my eyes.

"I don't know how to answer that question because I'm so much better than *okay*, I can't put it into words. You've changed my life, Charly."

I blink up at him, moved and a little curious about the fierce, almost nervous look in his eyes.

"I never wanted to need you," he continues. "It's a vulnerability that I didn't think I would ever be comfortable with. I wanted you. I still want you, and I always will.

"I've come to learn that despite what I thought I wanted, I do need you, and the vulnerability is a beautiful thing when it's with someone you trust." He kisses my knuckles, and gazes deeply into my eyes. "I need you, Charly, in the most elemental, basic ways. I can't see myself ever without you. You've brought such humor, love, and happiness to my life. I can't promise that it'll be a perfect life, but I can promise that I'll do everything in my power to make sure that it's a life we're proud of."

He lowers down to one knee and pulls a little blue box out of his pocket, and I'm stunned. It's hard to breathe. I want to jump up and down and cry like a baby, all at the same time.

"Please do me the honor of being my wife. Build a life with me, Charlotte."

I blink at him for a heartbeat, and finally, I nod vigorously and throw myself into his arms, holding onto each other on the floor of this pier.

"Is that a yes?"

"Yes," I say, surprised to see tearstains on his shirt. "Absolutely yes."

"Here, this is for you." I lean back and gasp at the gorgeous diamond he slides on my finger. It's twinkling in the starlight. "I hope you like it. If you don't, you can exchange it."

"It's perfect." I wrap my arms around his neck and hold on tight. "This is perfect."

EPILOGUE

~Beau Boudreaux~

Three Months Later...

"Leave it to Charly to have a wedding in London," I say and scrub my hand over my mouth. "I would never say this to her, but how are we supposed to leave the company for a week? I think Eli will have a nervous breakdown."

"It'll be fine," Savannah says calmly. We're in her office, trying to make arrangements so we can all go to London next week. "We have a strong team, and we're only a phone call away."

"Why couldn't she have just gotten married here?"

"Because she didn't want to," Van says and pats me on the cheek, hard. She's stronger than she looks.

Her phone rings with a call from her assistant.

"Yes?" Van says.

"There's a Mallory Adams here to see you."

"Oh, great. She can come in." Van smiles at me. "Mallory and I are going out for lunch."

"Is this the Mallory that rents the shop below my apartment?" I ask, just as the woman herself walks through the door.

"That's me," she says with a smile, and my tongue

immediately sticks to the roof of my mouth. I always pictured her as a matronly woman, in voodoo witch dresses and long dreadlocks.

I was wrong.

Her hair is long and red, in soft curls. Her eyes are wide, and a curious shade between blue and purple. She's taller than my sisters, but not by much, and she's curvy in all the right places.

There's nothing *matronly* about her.

She's fucking beautiful.

"Mallory, this is Beau," Van says with a wicked grin. "Also known as the pain in your ass."

"He's not that bad," Mallory replies as she approaches the desk. She holds an envelope out to me, and our hands brush as I take it, making her eyes dilate. "I thought I'd drop the rent by, since I was here anyway."

"Thank you."

Is that my voice?

"You're welcome." She takes a step back and her eyes roam all around my head and shoulders, and she smiles widely. "I like you already, Beau Boudreaux."

I raise a brow. "Really?"

"Mm." She turns her attention to Van. "Should we go?"

"Sure." Van grins and reaches for her bag. "I love what you've done with your hair."

"Thank you. It was time for a change."

Both women walk out of the office, and I still can't move, struck dumb by the surprise of Mallory Adams.

I'm going to have to visit her shop in the near future.

Don't miss out on Adam's story in the 1001 Dark Nights novella:

EASY FOR KEEPS
(A BOUDREAUX NOVELLA)
BY KRISTEN PROBY

Adam Spencer loves women. All women. Every shape and size, regardless of hair or eye color, religion or race, he simply enjoys them all. Meeting more than his fair share as the manager and head bartender of The Odyssey, a hot spot in the heart of New Orleans' French Quarter, Adam's comfortable with his lifestyle, and sees no reason to change it. A wife and kids, plus the white picket fence are not in the cards for this confirmed bachelor. Until a beautiful woman, and her sweet princess, literally knock him on his ass.

Sarah Cox has just moved to New Orleans, having accepted a position as a social worker specializing in at-risk women and children. It's a demanding, sometimes dangerous job, but Sarah is no shy wallflower. She can handle just about anything that comes at her, even the attentions of one sexy Adam Spencer. Just because he's charmed her daughter, making her think of magical kingdoms with happily ever after, doesn't mean that Sarah believes in fairy tales. But the more time she spends with the enchanting man, the more he begins to sway her into believing in forever.

Even so, when Sarah's job becomes more dangerous than any of them bargained for, will she be ripped from Adam's life forever?

ABOUT KRISTEN PROBY

New York Times and USA Today Bestselling Author Kristen Proby is the author of the popular With Me in Seattle series. She has a passion for a good love story and strong characters who love humor and have a strong sense of loyalty and family. Her men are the alpha type—fiercely protective and a bit bossy—and her ladies are fun, strong, and not afraid to stand up for themselves. Kristen spends her days with her muse in the Pacific Northwest. She enjoys coffee, chocolate, and sunshine. And naps. Visit her at KristenProby.com.

OTHER BOOKS BY KRISTEN PROBY

The Boudreaux Series:
Easy Love and on audio
Easy Charm and on audio
Easy Melody and on audio
Easy For Keeps

The With Me In Seattle Series:
Come Away With Me and on audio
Under the Mistletoe With Me and on audio
Fight With Me and on audio
Play With Me and on audio
Rock With Me and on audio
Safe With Me and on audio
Tied With Me and on audio
Breathe With Me and on audio
Forever With Me and on audio
Easy With You

The Fusion Series
Listen To Me and on audio

The Love Under the Big Sky Series, available through
Pocket Books:
Loving Cara and on audio
Seducing Lauren and on audio
Falling for Jillian and on audio

Baby, It's Cold Outside and on audio
An Anthology with Jennifer Probst, Emma Chase, Kristen Proby, Melody Anne and Kate Meader

CPSIA information can be obtained
at www.ICGtesting.com
Printed in the USA
LVHW030728280519
619123LV00021B/434/P

9 781633 500136